NO STONE UNTURNED

A CITY OF FOUNTAINS NOVEL

C.J. JOHNSON

PRESS

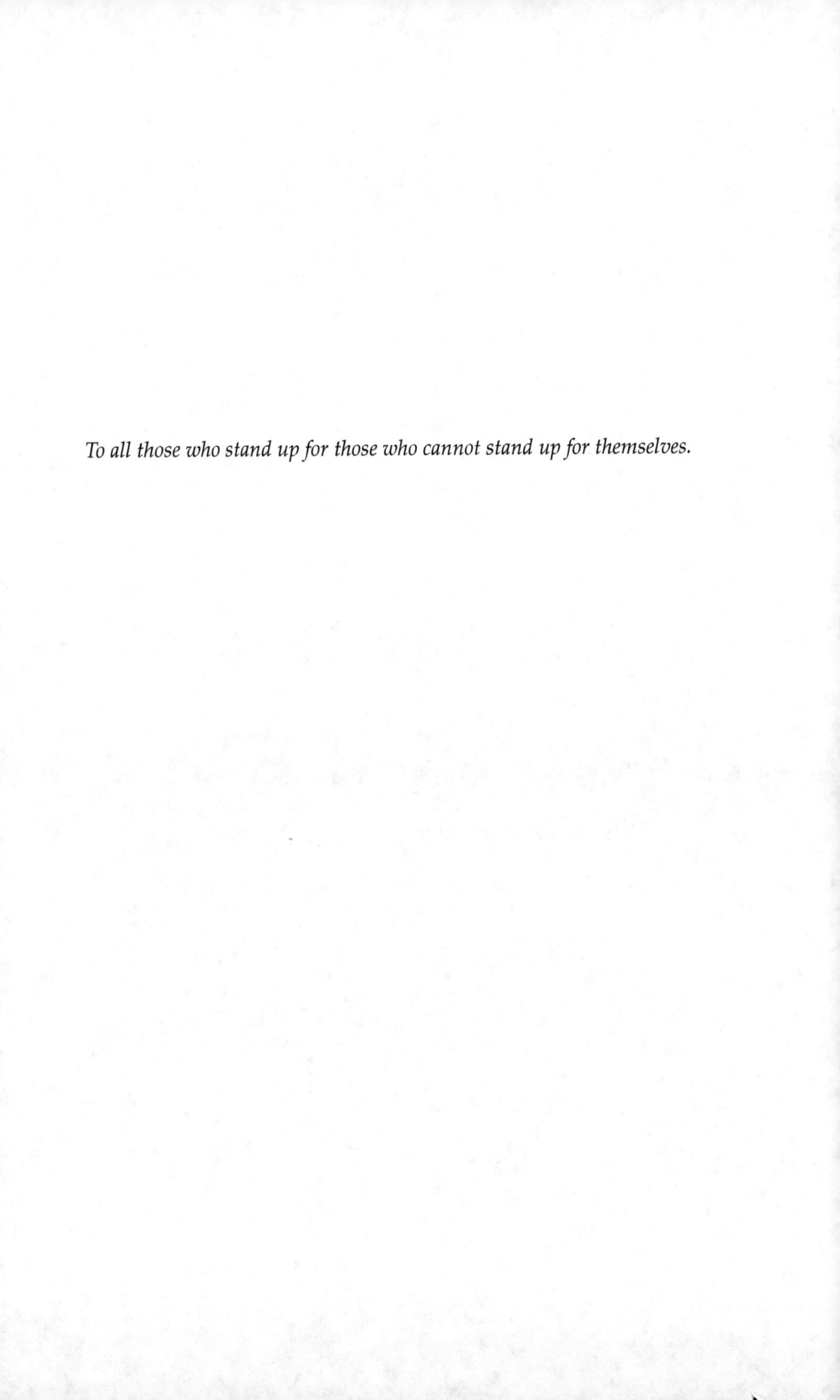

To all those who stand up for those who cannot stand up for themselves.

CHAPTER
ONE

THE SOUND of the howling wind was shrouded by the thump, thump of the music coming from the club. Laughter floated from the door as Sarah stepped out onto the sidewalk. Shivering, she suddenly wished she had brought her coat with her. With her arms wrapped around her body and her car keys clutched in her hand she began to walk.

"Where the heck did I park my car?"

As Sarah approached the corner it started to rain.

Behind her a deep, booming voice said, "It sure is cold tonight."

In a chivalrous manner, the man took off his coat and started to place it around Sarah's shoulders.

With a half-hearted laugh she replied, "You're not kidding. I forgot how cold winters could be in Missouri."

The man did not remove his arm from Sarah's shoulders after covering her with the coat.

"Can I give you a ride?"

"Um, no thanks. My car's just ov…"

In one swift movement, before Sarah could say a word, she felt her body pivot toward the car on the street.

"It's cold. I'll take you."

"No, really it's not far—I can walk."

With one hand on her shoulder and the other on the small of her back the man pushed Sarah toward the car. Gruffly he said, "Get in."

Stumbling on the curb, Sarah fell into the open car and felt the door slam behind her. She reached for the handle to open the door, but the handle wasn't there. Panic began to set in as she grabbed for her cell phone to call 9-1-1. The man wrenched the phone from her hand, opened his window, and tossed it. Sarah looked over her shoulder and saw pieces of the phone bounce off the pavement under the streetlight.

"There's my car," Sarah yelled, but the car continued past the parking lot.

"Shut up!"

Sarah clutched her purse close to her body. She felt the hard, rectangular shape of her other cellphone through the fabric. Slowly she moved her bag between her leg and the car door. Sarah carefully unzipped the bag and retrieved the phone. She placed it next to her leg, furtively glanced downward, and dialed 9-1-1.

CHAPTER
TWO

"WHERE ARE YOU TAKING ME?" Sarah's question was met with a grunt. She asked more emphatically, "Where. Are. You. Taking. Me?!"

"Shut the fuck up."

Sarah pushed the buttons on her cell phone again hoping the police would find her. She looked out the window, staring at the scenery. Sarah had been gone from Kansas City for nearly two years and nothing looked familiar. She had never seen this part of town. Was she nearing the Country Club Plaza or still in Westport?

"Why are you doing this?" Sarah asked.

Instead of answering her, he turned the volume up on the radio. The music thumped and vibrated the car seat. When they approached a stoplight, Sarah started to look around, trying to find a way to escape. Even if Sarah found a place to run, she didn't know how she would get out of the car.

The car began to slow as the man pulled into an empty parking lot. Sleet began to ping the windows and hood of the car. Sarah could see Christmas lights twinkling on the buildings in the distance. The man got out of the car and walked around the front towards the passenger side. Sarah scrambled to climb over the seat to the driver's side door. Before she could get the door open and climb out, the man was at her door. He had one hand on the top of the car and the other on the door frame.

Sarah saw the opportunity, clutched her little purse, ducked under his arm, and ran.

Sarah's swift exit startled him, but her stride was no match for his. She ran about fifty feet then felt his arm slide around her waist as he tackled her to the ground. They landed in a pile, face first, and slid around in the cold mud. The man began to yank at Sarah's clothing. She tried to scream but the words wouldn't come out. She wanted to fight back but was frozen in shock. The sound of a dog barking nearby seemed to startle the man. Suddenly he stopped groping her, pulled her up from the ground, and forced her back inside the car.

When he slammed the car door Sarah realized she still had her purse. She reached inside and pushed the redial button on her cellphone. The radio was loud, but she tried asking the man questions, hoping the call taker could hear her and track the call.

"Why'd you take me? Where are we going? What are you going to do to me?"

The man mumbled incoherent responses and turned the radio up even louder. Sarah tried to pay attention to where they were, but it seemed like he was driving aimlessly. After what felt like hours, the man pulled the car into an alleyway and parked.

CHAPTER
THREE

SARAH LEANED into the car door skeleton and tried making her body as small as possible. The man grabbed at her body and ripped the buttons off her blouse. Eventually he pulled up her skirt, climbed across the seat, and got on top of her. Sarah turned her head as he tried to put his mouth on hers. The man pulled back, grabbed her head, and tried to force her mouth onto his exposed body. Sarah tried to turn her head away as she gagged on the bile that rose in her throat. He continued to manipulate and pry her legs. Eventually he penetrated her and when he finished, he got back into the driver's seat, and began to drive.

Sarah laid against the seat feeling broken, unclean, and defeated. She stared out the window and cried silently, desperately trying to figure out where they were. She was beginning to doubt she would ever get away from him.

Sarah didn't know how long they drove before the car began slowing down. The man parked in the driveway behind a small house, turned to her, and said, "Try anything and I will kill you."

Sarah nodded and looked out the window for a street sign or a house number but couldn't see anything in the dark.

"Where are we?"

"Don't you worry about *where* we are. Just do what I say, and you'll be fine."

The man stepped out of the car and stared at her through the windshield as he walked in front of the car. She held her purse close to her body and waited for him to open the door. This time he blocked the opening to prevent her from running.

Sarah stepped out of the car and felt the moist, cold air against her skin. The sleet had stopped, and the air smelled like snow. The man gripped her arm tightly and pushed Sarah up the uneven driveway. His grip steadied her when she stumbled. The man pushed her onto the small back porch and opened the door into a dark kitchen. The only light in the room came from the clock on the stove.

Sarah felt it had been hours since she was at the club. Looking at the clock she thought, "*Is it really only 130?*"

The sound of a familiar sitcom came from a nearby room. The man increased the grip on her arm and growled, "Don't say a fucking word."

He led her into a small bedroom next to the kitchen and shoved her onto the bed. Sarah scooted herself to the top of the bed, pulled her knees up to her chest, and pressed her back into the wall. Then she waited.

From a distant room, a woman's voice asked, "Tre, is that you?"

"Don't say a word. Don't. Move."

Tre walked out of the room, shutting the door behind him. Sarah could hear him talking to someone but couldn't quite make out *what* he was saying. She dialed her cell phone, hoping she could tell the call taker enough that they would come look for her. He walked in just as she hit the send button. She disconnected the call and quickly shoved the phone back into her purse.

Tre didn't say a word. He undid his pants, pulled her skirt up, and pushed himself inside her. She cried and tried to push his heavy body off hers, but he was too strong. When he was finished, he stood up and said, "Let's go."

Sarah sat up and tried to straighten her clothes. Her trembling fingers fumbled to find buttons that weren't there. Tears fell silently down her face.

"Come on," Tre grunted.

He led Sarah out the way they had come, but once outside he steered her toward a different car. She was suddenly grateful she had kept the purse she clutched next to her side.

Her fingers traced the outline of the hidden phone.

CHAPTER
FOUR

"WHERE ARE YOU TAKING ME TRE?"

"How do you know my name?" he asked gruffly.

"I heard it before. At the house. Where are we going?" Sarah asked.

"I've got things to do." With those words, he turned up the volume on the radio.

Sarah watched the houses pass by outside the window. After a few blocks, they turned onto the highway and drove away from the city.

"Why don't you let me go?" Sarah pleaded. "I promise I won't tell anyone. I just want to go home."

"Shut up."

Sarah turned back towards the window, bit her lip, and watched for landmarks. Eventually the city lights faded, and the exits became less frequent. The further from the city they got the more terrified Sarah became. It suddenly struck her that he was taking her to the country. He was planning to kill her and dump her body where she wouldn't be found.

Sarah reached for the door handle and to herself she thought, *"If I'm going to die, I'll take my chances and jump."*

When the car began to slow near an exit, she removed her hand from the door handle, and asked, "Are you going to kill me?"

"Bitch if I was going to kill you, you'd already be dead."

Sarah took small comfort in his words. Tre pulled into the deserted parking lot of a small gas station. Parking near the door he said, "If you try to get out it'll be the last thing you do."

Tre lifted his shirt to show the grip of a handgun sticking out of his waistband.

Sarah watched Tre walk into the store and go towards the cooler. When she was certain he couldn't see her, she grabbed her cellphone and dialed 9-1-1. Again.

"Grandview 9-1-1."

"He won't let me go. I'm scared. He raped me. He said he would kill me."

"Where are you?"

"I don't know. A gas station. On the Plaza?"

With surprise the operator asked, *"Where?"*

"I don't know."

"What does he look like?"

"I've got to go. He's coming. Please! Help me!"

Sarah shoved the phone back into her bag just as Tre opened the car door. She wondered to herself if they would find her this time. How many times had she called 9-1-1?

Tre pulled out of the parking lot and asked, "Can you get money?"

Sarah looked at him questioningly. She had just gotten paid so she had a little money in her account, but she didn't know how much her bank would let her get out at the ATM.

"Maybe," was her meek reply.

Gruffly Tre said, "You better hope so."

Sarah did.

Tre pulled back onto the highway and drove north, back towards the city. Sarah tried to focus on landmarks, signs, anything that would help her identify where she was. When the highway split, Tre took the road opposite the one they had come and sped up. Within minutes, she noticed lights and exits leading towards businesses. Eventually she saw what looked like a shopping center.

Tre took the exit and asked, "Do you have your debit card?"

Sarah nodded in the dark.

"I asked if you had your card."

"I have it."

A few blocks later Tre pulled next to a bank ATM in a strip mall parking lot.

"How much can you get?"

"I...uh...I don't know," Sarah stuttered.

"What's your number?"

"I'm not sure. I just push it in. Can you just let me try it?"

"Bitch you better not be trying nothing. Get over here and put the number in."

"Uh…uh...okay."

Sarah inserted the card, looked in the camera, and mouthed the words, *"Help me."* She entered her PIN and requested the maximum amount.

"Don't hold out on me bitch," Tre growled as he counted the cash.

"I can try again," Sarah softly answered.

"Do it."

Climbing over his lap, she typed in the PIN, looked in the camera, and again mouthed the words, *"Help me."*

The machine declined her request. She knew it would but recognized there was no need arguing with him. She knew it wouldn't end well.

Pushing her back into the passenger seat, Tre pulled away from the machine. Moments later he was back on the highway, heading back towards the city.

"Will you please let me go? I promise…"

"Shut up."

Sarah sat back in the seat, rested her head against the headrest, and resigned herself to her fate. Tears fell from her dark eyes and down her cheeks. Silently she began to say the Lord's Prayer.

Aloud she whispered, "Please let it be quick."

CHAPTER
FIVE

SEVERAL MINUTES PASSED before Sarah said, "Tre, I really need to go to the bathroom."

Tre grunted.

"Look, if you don't stop somewhere I'm going to wet my pants. Please?"

He drove a few more blocks before pulling into another gas station. Sarah scanned the neighborhood outside the car window. The street was empty, but the parking lot was well lit. The nearest house was half a block away and she didn't see any other businesses. There was nowhere for her to go so she waited.

Before he got out of the car Tre said, "If you try anything inside the store, I'll kill you."

Sarah's shoulders curved inward as she shrunk away from him. The steely gaze of his eyes caused an involuntary shiver to run down her spine. She stepped out, looked around, then walked to the front of the car where Tre was waiting.

Tre shoved her through the store door.

"Hey Tre," said the clerk. "How's your momma?"

Before Tre could answer, Sarah timidly asked the clerk, "Where's the bathroom?"

The clerk gestured towards the back of the store, "Back there."

Sarah held her blouse closed and clutched her purse tightly to her body. She shuffled towards the partially opened bathroom door.

Behind her she could hear the clerk ask Tre, "Who's that girl? What's wrong with her?"

Tre mumbled a response.

"She looks scared Tre. Like she doesn't want to be with you. Why don't you just let her go? Why're you messin' with her?"

Sarah could hear Tre mumbling – something about 'those white bitch- es.' She hoped the clerk would talk some sense into Tre. Maybe he'd just leave her there. Or maybe the clerk would do something to help her. Maybe the clerk would help her get home.

Sarah locked the door and dialed 9-1-1. When the operator answered she whispered, "I'm at the Fast Stop. I've been raped."

Suddenly she could hear Tre stomping towards the bathroom. She hung up her cellphone when he started kicking the door. The clerk yelled at him to stop but Tre continued to kick. Sarah watched as the pins loos- ened at the hinges. She shoved the phone back into her purse, turned the water on, and washed her hands. Sarah splashed water on her face, removed a five-dollar bill from her purse, and wrote "please help me!" She shoved the bill back into her purse and slowly opened the door.

"What the hell were you doing in there?"

"I, uh, was just, uh, using the bathroom." Attempting to act like nothing was wrong she asked, "Can I get a bottle of water?"

"Hurry up," he growled.

Sarah walked to the cooler slowly, hoping the clerk would do some- thing. She picked up a bottle of water and shuffled back to the counter.

"A dollar nine," said the clerk.

Sarah placed the five-dollar bill on the counter and prayed the clerk would read it and do something. Sarah made eye contact with the clerk, lowered her eyes to the bill, and then quickly raised them back to the girl. The clerk gave her the change, picked up her magazine, and went back to flipping pages.

"Tell your momma I said hi," the clerk said.

With a grunt Tre grabbed Sarah's arm and led her out of the store. Sarah hesitated in front of the store and surveyed her surroundings poised to run.

Tre stood at the front of the car, raised his shirt, and said, "Get in the car bitch."

Sarah looked back to the store clerk then got into the car. The clerk looked up just as Tre raised his shirt, then quickly looked back down. Once she was sure they were gone the clerk pulled the bill from the register and looked at it. She read the words written across the paper, picked up the cordless phone, then returned it to its cradle. She picked up her magazine and stared at the page.

CHAPTER
SIX

THEY WERE SOON on the highway again. Tre drove north on the empty road and after what seemed like minutes exited onto another side street. The houses turned to businesses and Sarah began to recognize the store fronts. She thought they were on the same road earlier in the evening when she went to meet her friends. If so, Tre was heading back to Westport. The car began to slow and sputter before finally coming to a stop in the middle of the street.

Tre looked at her and growled, "Stay here."

Sarah watched Tre get out of the car and knew this was her only chance to get away. If she didn't make a run for it, he might kill her. She waited until he lifted the hood of the car then slowly opened the door, praying he wouldn't hear it creak. She crept out of the car then began to run. Sarah could hear him yelling but didn't turn around to see if he was following her.

Sarah didn't know where she was going other than away from him. Sarah darted through a yard, slipped on the wet leaves, and landed face first on the ground. She scrambled back to her feet and continued to run towards a better lit area. Sarah glanced over her shoulder and looked to see if he was following her. She couldn't see him but didn't stop running. Suddenly Sarah could see businesses and lights ahead. She didn't know what time it was but hoped someone would still be out.

Once she was on the street with businesses surrounding her, she pulled her cellphone from her purse. Sarah pressed the numbers quickly, from memory, and when she heard his voice, she choked back a sob.

"Daddy…help me."

Clearing his throat, he asked, "Where are you, Sarah? Are you okay?"

The sobs overcame her. Sarah struggled to get any words out.

"Sarah, are you okay?"

"Daddy, I'm so scared."

Sarah's father jumped out of the bed, began to search for his glasses, and asked "Where are you baby girl?"

Seeing a security guard, she yelled, "Please help me!" Sarah stumbled over to the guarded and handed him the phone. "Can you please tell my daddy where we are?"

The security guard gave Sarah's father the address.

"Will you please stay with her until I can get there?" he asked.

"Yes sir. I'll make sure the police get called too," the security guard replied.

Sarah sat down on the curb and wept. Her body hurt everywhere but she was finally safe. Her dad was coming. Tre couldn't hurt her now.

CHAPTER
SEVEN

THE SHRILL RING of the telephone pierced the night. Breathing heavily, Detective Francesca "Frankie" Thomas, struggled to extricate herself from the tangled sheets to silence the sound. Grabbing the phone, she grunted, "Dammit!"

Looking at the caller-id she answered, "Detective Thomas."

Frankie wrapped the sheet around her taut, naked body, and grabbed the pen and notepad lying on the bedside table. The only light in the room came from the alarm clock next to the bed.

Frankie turned the bedside lamp on as she peppered the caller with questions, jotting the answers onto her notepad.

"Where is she now? Is there anyone in custody? Where are you?"

Frankie glanced at the clock, "I should be there in about thirty minutes. No, I'll call Crime Scene en route."

Frankie disconnected the phone, laid back onto the bed, and hit the pillow with her hands. "Dammit."

The howl of the wind echoed in the dark room. Derek rolled over, lifted himself up onto his elbow, and placed his other hand across her abdomen. The sheets slipped to his narrow waist as he leaned down and kissed Frankie gently on the nose.

"Tell me it ain't so."

"Sorry babe. Duty calls. Trust me, I'd much rather stay here tangled up in these sheets with you."

Frankie gently traced the pink scar on Derek's side with the tips of her fingers, remembering. She sighed, sat up in the bed, and got dressed to leave.

"Where're you headed? Is it still raining?"

Frankie gathered her things, as she answered, "Westport. Kidnap and rape. A security guard found a girl wandering in the streets and called 9-1-1. They sent her to County Hospital, but officers are still on the scene. I'm going to go there first then head over to the hospital. There's no one in custody so I'm betting it'll only take three- or four-hours tops."

Derek followed Frankie to the kitchen, walked up, and stood behind her. Frankie grabbed her holstered gun from the table and slid it over her belt.

"Famous last words, but just in case you need an incentive to hurry back..."

Standing a full head taller than Frankie's five feet Derek leaned down and brushed the nape of her neck with his lips, letting them slide downwards towards her collarbone. His hands encircled her waist.

An involuntary moan escaped Frankie's lips as she said, "Seriously, I have to go...but I'll be back."

Derek turned Frankie to face him and covered her mouth with his, smothering the sound of her words. When he was certain he had left her aching for more he released his grip and said, "Wake me up when you're finished." Derek winked and squeezed her butt when she turned to walk towards the door then added, "Feel free to be creative."

Walking out the door, Frankie touched her fingers to her lips and mumbled, "Absolutely."

CHAPTER
EIGHT

FRANKIE DROVE to Westport in silence. Derek lived at the northernmost edge of the city, but the twenty-minute drive went quickly. As she listened to the chatter on the police radio her mind began to wander. It had been over a month, but she could remember the day like it had just happened.

A local gang member had been accused of murdering a four-year-old girl in a drive-by shooting. Derek was a county prosecutor and a jury had just handed down a guilty verdict. He and his co-counsel, Jessica Moon, were leaving the courthouse together when an SUV rolled up. The pair were standing by Derek's car when the shooter laid down fire hitting Derek and Jessica multiple times. Frankie's old patrol partner, Mac, was the first on the scene and once the scene was stable, he called her.

Frankie had just gotten a break in a rape case involving an organized crime family, but as soon as she could she broke away and went to the hospital to check on Derek. As fate would have it, when Frankie was leaving the hospital her neighbor, Bruce was being wheeled into the Emergency Department. One of the men involved in her case had attempted to kidnap her daughter, but Bruce intervened and was shot in the process.

Frankie solved her case and Bruce was recovering nicely, but something inside her died that night. For the first time in her career, she was beginning to wonder if it was worth it.

When Frankie finally got back to the hospital to see Derek, he was coding. She watched the nurses and doctors surround his body and attempt to bring him back to life after he arrested. Frankie stood outside of his room, alone and frightened; wondering if he was going to live or die. It would be hours before anyone would tell her he was going to be okay. Derek and Jessica were touch and go for several days but fortunately both lived, and the shooter was in custody awaiting trial.

The closer Frankie got to the City of Fountains the clearer the skies became, and the memories were packed away. The streets were empty except for a few stray cars. The lateness of the hour and the coldness in the air kept people inside who would otherwise stroll the streets at night. Frankie slowed her car when she saw the rotating blue and red lights marking the crime scene.

CHAPTER
NINE

FRANKIE LEANED against the patrol car taking notes as Officer Jack Meyers described what occurred prior to her arriving. Frankie had known Meyers since she graduated from the Police Academy. He had been her field training officer and put her through the ropes to make sure she could handle herself once she finished break-in. They had forged a close friendship and continued to be partners until the next class produced a fresh set of recruits.

"He's new. I think he's been out of the academy maybe three or four days. Poor kid stumbled all over himself," laughed Meyers.

"Make sure you help him write the report. I know boots need practice handling these types of calls, but their reports tend to be poorly written."

"You were new at one time too kid," chastised Meyers.

"I know, but I had a hard ass for a field training officer, so my reports were always good." Frankie winked at Meyers.

"Hmm, I guess that's true. I'll tell his FTO to make sure the report is done right."

"Thanks. What's the victim's name?"

Looking at his notes Meyers answered, "Smedley. Sarah Smedley." He looked at his feet, then back up at Frankie. Almost under his breath he said, "Damn. This one's legit. She looked so scared, and her eyes were... empty. Her hair was all over the place and full of mud and leaves. The buttons on her blouse were missing too. What really got me was she was walking around holding her panties in her hand."

Frankie took note of what Meyers was saying, then asked, "Where's her car?"

Meyers gestured over his shoulder to a lot empty but for one car. "It's that one over there but by all counts he was never near her car."

"Do we have a description on him?"

"Black male over six feet. The Vic's pretty tall and she said he was taller than her and built like a football player. She described him as having a light complexion and light eyes."

"Description on the car?"

Meyer flipped through his notes and said, "That's a weird thing. She said there were two cars. The last one was a black Chevy Capris with a temp tag."

"Two cars?"

"Yeah. He forced her into a red sedan over there," Meyers pointed towards the curb in front of a bar about fifty yards away. "But at some point in the night he switched cars."

"Did the rape occur inside the cars or at some other location around here?"

"There was more than one rape at more than one location, but she didn't seem to think any of them were around here. At least one occurred in the first car, but we don't know where it is."

"Where did Sarah say she first come into contact with him?"

Jack pointed to the sidewalk in front of the comedy club across the street, "Over there. She was walking from the dance club towards the corner, trying to find her car. She was turned around and couldn't remember where she parked."

Frankie scanned the area then stood quietly looking at the notes on her notepad. The storefronts were dark so she wouldn't know if there were any surveillance videos available until the next day.

Frankie grabbed the camera she kept in her bag and started taking photographs of the area. She was almost finished when something caught her attention. Lying on the street, halfway to the corner, was a cellphone case. Frankie snapped a couple photographs and with a gloved hand, picked it up off the ground. The light blue case had a mermaid with a crack that split it in half.

"Hey Jack!"

"Yeah."

Showing him the phone case, Frankie asked, "Does this mean anything to you?"

"Not really," he said. Scanning his notes he added. "Wait. She said he threw her phone out of the car. I guess it could have come from her phone, but I don't see one laying around anywhere."

Frankie dropped the phone case into a paper envelope, "Hmm, me either."

Once she was sure she had all she needed Frankie turned to Meyers and told him he could release the scene.

"I'm going to head to County to talk to her. Can you please make sure the recruit gets his report in the system before the end of his shift?"

"Will do Frankie."

FRANKIE WALKED through the doors of the Emergency Department and stood frozen in place. The sounds and smells of the busy place were muffled as memories enveloped her. Bruce coming in on a gurney with her daughter Dani following, her clothes tattered. The look of fear on Keith's face when he walked through the doors holding her son Tyler's hand. The site of medical personnel working to resuscitate Derek when he coded. The sounds of the machines rang in her ears. Frankie jumped at a touch on her shoulder.

"Can I help you?" asked the charge nurse.

Frankie wiped the tears that had escaped her eyes, "I'm here to talk to Sarah Smedley. She was brought in for a forensic exam."

They walked to the nurse's station where the nurse checked the computer, looked up, and said, "Looks like the doctor already cleared her. They moved her to the forensic exam room. It's 6b – down the hall."

"Thank you."

The walk to 6b was familiar. Frankie was about to knock on the closed door when the forensic nurse, Jennifer Jacobson, walked out. Jennifer was a short, stout nurse who had worked in the Emergency Department for over thirty years and had built the forensic program from the ground up. She was a typical Emergency Room nurse with zero tolerance for nonsense. Jennifer was a force of nature with a big heart who had been known to handle a belligerent drunk sternly one minute then move heaven and earth to help a victim of domestic or sexual violence the next. Jennifer spent many a long night with victims trying to make an invasive, potentially humiliating, experience as tolerable as possible. Frankie had learned so much about compassion, forensics, and people by watching and listening to Jennifer. Over time she had become both a mentor and friend to Frankie.

"We haven't started the exam yet. You can go on in and talk to her. I collected her clothes and swabbed her mouth so she could have some water and a blanket. Beth is with her. We'll finish up when you're done."

"Thanks Jen," Frankie said.

Frankie stepped inside the small, sterile exam room. The face greeting her from the exam table was red with streaks of mascara dissecting her cheeks. Sticks, leaves, and dirt protruded from Sarah's shoulder-length, raven-colored hair. Dried blood created a crusty glue that held hair against her olive skin. Frankie noticed traces of dirt on Sarah's nose, chin, and ears. She was long and lean but didn't appear frail. Her hands were dirty, and her nails were chipped and broken.

"Sarah?"

She opened her eyes and acknowledged Frankie's presence in the room.

"My name is Detective Frankie Thomas. I work for the Kansas City Missouri Police Department, and I'll be the detective working your case."

Sarah searched Frankie's face; her eyes were wild with fright.

"Do you mind if I sit down?"

Sarah nodded her head in agreement.

Frankie pulled the digital recorder out of her pocket, moved the stool closer to the side of the bed and asked, "Can you tell me what happened?"

Sarah sighed and shivered involuntarily. Looking towards the advocate sitting next to her, she quietly asked, "May I please have another blanket?" Looking back at Frankie she asked, "Where do I begin?"

"Just tell me what you remember, how you remember it. Maybe start with when you got to Westport."

CHAPTER
ELEVEN

"I just moved back to Missouri a few weeks ago. I'd been living in Seattle the last five years and my friends wanted to take me out as a welcome home. I had to work late so instead of riding together I met them at the bar. It was probably 7:30 or so when I finally got there. I moved away when I was eighteen, so I'd never been to any of the clubs in Westport and was excited. I was raised not to drink alcohol. My mom and dad didn't really approve but I'm twenty-three so there wasn't a lot they could say.

"We started out at Latitudes. I had a couple drinks and shared some appetizers with my friends. Everyone was having fun. We were reminiscing and catching each other up on our lives. No one wanted to see the night end so about 10 o'clock we decided to go to the Pub to dance. It was so much fun. We danced nonstop for a couple of hours. I started getting hot and a little lightheaded, so I stepped outside to get some air. I noticed there was an empty parking space across from the Pub and it hit me that the parking lot across from Latitudes, where I parked, had signs that said two-hour parking. I didn't want my car to get towed and I can't afford a ticket, so I decided to go move it.

"I thought the parking lot was closer than it was. I didn't think it would take long and didn't tell my friends where I was going. Since the lot was close to Latitudes, I had left my coat in the car. It was cold - the wind felt like a knife cutting through me. I was about to go back inside to borrow a friend's coat when Tre started talking to me. He was making small talk and offered to give me a ride. I told him no, but he put his coat around my shoulders and shoved me into a car."

Sarah paused, took a drink of water, and blew her nose. She attempted to wipe away the tears falling down her face, took a deep breath, and slowly exhaled before continuing.

"Once I was inside the car, I reached down to open the door to get out. Only," Sarah stifled an audible moan of distress, "The handle was missing. Actually, the whole door panel was missing. Then he drove past the parking lot. I saw my car and told him to stop. I told him my car was in that lot, but he told me to shut up. That's when I knew I was in serious trouble. I wasn't sure where he was going to take me or what he was going to do so I grabbed my phone and tried to dial 9-1-1. That really made him angry. He grabbed the phone from me and threw it out the window. I watched it break into pieces on the road."

Sarah laid her head back onto the pillow and closed her eyes. Frankie waited patiently, knowing better than to rush the process. The missing advocate silently entered the room and placed the warmed blanket over Sarah.

Softly, Sarah said, "Thank you."

Beth touched Sarah's hand, nodded her head, and sat on a chair.

Sarah looked over at Frankie, gave a sideways smile, and smirked, "But he didn't know I had another phone. I didn't want him to see it so when he wasn't looking, I moved my purse between my leg and the door. I slipped the phone out of the bag and pressed it under my leg slightly so I wouldn't have to hold it. I pressed 9-1-1. I really thought the police would find me. He had the music up pretty loud, but I thought the operator could hear me and would send a car to look for me." Wistfully Sarah whispered, "But no one came."

"Sarah had you ever seen this man before?"

Shaking her head, Sarah said, "No."

"Sarah, can I ask why you have two cell phones?"

"I work for a cell phone company. They pay for me to have a phone as part of my benefits. I still have a contract with another provider, so I keep it on in case my other phone dies."

"Makes sense. Did you have a case on the phone he threw out of the car?"

"Yeah."

"What did it look like?"

"It was light blue with a mermaid on it. I don't think it would protect the phone, but it was cute."

"Thank you. What happened next?"

Frankie listened intently as Sarah shared her experience. She told the story in fragments, not in a linear fashion. Frankie made notes while she listened, paying special attention to her demeanor. Sarah's tears and trembling hands told of the fear she felt. When Sarah finished, Frankie softly exhaled. She watched as Sarah wiped more tears from her face.

"He drove all over the place again. It was like he wasn't sure where he wanted to go. At one point, he stopped at a gas station. I don't know for sure where it was, but I think it was near the Plaza again. He got out of the car to go inside so I called 9-1-1. Again. I thought for sure the police would find me this time."

Frankie noticed a pattern. Sarah called 9-1-1 and no one responded. She understood why – the call-takers didn't have the technology to ping the cell and may not have been sure it wasn't a prank or a misdial. Especially with loud music and no one talking. But Frankie also understood the frustration Sarah must have felt.

"He just drove around with the music blaring. I held the phone by my leg and dialed 9-1-1 again. I kept thinking I would see police cars come up behind us. But nothing. He was acting really weird. Disorganized. At one point I finally told him I had to go to the bathroom. At first it was like he didn't hear me or just didn't care, but he eventually stopped at another gas station. Before I got out, he told me if I said or did anything he was going to kill me. When we got inside the clerk called him by name. It scared the heck out of me, but there was a part of me that was hopeful. Maybe, since it was a woman, she would help me."

Sarah stopped, took a deep breath followed by a long drink of water.

"He kind of kept his arm on me as we went inside. I asked her where the bathroom was. She pointed to the back of the store. While I was inside, I could hear him talking about 'those white b-words.' He was really angry. The clerk was talking to him about me not looking like I wanted to be there, so I thought maybe she was going to help me. Once I locked the door, I called 9-1-1. I told the lady that answered I had been raped and was at a gas station, but I didn't know where. I really believed this time someone would come. While I was talking to 9-1-1 he started kicking on the door. I didn't want him to catch me with the phone, so I hung up and turned the water on. Then it dawned on me, I could write a note on money. If he would let me buy something I could pass it to the clerk. I grabbed a five-dollar bill and wrote 'please help me' on the back and shoved it back into my purse. He was still kicking the door but before he could break down the door, I opened it up. I just looked at him like, 'what?' He let me buy some water and when I gave the girl the bill, I tried to give her a look so she would look at the message. She just snatched the money and gave me my change. I didn't know what else to do. He grabbed my arm and forced me outside to the car.

"Eventually he took me to an ATM and told me to withdraw all my money. I just got paid but my bank only lets me take out $300 a day. I took out as much as I could and gave it to him."

"Do you know where the ATM was? Or what bank it was?"

Sarah laid against the bed, slightly pensive, and after a few moments said, "I think it was Bank of …" Sarah paused before exclaiming, "Wait, get my purse! I got a receipt and shoved it in my purse."

Frankie couldn't believe it. ATMs have cameras and with any luck they would have a picture of the suspect and the suspect's car in a few hours.

Sarah handed the receipt to Frankie, "Here you go."

Frankie looked at the receipt. Bank of America. The dollar amount confirmed what Sarah had said. The location numbers on the receipt should lead them to the address of the ATM. Frankie just hoped Bank of America would give over the video or photographs quickly.

"Tell me about what happened after you left the ATM?"

"Something seemed different. He was still driving around but then I started to recognize buildings. After a while the car started sputtering and acting weird, and then finally stalled out. He told me to stay in the car while he checked to see what was wrong. When he got in front of the car with the hood up, I opened the door and started to run."

CHAPTER
TWELVE

SARAH WAS BREATHING HEAVILY, as though she were running a race. She asked for more water, took a long drink, and hesitated before beginning again.

Frankie sat and waited, comfortable with the silence while Sarah processed what happened.

"I don't know how long I ran but I finally realized he wasn't following me, so I stopped to call my dad. A security guard found me wandering around. He talked to my dad so he would know where to come pick me up. One of them called the police."

"I think I know the answer to this but, Sarah I have to ask you a question. When you got away, why did you call your dad instead of 9-1-1?"

Sarah took another long drink of water. Softly she answered, "I had called 9-1-1 several times and no one came. I was scared. I thought he was going to come find me and kill me. I knew if I called my dad he'd come. He'd protect me."

Frankie nodded in understanding.

"Do you remember the name of the gas station where you got the bottle of water?"

"No, but I'd probably recognize it if I saw it again."

Frankie looked at her notes and asked, "Did you see him at Latitudes or the Pub? Or anywhere else tonight?"

"No."

"Earlier you mentioned 'Tre' started talking to you. How did you know his name?"

"When he took me to the house, I heard someone call him by name. The store clerk called him by Tre too."

"Okay. Can you tell me what Tre looked like? What was he wearing?"

Sarah laid her head back on the pillow and closed her eyes. Frankie watched her hands begin to tremble. Sarah's eyes moved back and forth under her eyelids.

After a few moments, she answered.

"He was tall. I'm 5'10" and he was a head taller than me. He was big but not fat. More muscular. Like a football player. He was strong. He was black, but not real dark. He had real short hair and I think he had light colored eyes."

"How old do you think he was?"

"*My age?*" Sarah said in more of a question than a statement. "I'm 23. He was probably close to my age. Within a couple of years at least. He had on blue jeans and a dark colored hoody."

Before Frankie could ask any additional questions, Jen opened the door.

"Are you about done Frankie?"

"Yeah, I think I have what I need Jen." Turning to Sarah, Frankie asked, "Do you have any questions for me?"

Sarah shook her head. Frankie gave Sarah all her contact information and told her she'd call her in the next few days. As she gathered her things to go, she heard softly, "Thank you Detective Thomas."

Frankie looked over her shoulder and nodded then walked out the door.

THIRTEEN

FRANKIE WALKED to her car slowly. She looked at her watch while she placed her bag in the passenger seat. 4 A.M. She stretched her back and walked around to the driver's side. Once inside the car she made a list of things she needed to follow-up on.

"What the hell is wrong with people?" she asked aloud.

Once she finished her list, Frankie pulled out of the garage, and headed back to Derek's house. This was the first weekend she had stayed with him since he had been released from the hospital. Her children, Danielle and Tyler, were staying the night at her dad's house so she had no reason to go home. She listened to the officers' chatter on the car radio and drove with purpose.

Derek's black Lab, Bear, greeted Frankie at the back door with a deep bark.

Patting his head, she said, "Shh Bear, It's just me."

Frankie dropped her bag on the chair and laid her holstered gun on the kitchen table. She was tired but didn't think she'd be able to sleep, and Derek needed his rest. So, instead of going back to bed she grabbed a bottle of Bud Light, a throw blanket, and sat on the couch. She rested her head against the back of the sofa and sighed as she inhaled the familiar smells of leather and Derek's cologne. In the silence, Frankie sipped the cold drink and thought about Sarah's story. Bear jumped onto the couch, curled up next to her, and laid his head on her lap. Frankie smiled and stroked the dog's soft fur and felt the stress leave her body.

She didn't know how long she sat there before she heard Derek shuffling down the hall. Bear's ears perked up at the scent of his master, but he didn't move from Frankie and the attention she was giving him.

"Hey babe, are you okay? I thought you'd wake me up when you got back."

Frankie thought she heard a spark of disappointment in Derek's voice.

"I'm sorry. I haven't been here long. I just needed a minute to unwind."

Derek sat down on the arm of the sofa, put an arm around Frankie, kissed the top of her head and asked, "Want to talk about it?"

She laid her head against his chest and sighed.

"You'd think I'd get used to these stories by now."

Derek rested his chin on the top of Frankie's head and said, "I hope you never get used to them."

Light began to filter through the blinds while they sat in silence; each lost in their thoughts. Frankie stroked Bear's fur and Derek gently stroked her arm. After a few minutes, he stood up and took Frankie by the hand.

"Come here."

Derek led Frankie to the kitchen and opened the blinds covering the French doors. He pulled her body in front of his and wrapped his arms around her. Frankie leaned into Derek's embrace, resting the back of her head against his chest. She covered his hands with hers and together they watched the sun rise just beyond the pond.

"Mmmm. Just what I needed."

Kissing the top of Frankie's head Derek mumbled, "Me too."

The two stood in silence watching the sun as it continued to ascend. Frankie's thoughts centered on where to begin with her case and Derek tried to forget the nightmare that woke him. This one was particularly vivid. He felt the sting of the sand hitting his face. He heard the blades from the helicopter chopping the air overhead and smelled the rancid odor from the sewer that flanked the base. In his dream, he looked up and saw the face of his best friend Kyle in the helicopter, then heard the explosion. He felt the heat of the fireball on his skin and the loss of his friend in his gut. When the first piece of metal hit the ground, he bolted awake in a cold sweat.

Several years had passed since Derek witnessed the helicopter crash that killed his best friend in Afghanistan. The nightmares had been brutal right after the accident, but over time they had lessened. After he was shot, they came back with a vengeance. The doctors told Derek he had died. Actually, they said he was dead for more than three minutes. This fact was never far from his mind. Now when he slept, *if* he slept, he often woke up screaming or in a cold sweat. In his dreams, he was either in Afghanistan or lying in the parking lot behind the courthouse. Derek jumped at Frankie's slight turn away from the door.

"Are you okay?"

"Huh? Yeah, I'm fine. You surprised me when you moved that's all." Derek hoped Frankie accepted his excuse at face value. He let his arm fall from her shoulder as she turned to walk back towards his bedroom.

"Okay. I'm going to go jump in the shower," Frankie said.

"Want some company?" Derek asked.

Frankie winked at Derek and motioned for him to follow her.

CHAPTER
FOURTEEN

"MOM! WHERE ARE MY SHOES?"

"I can't find my book bag and I need this field trip paper signed."

"I need lunch money, mom."

Frankie took pleasure in the sounds of morning at the Thomas household and dreaded the day when it would be silent. She donned her cold weather running gear, laced her sneakers, and put the leash on her Golden Retriever Isabelle.

"Tyler, your shoes are in the basket by the door. I put lunch money in your bag. Danielle your book bag is hanging on the back of *your* door. Give me the paper so I can sign it. Why didn't you give it to me last night? You know the rules."

"I forgot," Danielle got her bag and thrust the paper at Frankie, "Can you just sign it?"

"Watch your tone, Danielle Elizabeth. It's too early in the morning."

Dani snatched the signed paper, shoved it in her bag, and grumbled, "Yes ma'am."

Tyler looked up at Frankie expectantly, "Mom, are you working tonight?"

She knelt to meet him at eye level, "I am bud, but then I'll be off the next couple of days. Okay?"

With a disappointed sigh he said, "Okay."

Dani put her arm around her brother and said, "Come on little brother. Let's get moving. How about I meet you at the bus stop and walk home with you today?"

Tyler's eyes lit up with excitement, "Really?"

Laughing she ruffled his hair and said, "Yeah really."

"Ye-us!" Tyler lifted his knee and pulled his fist down from the air in excitement.

Frankie smiled at their exchange. She caught Dani's eye and mouthed, "Thank you."

Dani nodded and pushed Tyler out the door. Frankie and Isabelle followed close behind.

After dropping the kids off at their respective schools Frankie took Isabelle to the park for a run. She didn't normally like to run in the cold but wanted some fresh air. With Daughtry blasting through her headphones, she let the music set her pace. With each step, she felt the stress leave her body. After two laps Frankie's thoughts turned to her latest case. Mentally she started going through the list of all the follow-up she needed to do.

Forty-five minutes later Frankie was filling the dog's water bowl and putting a roast in the crockpot for the kids' dinner. HGTV provided the background to her morning chores. By noon she had laundry started, her clothes ironed for work, and a clean kitchen.

Frankie was at her desk by 3pm reviewing the recruit officer's report. Mia walked in just in time to hear her say,

"What the hell?"

"Good afternoon to you too."

"Oh, hey Mia. I'm just trying to figure out who the hell approved this report. A boot wrote it and it's awful. Jack Meyers was on the scene. His description and what's in this report aren't even remotely close."

"Didn't Meyers used to work in SVU?"

"Yep. I'm going to call the field training officer and see if he can get it fixed." Frankie started dialing the patrol station's front desk while saying to Mia, "What does your night look like?"

"I was planning to catch up on reports. What'd you have in mind?"

"I'm going to pull the locations linked to the 9-1-1 calls on the case I caught this weekend. Want to go hunting with me?"

"Sure."

Frankie ran a query in the computer aided dispatch system using the victim's two cell phone numbers. The first one hit on a tower in Westport which coincided with what the victim had told her. The remaining calls were all from the second cellphone and scattered all over the City of Fountains. On a lark, she called Belton and Grandview Police Departments, jurisdictions south of the city, and asked them to run a query as well. Grandview found a phone call originating in their city and promised to email it to her.

Frankie reviewed the calls and the notes she made during the victim interview. Some of the locations matched Sarah's statement but others were out of order. She made a note to follow up with her to clarify. Frankie always started by believing the victim and let the facts drive the investigation. The inconsistencies in Sarah's statements could be related to the trauma experienced and its effect on memory. Traumatic memories often held gaps and were rarely revealed in chronological order. Distance and time were frequently distorted. Some of the gaps in memory could be repaired with a couple of sleep cycles, but some memories would be lost forever.

Twenty minutes later Frankie and Mia were in the car with a photograph of the victim and a list of locations to check.

"Let's start at Latitudes. Maybe the bartender or bouncer saw her talking to someone before they went dancing."

"Do we have a description on him?"

"He's a black male, 23-25 years of age. 6'02-6'04" tall with short hair and light eyes. He was wearing blue jeans and a dark hooded sweatshirt."

Mia jotted notes as Frankie drove.

"Did he give her a name?"

"No, but she said the gas station attendant called him 'Tre.'"

"Well, that's a start I guess."

"Yeah, I guess. This case has me fired up."

"Don't they all?" teased Mia.

"True enough. But this one really got to me. This girl called 9-1-1 eleven times. Eleven. Yet no one came to her aid. When she finally got away from him, she didn't call the police she called her dad."

"Of course, she did, Mia sighed. "She knew he'd come."

Mia was a talented detective with good instincts. Taller than Frankie at 5'6" she had short, spiky red hair, fair skin with freckles, and Irish blue eyes. Her hairstyle matched her personality – she was full of fire and spunk. Mia matched Frankie in her passion for the underdog, often championing those who couldn't stand up for themselves. But Frankie knew better than to let Mia's sweet disposition and compassion fool her; she could hold a person to task, setting them straight without blinking an eye.

Frankie had been assigned to be Mia's training detective and in typical "Frankie fashion," Mia was baptized by fire. This meant working many late nights and challenging cases. As a result, the two bonded. They were not only work colleagues, but best friends.

The Sex Crimes Unit did not have assigned partners but after the training period was over, Frankie and Mia continued to work most shifts and cases together. The two frequently bounced ideas and theories off each other, even if they were not working the case together. Their Sergeant often threatened to separate them because it seemed trouble always found them. But as much as he threatened, they knew he was just teasing. They made a good, effective team and put together strong cases for prosecution.

CHAPTER
FIFTEEN

FRANKIE PARKED the unmarked police car in front of Latitudes; the bar where Sarah said she started her evening.

"Let's hope some of the same folks from Saturday are working."

The pair quickly walked to the entrance of the bar, holding their jackets closed to block the cold December wind. The bar was relatively empty but wouldn't stay that way for long. It was the last Monday night football game of the season, and the Kansas City Chiefs were playing. With five big screen televisions the bar would fill up quickly.

The bartender, who was leaning on the bar talking to one of the cocktail waitresses, looked up and said, "Afternoon."

Frankie and Mia approached the pair and introduced themselves. The waitress turned and walked away. Mia nodded to Frankie and followed the waitress.

Frankie looked back to the bartender and asked, "Were you working Saturday night?"

He stood up straight and said, "I was here. Why, what's up?"

"A girl was kidnapped Saturday night, and she said her night began here." Frankie pulled a folder from her bag, handed the bartender a photograph, and asked, "Do you remember seeing this woman?"

Holding the photograph, he said, "There were a lot of people in here Saturday night."

Frankie didn't immediately reply.

"She looks familiar though. Was she here with a group?"

Frankie nodded.

Rubbing his chin, the bartender said, "Yeah, I think I remember seeing her. She came in after her friends. Their waitress was busy with another table, so she came to the bar for a drink. Did you find her?"

"Yeah. Do you remember seeing anyone in the bar watching her?"

"Detective, this place was packed, and you want to know if I remember someone watching *that* girl?"

Frankie didn't reply but maintained eye contact.

With an exasperated exhale the bartender answered, "No. I don't remember seeing anyone *watching* her. In fact, I don't remember seeing her after she got the drink."

While Frankie talked to the bartender about surveillance footage Mia cornered the waitress who had walked away.

"Ma'am."

The young girl turned around to face Mia.

"Yeah?"

"Were you working Saturday night?"

"For a while. Why?"

Pulling a photograph from her bag she asked, "Do you remember seeing this girl in the bar?"

Looking at the woman in the photograph she asked, "Is she okay?"

"She will be. Did you see her Saturday night?"

"Yes, but not here. What happened to her?"

Mia hesitated before answering, "She was kidnapped. Where did you see her?"

The waitress began to fidget. She ran her fingers through her hair and stared out the window. Mia watched an involuntary shiver run down the girl's spine.

"After I got off work, I decided to go to Kelly's to meet some friends. I stopped outside to have a cigarette before going in. That's when I saw her."

CHAPTER
SIXTEEN

FRANKIE APPROACHED Mia and re-introduced herself to the waitress.

"And you are?"

"Nora. Nora Cavanh."

Mia looked at Nora and asked, "Will you tell Detective Thomas what you just told me?"

Nora sat in the chair and laid the cloth napkin she had been holding on the table. Mia and Frankie sat opposite her and waited.

"I left work around 11 or so and decided to meet up with some friends for a drink at Kelly's before heading home. I wanted a cigarette before going inside so I stood on the sidewalk and talked to the bouncer while I smoked. I don't know for sure what exactly caught my eye, but I saw that girl. She was walking next to a guy, but it didn't seem like she was *with* him. You know what I mean? Then..." Nora looked down and began smoothing the wrinkles in the napkin.

Mia spoke softly, "What happened?"

Nora continued to look down at the table.

"They were walking, and he put a coat around her shoulders. At first it seemed innocent. Sweet even. But then when they got next to the car...." Nora looked up from the table. "It looked like he pushed her inside. She didn't yell or do anything, so I figured they were a couple and had gotten into a fight or something. But…"

"But…?"

"When they drove by, I got a look at her face. She had this…this look. Like she was… was scared. I watched them turn on Pennsylvania and go towards Latitudes. When they got by the parking lot across the street from the bar, I saw something fly out the window."

Frankie perked up and asked, "Did you see what it was?"

Nora reached out, grabbed the napkin, and began to wring the fabric in her hands. After a moment, she laid it back onto the table, and smoothed it out again. Nora reached into her apron pocket and produced the remains of a cell phone. She gently laid it on the napkin.

Frankie looked at Mia and raised her eyebrow as if to say, *"Could this be the phone that matches the case I found?"*

Mia gave her a knowing nod.

"I stood there for a minute and waited to see if anyone noticed, but if they did, they didn't do anything. I almost didn't either, but curiosity got the best of me. I waited until the car was out of sight then went and picked it up. It's been in my apron ever since."

Frankie removed a pair of gloves and a manila envelope from her bag. After inspecting the damage, she placed the broken device into the envelope.

"Nora, what do you remember about the car?"

"It was dark. I think it was red but could have been maroon. It was definitely a 4-door, probably late 80's or early 90's. It might have been a Buick. My brother works on cars so I'm familiar, but like I said, it was dark. One of the headlights was out and it didn't have any license plates. It might have had a temporary tag, but I'm not sure."

"What about the man. What did he look like?"

"He was tall. Black. Short hair. Clean cut. Big – athletic. I couldn't see his eyes. He was probably in his 20's. He didn't look out of the ordinary, you know? Like, not an old guy or a teenager or anything."

"Do you remember seeing him at Latitudes?"

Nora paused and gave the question careful consideration before answering.

"No, I don't think so."

"Had you ever seen him before Saturday?"

"No, he didn't look like any of my regulars."

"What about her?" asked Mia.

"No. I would have remembered her. She was pretty, in a non-assuming way."

"Is there anything else you can think of that might be important for us to know?"

Nora shook her head.

CHAPTER
SEVENTEEN

BEFORE THE CAR door closed Mia's cellphone began to ring. "Sex Crimes, Boden." She grabbed her notepad and began to write feverishly. "Where are they taking her? Okay. We'll head that way."

Frankie waited for Mia to disconnect the call before she asked, "Everything okay?"

"Yeah. I mean, no." She turned her body to face Frankie, "Do you remember Allie Wheaton? The girl who talked like a valley girl and wore a wig?"

"Mhm."

"That was Shane on the phone. He said Allie was hit by a Metro bus. She's alive but was unconscious on the scene. He wasn't sure how bad her injuries are. The ambulance is taking her to County."

"How the hell did she get hit by a city bus?"

"He didn't give any details. I think they had just loaded her when he called. He found my business card in her jacket pocket and was hoping I had contact information for her family."

"She was pretty transient. Did she ever give you any names or numbers for her family?" Frankie asked.

"I'll have to check. I think she gave me her grandparents' phone number, but they are out of state. You mind running by County to see how she is?"

Frankie nodded and asked, "Where'd it happen?"

"77th and Prospect. Maybe we can run by the scene after we check on her."

The drive was quiet, both detectives lost in their own thoughts. Frankie and Mia had interviewed Allie a few months prior on two separate cases. One of them was resolved quickly, but the second was still ongoing. Allie had been picked up by a man and raped and Frankie was pretty sure the man was the same one in a series of rapes they were working. Allie was not homeless, but moved from house to house, staying with friends until her welcome ran out. She was young but had seen more than she should have in her short life.

Mia led the way into the Emergency Department where the charge nurse directed them to trauma room 2. Frankie and Mia stood in the doorway watching the doctors treat the young girl. Her tiny body, that once seemed sturdy, now looked frail. Her wig was lying on the floor next to spent latex gloves. Her smooth skin, once the color of rich espresso, was now gray. Her eyes were closed, and her lips had lost all their color.

Once the doctors finished and stepped away, Mia and Frankie stepped inside the room. Mia gently touched Allie on the shoulder. Her eyes fluttered, then opened. Frankie looked into eyes the color of melted caramel.

Allie looked at both detectives and asked, "Why...why...are you...here?"

Mia smiled, "They found my card in your pocket and thought I might have an emergency contact for you. We wanted to make sure you were okay. Can you tell us what happened Allie?"

"I...I... don't...know. I was...waiting...for the...bus and I...I...saw...that...car." Allie's eyes closed. After a few moments she added, "I...think...I might...have...been...pushed."

Mia looked over at Frankie and said, "We'll look into it Allie."

Allie lifted her lips in a slight smile, closed her eyes, and murmured, "Thank you."

"Do you want me to call your grandparents Allie?"

Mia watched her head move slightly to the left and right. Her movement was almost imperceptible.

Once they were inside the car Frankie said what Mia was thinking, "You think it's related to her rape?"

"I don't know, maybe. It's worth looking into. Let's go down to 77th and Prospect."

ON THE WAY to the scene, Frankie asked Mia, "Did Allie ever tell you why she left home or why she got out of the Navy?"

Mia shook her head then said, "Not entirely. One night I went over to have her sign a summons on the case with her neighbor and she was pretty chatty. Did you know she was from North Carolina?"

"No, what part?"

"Greensboro? Greenville? Green-something. Her grandmother is a professor and her grandfather's an attorney. Or maybe a banker? Or...I can't remember, but he's a professional. She never said why she lived with them growing up, but she said they were good people.

"Allie enlisted in the Navy right out of high school. Her first duty station was in California. I asked her about her life there and she said it was the first time she'd ever lived away from home. She was training to be a corpsman."

"Seriously?" Frankie was surprised to hear Allie had an interest in the medical field.

"Yeah. She hadn't made a lot of friends so when this guy from work invited her to a party she went. She wouldn't tell me much, just that something happened at the party. She tried to run away from the guy that invited her but ended up going through a plate glass window. They were on the second floor. She didn't remember anything until she woke up in a hospital room at Balboa Medical Center. They told her she was lucky there had been a pool to break her fall. She was in the hospital for a couple weeks and ended up getting separated from the service."

"Do you think she was raped, drugged, or both?"

"At least raped. She told me the last one we talked to her about was her eighth rape. I looked in the database and we only have the two reports. I didn't ask for more details."

"Geesh. How the heck does she get out of bed in the morning?"

"Right?"

Frankie parked just outside of the yellow crime scene tape. Ducking underneath the tape, she and Mia found the traffic investigator in charge of the scene.

"Hey Tucker. How've you been?" Frankie shook hands with the officer.

"Hey Frankie. Mia. What are you guys doing here? Slumming?" Tucker laughed.

"No. The girl that was hit? We're working a couple cases with her. We think she's part of a series. Do you know what happened?" Mia asked.

"It's still early, but I'm thinking about calling the Assault Squad to see if they want to come out."

Mia looked to Frankie, then asked Tucker, "Why?"

"A couple witnesses said they saw the girl waiting for the bus. She was standing outside the shelter when some dude came up behind her. The witnesses said it looked like he pushed her."

"We went to see her at the hospital. She told us she'd seen the car from her rape while she was waiting for the bus. She also said she thought she'd been pushed."

Tucker started to say something but stopped. He looked from Frankie to Mia and asked, "Were you planning to write a report on your contact with her?"

Mia quickly answered, "Of course."

Tucker gave Mia the report number and all the information she needed to complete her report then went back to sketching the scene. Once they were inside the car Frankie asked, "Were you really planning to write a report?"

Smiling Mia said, "Maybe."

CHAPTER
NINETEEN

"HEY BABY. LOOKING FOR A DATE?" Josie Brewster leaned into the passenger window of the car.

"Mmhmm. Why don't you get in so we can talk?"

Cocking her head to the side she gave him a sideways glance and opened the car door. The supple leather seats felt indulgent on the skin underneath her short skirt. Josie turned to face the man as he pulled the car away from the curb. The short, bristly facial hair did little to cover the pock marks on his cheeks.

"Where are you headed?"

"Wherever *you* want to go baby," Josie replied. "You smoke?"

"No, but I'll get you something if you want."

"Sure baby. Go down Prospect. My guy usually hangs out near the Green Duck."

Josie leaned her head against the window and let her eyes scan the car. She hoped to find some loose change or something she could take and sell. It was getting cold, and she needed to get enough from this guy to be able to stay in a hotel instead of on the streets. Josie noticed a card with a photo hanging from the rearview mirror. Just as she read the first name "Allen" the man grabbed it and shoved it into his pocket.

"What do you want from me tonight?"

"Head."

"You're in luck baby. 20 and a rock and I'll take good care of you."
Allen grunted.

"Pull into the lot. I see Darius. You got a 10?"

Allen pulled a ten-dollar bill from his pocket, handed it to Josie and said, "It better be worth it."

Josie stepped from the car, turned around, and said, "Don't worry baby. It'll be the best head you've ever had."

After Josie got the rock of crack she returned to the car and pulled a glass pipe from her purse. She was so intent on loading the pipe and not losing the drug that she didn't notice where Allen was driving.

He was silent as he made a random series of turns. When she was finished loading her pipe, Josie pulled out her lighter and lit it, inhaling the drug deep into her lungs. The car came to a stop in a dark alley lined with abandoned houses.

Allen's once amiable tone turned brusque, "Get in the back seat."

"Just a second baby. I'm almost done."

Allen grabbed Josie by the hair and pulled the tiny woman's body off the passenger seat. The pipe dropped from her hand onto the floorboard of the car.

"Bitch, I don't care if you're done or not. I said get in the backseat," Allen's face contorted in rage.

Josie had seen that look before. Terror crept up her spine. She slowly climbed over the console between the front seats to get into the back. The man was too large to climb over the seat; instead, he got out of the car and let the driver's side door slam shut. Josie pulled at the door handle closest to her, but it wouldn't open. She fumbled with it until Allen opened the opposite door.

"Please don't hurt me," screamed Josie.

"Shut up bitch!" Josie's head jerked back with the force of Allen's hand slapping her.

Josie grabbed her face and whimpered, "What do you want?"

Allen grabbed her clothes and pulled them from her body. Josie was frozen in fear. Unable to move. She felt the man's large hands on her body. She felt him penetrate her and when he was finished, he drug her limp, naked body from the car. He left her lying in a heap before getting back into the driver's seat. Josie watched as her clothes flew out the window and onto the ground.

Josie sat in the alley and stared at the car as it pulled away. She held her torn shirt close to her body and repeated to herself, "7BH. 7BH. 7BH."

TWENTY

"WHAT'S NEXT ON THE LIST?" asked Mia.

She and Frankie had been driving around the areas where the 9-1-1 calls originated hoping to find the gas station with the clerk who knew Tre. They had been to three convenience stores, but no one knew him.

"It looks like one of the calls came from the area of 75th and Oak Street. There's a Fast Stop convenience store a few blocks away on Holmes – maybe someone there knows Tre."

The parking lot was empty when they parked the car. Frankie noticed a couple of cameras on the outside of the building and silently hoped their surveillance system worked.

The young clerk barely looked up from the magazine she was reading when Frankie and Mia walked inside.

Before Frankie could introduce herself, she asked, "Is this about Tre?"

Frankie raised an eyebrow at Mia. She removed a photo of Sarah from her bag. "Have you seen this woman before?"

The clerk held the photograph in her petite hands and stared. She handed the photo back to Frankie and looked past her, out the window.

"Yeah, I've seen her."

"When?" Frankie tried to mask her excitement.

"She was in here Saturday night." The clerk paused before asking, "Is she okay?"

Frankie avoided the question, "What's your name?" With hesitation the clerk answered, "Cheyenne."

"What happened when she was here?"

"She asked to use the bathroom. I was talking to Tre but then he got really weird and started kicking the bathroom door. I screamed at him to stop. I didn't want the manager to get mad if he broke the door."

"Did he stop?"

"Not until she opened the door."

"Did you notice anything about her clothes?"

Cheyenne paused for a moment then said, "She was holding her shirt closed. I didn't think anything about it at the time, but it was weird."

"What do you know about the guy she was with?"

Before Cheyenne could answer the question two loud teenage boys came in and walked towards the cooler. They dropped a bag of chips, a soda, and a can of Colt 45 onto the counter.

One of the boys demanded, "Get me a Black and Mild."

Frankie and Mia stepped back from the counter and waited while Cheyenne rang up the chips and soda.

Cheyenne nodded in the direction of Frankie and Mia, "Boy you know you ain't old enough to buy a cigar much less a beer. Now get out before I call your momma and tell her you were in here."

The boys laughed, took their bag, and walked out the door. Frankie couldn't be sure but thought she saw one of the boys raise his middle finger when he got past the back of their car.

Laughing out loud Frankie asked Mia, "Did you see that?"

Mia nodded, "I keep waiting for kids to get more creative."

"They ain't bad boys. Just like to push things," Cheyenne explained. "They're in here almost every day."

Frankie turned back to Cheyenne, "You were about to tell us about Tre."

She took a deep breath, "Is he going to know you talked to me? That guy's not right."

"We'll do what we can to protect your identity."

With a sigh Cheyenne said, "His name is Treyvon. I think his last name is Stockton, but I'm not 100% sure. Everyone calls him Tre. He used to live around the corner, but I think his momma moved. Miss Stockton's nice. She used to bring me food sometimes when I worked the late shift or on a holiday."

"Do you know Miss Stockton's first name?"

"I'm not sure. Aurelia maybe?"

"Do you know where they moved?"

Cheyenne paused before answering, "No. You might check with the pastor at the church on Paseo. He'd probably know where she is. She was pretty involved there. I think she may even still go there."

Before Frankie could ask any additional questions, the unit cell phone rang, "Sex Crimes, Detective Thomas."

Mia began collecting Cheyenne's contact information.

"Okay. We'll be there in about fifteen minutes." Frankie disconnected the call, turned back to Cheyenne, and asked, "Is there anything else you can remember that might be helpful?"

Cheyenne started to fidget. It was apparent there was something more she wanted to tell them. As Frankie was about to say something Cheyenne turned to the register and opened the drawer. She lifted the cash drawer and pulled out a five-dollar bill. Sliding it across the counter she said, "That girl paid for her water with this."

It took Frankie a moment before she realized it was the bill Sarah told her about at the hospital. She read the words aloud, "Please help me."

Frankie could feel the heat of anger rising up her neck. Sarah asked this woman for help, and she did nothing. Frankie's blood boiled and her chest constricted in anger but all she said was, "I'm taking this as evidence."

"What do I tell the manager when my drawer is short?"

"Give them the case number and tell them to call me if they have any questions. Do you have access to the surveillance system?"

"No, but my manager will be here in the morning. He can get it."

Frankie handed Cheyenne her business card. Through gritted teeth she asked, "Can you please ask your manager to pull all of the surveillance of that girl and Tre?"

Cheyenne nodded and asked, "Is she okay? She's not dead or anything is she?"

"Why would you ask if she was dead?"

Fidgeting with the pen on the counter Cheyenne said, "She seemed so scared. I told Tre he should just leave her here. Tre can be a real creep and she didn't act like she wanted to be with him. But he wasn't holding onto her. And then she left with him, so I figured I got it wrong."

"She's not dead." With that Frankie turned and walked out the door.

TWENTY-ONE

"WHO WAS THAT ON THE PHONE?" Mia asked as she fastened her seatbelt.

"Mac. They caught a case at 24th and Bellefontaine." Frankie grabbed her cellphone and called the Crime Scene Unit while she drove. "Sounds like it might be the same guy that attacked Allie."

"Seriously?"

"Yeah. *And* the vic got a partial plate."

"Damn, maybe we finally caught a break."

Frankie thought about the case while she drove.

"What are the chances it's the same guy?" Mia's spoke the words Frankie was thinking.

Frankie turned towards Mia with her answer, "I'd say pretty good."

The drive was short. The blue and red lights on scene were visible before the people that stood in front of them.

"Damn," exclaimed Mia.

Before Frankie could say anything, she saw the petite woman sitting on the back of the ambulance. She had blood trickling from a cut below her swollen eye. The medic was examining the wound while the officers strung crime scene tape.

"Hey Mac!" Frankie slapped the back of her old patrol partner.

"Hey Frankie. I wondered if you were working tonight."

"Always." Frankie smiled. "I talked to the recruit. He said the victim got a plate number?"

"A partial. 7BH. Missouri. Guys are out looking for it now, but it sounds like this guy took off pretty quickly. He threw her out of the car after he raped her."

"Sound familiar?"

"Yeah – how many women has this guy attacked?"

"I think this makes three – if it's the same guy."

Frankie walked towards the medic and the woman he was treating.

After she introduced herself, she asked, "Does she need to be transported?"

"She should definitely be seen by a doc, but you can take her if she'd prefer," replied the paramedic.

"Ma'am, would it be okay if my partner and I take you to the hospital after we talk?"

Josie nodded.

"Okay, let's go to headquarters and get a statement, then we will take you to the hospital."

CHAPTER
TWENTY-TWO

FRANKIE ESCORTED Josie to an interview room to get her statement while Mia started the recording equipment.

"Can you tell me what happened tonight?"

"I was hanging out up on the Avenue." Josie looked down at the table and became quiet.

"Josie, you can tell me what you were doing. I'm not going to arrest you if you tell me you were trying to make a date or score drugs."

Looking up she softly asked, "For real?"

Frankie nodded.

Josie looked around the bland room then back down at the table. After a moment, she looked up and sighed, "I was trying to make a date and maybe score some crack. If I had enough money left over, I was going to get a room for the night. It's starting to get cold, and I didn't want to sleep outside."

She paused and waited to see if Frankie or Mia would say anything.

"This guy pulled up by where I was standing and sort of motioned for me to come over. I asked if he was looking to party, and he offered me a ride. Everything was cool at first. He bought me a rock and while I was loading my pipe he drove to this alley."

Josie stopped and took a deep breath.

"He told me to get into the back seat. I told him I wasn't finished smoking but, it was like…he changed. He seemed angry suddenly. He grabbed me by the hair and forced me into the back seat. He was too big to climb over the seat, so he opened the back door. I tried to open the door by my head, but it wouldn't open. He got into the backseat and on top of me, trying to stick me. I kept moving around, trying not to let him get it in but that just made him madder. He was already having some trouble getting it up and that really made him angry. The more he tried the more difficult it became. Then he punched me and started calling out my name saying I wasn't doing what he paid for. But he never gave me any money. And we didn't agree to what he took.

"When he finished, he put his thing up, and got out of the car. He reached in and pulled me out of the backseat by my hair. Then he just left me on the side of the road like I was a piece of garbage. When he pulled away, I got a glimpse of the license and said it to myself repeatedly."

Josie grabbed a tissue and wiped her nose. Her eyes were filled with tears but not even one fell.

"Tell me about the car."

"I'm not sure what you want to know."

"What was the inside like?"

Josie rested her chin on her hand in thought. Softly she said, "It was nice. The seats were leather and felt nice against my legs."

"Did anything about the car stand out to you?"

"I kind of looked around the car. I was hoping he had some loose change or something I could boost. Like I said, I really wanted to stay in a room tonight. Maybe take a hot shower or bath. He caught me looking at this thing with a name on it hanging from the mirror and snatched it."

"Did you see the name?"

"Allen, maybe?"

"Was there anything else you remember or want to add about the car?"

Closing her eyes, she answered, "The radio. It had lights that moved on the front. It was fancy and kind of stood out."

Frankie let Josie catch her breath while she reviewed her notes. When she was finished, she looked up and asked, "Tell me more about the doors."

"What do you mean?"

"You mentioned you couldn't get it to open…"

"Yeah, it was like a cop car. The back door wouldn't open from the inside."

"Was the door damaged in any way?"

"No. The handle just wouldn't open the door."

Frankie made notes on her tablet and asked, "What did he look like?"

Josie tapped her fingers on the table, "He was tall. His head almost hit the roof of the car. He was big. Not fat, just big. He was light skinned."

"Did he have any facial hair?"

Putting her fingers to her lips she said, "Maybe a little. He had marks on his face too."

"What do you mean by marks?"

"Like craters in his skin."

"Can you tell me where you bought the crack? I'd like to see if they have any surveillance of him or his car."

Josie hesitated, "I don't want to get my dealer in trouble."

"We aren't interested in him Josie. We just want to find the guy that raped you."

Jose didn't immediately answer. She looked to her hands as if they could give her guidance. Finally, she said, "The Green Duck. He usually hangs out around there. I don't know if they have cameras though."

"Thanks Josie. Is there anything else you think we need to know?"

Josie shook her head.

"Are you willing to get a forensic exam done at the hospital?"

"I can't pay," Josie mumbled.

"You can get the exam for free and they will let you shower after. We'll give you a ride down to County and then they can give you a cab voucher to a shelter."

Josie nervously asked, "Do you think it will matter? I mean, who's going to believe me over him?"

"I think it's important. They will check you out medically and make sure you're okay. Plus, they will collect any evidence they find. And Josie?"

Looking up from the table she said, "Hmm?"

"We believe you."

Josie let the words sink in before saying, "Okay, I'll go."

Frankie and Mia escorted her to the car, making small talk during the ten-minute drive to County Hospital. Mia watched Frankie's steps slow the closer she got to the ER entrance.

Speaking softly, she asked, "Frankie, are you okay? I can take her in if you want to wait out here."

"I'll be fine. I was here a few nights ago – it's not like I can avoid this place forever."

Frankie informed the receptionist why they were there and within minutes Josie was escorted to a private room.

Mia touched Frankie's shoulder as the two walked back to the car and said, "It'll get easier."

"I know," was Frankie's soft reply.

"How do you want to attack this case?" Mia asked.

"Let's review the other cases we have and see if we can put them together. Maybe do a search and see if we can find any cars matching the license and description."

Parking the car Frankie said, "I'll be up in a minute."

She retrieved her cell phone and dialed. A single ring was met with Derek's throaty, "Hey, are you okay?"

"Yea, I just wanted to check on you."

"Are you working late?"

"Yeah, it's looking that way."

"Okay. Stay safe babe."

"Always."

Mia was surrounded by case files and making notes on a dry erase board when Frankie walked into the room. Hearing her, Mia stopped writing and turned, "How's Derek?"

"He's okay. I think I woke him up."

"Are you?"

"Am I what?"

"Okay. A lot has happened over the last couple months. Your dad. Bruce. Dani. Derek."

Walking over to the window, Frankie looked towards the courthouse and the buildings beyond. Mia was right. A lot *had* happened. Her dad had a heart attack and almost died. Frankie's neighbor Bruce was shot saving her daughter from a would-be-kidnapper seeking revenge against her. Derek was shot by a gang member. And, somehow, she was supposed to go on like nothing had happened. She had to be strong for everyone. Frankie took a deep breath, blinked the tears from her eyes, and then turned around to face Mia.

"I'm fine."

OFFICER ANTHONY "MAC" McClendon was angry. He and his partner, Maria Payne, had been looking for the car used in the rape for over an hour with no luck.

"He couldn't have just disappeared Payne."

"He'll show up – he can't lie low forever."

Mac made a sudden right turn, "Look, there he is!"

"Hang back Mac. You don't want to spook him."

Picking up the mic, Mac said, *"242 we are following a car possibly used in the rape at 24 and Bellefontaine."*

"242, what's your location?" the dispatcher asked.

"62nd and Prospect, south bound. Gold Honda, Missouri license 7 Boy Henry Young 8 8. Occupied one time."

"242 is following a car possibly used in a rape at 24th and Bellefontaine. Anyone else in the area?" the dispatcher asked.

"He's heading west on 63rd St. We just passed Park. We're coming up on Woodland. He's heading south on Woodland," said Mac.

"215, I'm about three blocks away."

The dispatcher said, *"Copy 215. 242, location?"*

"Meyer and Woodland. He's signaling east. Copy a car check. Meyer and Woodland east bound. Gold Honda Missouri license 7BH Y88. Hold the air."

"Copy. Holding the air at Meyer and Woodland," the dispatcher said.

"He's not stopping. He's heading southbound on Paseo."

"240 to dispatch, is 690 flying tonight," asked Sergeant Seever.

"Looks like he's going to keep heading south on Paseo. He's coming up on Gregory," Mac said.

"The helicopter's not flying tonight 240," said the dispatcher.

"We're about two blocks behind," Mac advised.

"He just blew the light at Gregory. He's heading eastbound and just about t-boned a car," said Sergeant Seever.

The radio was silent for a few moments.

"He's heading south on Prospect. We are coming up on… wait, he dumped the car. 77th and Prospect, south bound. Black male on foot, running west behind the houses."

"242 and 215 set up a perimeter," directed Seever. *"Dispatch, start the K-9 unit."*

Mac, Payne, and Seever parked their cars and started their search. Sirens signaled other cars were en route to their area. They crept through the yards slowly and quietly, hoping to find the man hiding in the shadows.

"He couldn't have gotten far," Mac said.

"242, we just got a 9-1-1 call about a possible burglary in progress at 2615 E 75th Street. Caller said an unknown party was trying to get into the house through a basement window," advised dispatch.

"242 we'll respond to the location."

"240, show me out with 242."

The officers approached the house at an angle. They were preparing to clear the corner to the backyard when Mac noticed a shadow coming out from behind the house.

"Show me your hands!" Mac shouted the directions to the man whose hands were shoved in his pockets. *"Show me your freaking hands!"*

Slowly Mac saw hands raise in the air. Seever and Payne kept their weapons trained on the man as Mac approached to handcuff him.

"You can clear the air. One in custody," said Seever.

"The air is clear at 2342."

CHAPTER
TWENTY-FOUR

THE SOUND of the phone ringing caused Frankie to jump, "Shit, I thought I forwarded the phone when we got back."

"If it's a scene we're calling Coleman out. He's on call," announced Mia as she picked up the phone.

"Agreed."

"Sex Crimes Boden. Okay. How do you know it's him? Okay. How far out are you? Copy. Yeah, we'll be here. One of you can stop at the fourth floor to get the paperwork you'll need to hold him. Tow the car to the #2 garage."

"Let me guess, we have one in custody."

"Yep. Looks like they got the guy that picked up Josie. They'll be here in about ten minutes," said Mia. "You can thank Mac. He's been out looking for this guy since we left them."

Frankie smiled, "Of course he was."

As if on cue, Mac walked into the squad room with a smile on his face and asked, "Did I screw up your plans for the night?"

"Actually…" started Mia.

"Where'd you get him Mac?" interrupted Frankie.

Mac told the pair about the car chase and eventual capture.

"We need you to stay here and get your reports done," directed Mia.

"Of course. Planning on a late night?"

"Yeah. I just hope she can ID him," said Frankie. Picking up the phone she got the Emergency Department charge nurse and said, "This is Detective Thomas with KCPD. Is Josie Brewster still there? Okay, can you please ask the nurse to hold her until I get there? It'll be about twenty minutes? Thanks."

Mia got Mac the paperwork he needed while Frankie put together a photographic line-up. Walking out the door she said, "Wish me luck!"

Frankie could hear Mia and Mac yell, "Luck" as she got onto the elevator.

The drive to County was brief and when Frankie walked through the doors she only hesitated for a moment. She entered the examination room and could tell Josie was starting to get impatient. Without explanation Frankie asked, "Do you think you would be able to identify the man who attacked you?"

Josie fidgeted on the table, "I think so. Do you have him?"

Frankie kept her voice calm as she explained the process, "I'm not sure. I have some photographs I'd like you to look at. If you recognize the man, I want you sign the photograph and tell me where you know him from. If you don't recognize anyone, it's okay. We'll keep looking."

Nodding Josie answered, "Okay."

She looked at the photographs in silence. When Josie got to Sawyer's photograph she said, "That's him! That's the motherfucker that raped me. That's him!"

She leaned back on the bed and hit the pillows with her clenched fists. Her face contorted in a rage. Josie asked, "What happens now?"

Frankie explained the next steps.

Josie said, "He had a name tag hanging from the mirror of his car but grabbed it and put it in his pocket. Did they find it?"

"I'm not sure, but I'll check." Frankie grabbed her cellphone and dialed Mac's number.

"Hey Frankie, did she ID him?" Mac asked.

"Did he have anything in his pocket when you picked him up?"

"Just a wallet and a name tag."

"You don't say," replied Frankie. "Thanks. Tell Mia we have a positive ID. I'll be back shortly."

Josie looked at Frankie and asked, "Well?"

"He had a nametag in his pocket."

"How long can you hold him?"

"24 hours. Unless they charge him. Then he'll have to make bond."

Josie exhaled with force. Frankie thought she saw a glimmer of tears in Josie's eyes.

THE TABLE in the squad room was littered with case files. Mia had filled the dry erase board with notes attempting to connect other cases to the man in custody.

Looking towards the board Frankie asked, "What do you have here?"

"Josie gave the first three on the license plate at 7BH. I pulled Allie's case file, and she gave us a license plate of 78H Y8B."

"It would be easy to mistake a B for an 8," interrupted Frankie.

"Absolutely. And they both said his name was Allen. The guy we have in custody is Allen Sawyer. What did Brooklyn's mom say about the guy that raped her?"

Brooklyn was one of the teenagers Frankie mentored through her organization, VISION. A couple of months prior her mother, Asia, had been picked up by a stranger, beaten, and raped. Frankie and Mia took her to the hospital for a medical exam, but she wouldn't make a police report.

"She didn't. But I can try to reach out to her again. It looks like we have at least two victims with this guy. Maybe three if Asia can ID him. Let's get the Perpetrator Information Center to query for any reports that have a similar pattern. He picks them up around Independence Avenue and drives to a secluded place where he rapes and dumps them. It doesn't appear that he kidnaps them – he lures them into his car with charm or money then flips the switch as soon as they are comfortable."

"I'll email PIC and see what they can send us. Crime Scene is en route to process him."

Before Frankie could respond a booming voice rang out, "Frank-eeee."

Smiling she turned to see a mountain of a man walking through the doorway, ducking his head to clear the jamb.

"Rhino!" She stood up to half-shake hands, half-hug the bear-sized man. Joel Pallerhinoshki earned the nickname Rhino when he played football for the University of Missouri; partially from his size and partially because no one could pronounce his last name correctly. He and Frankie had been friends for years, working cases and volunteering on community projects together.

"How's it going Mia?"

"Hey Rhino! How's your family?"

The trio made small talk briefly before turning back to the business at hand. Rhino pulled his notepad from his bag and asked, "What do we have?"

"Allen Simon Sawyer. Black Male. Date of birth 1/24/67. Investigative hold for rape. Case number is 075218. Victim is at County getting a kit done." Frankie rattled off the details she knew Rhino needed for his reports. "We are pretty sure he's connected to one of Mia's cases and possibly others."

"How many?"

"Not sure. Mia's going to contact PIC and see if they can send us a list of reports that fit this guy's description and MO."

"Did he give consent, or did you have to get a warrant?"

"Consent. You ready?"

Rhino winked at the women and replied, "I'm always ready."

CHAPTER
TWENTY-SIX

FRANKIE WENT to the detention unit on the 8th floor to retrieve Allen. After a few minutes of small talk with the detention officer, Allen was removed from the holding cell and released to Frankie to be escorted to the 4th floor interrogation room. Allen towered over her, but Frankie had a firm grip on his arm that let him know she could handle herself if he tried anything stupid.

As the elevator doors closed a deep voice quietly said, "You know I'm not going to talk to you, right?"

"Right now, we just want to execute the consent to search you signed."

The elevator doors opened and Frankie escorted Allen to the interrogation room where Rhino and Mia were waiting.

Rhino explained the process of evidence collection to Allen.

"Did the detention officers take your clothes upstairs?"

"Mmhmm."

Rhino methodically went through the collection, carefully packaging and labeling each envelope and tube. Once he was finished Frankie directed Allen to sit, advising him she and Mia would be back shortly.

"Do you want some water?"

"Yeah."

"Okay, give me a few minutes." Frankie shut and locked the door from the outside.

"Do you think he's going to talk? He was pretty quiet while I was scraping and swabbing."

"Dude, I don't think he's used to guys being bigger than him. He was scared as hell when he saw you hulking there!" said Mia with a laugh.

"I do have that effect on people," chuckled Rhino.

"I've got the docs we need. Rhino, do you need anything else from us?" Frankie asked.

"Nope, I'm good. I'll send Ash by to get the kit from County tomorrow night."

"Good deal. Thanks again for coming down."

"Anytime," echoed down the hall as he walked down the hall towards the elevator.

Frankie looked at the board where Mia had been making notes. Picking up her file folder she nodded to Mia and asked, "Ready?"

Mia grabbed her case folder and followed Frankie to the interrogation room.

Slapping the case files on the table Frankie and Mia sat down across from Allen. Frankie pulled out a few forms and started collecting basic biographical data. Allen was hesitant at first but eventually began to answer. Frankie used every question to make small talk. She wanted to set him at ease; get him to let his guard down.

"You were in the Army? How long?"

"Yeah. Uh, about twelve years."

"Really? Where was your favorite place to be stationed?"

"Hmmm. I don't know. I liked Germany but North Carolina was okay too."

"I've never been to Germany. Did you travel a lot while you were there?"

"Pretty much. I was a train ride from everything."

Frankie went to the next set of questions, continuing to distract Allen from the real reason they were there. After about twenty minutes she pulled the Miranda Waiver from her folder and asked him to read it aloud.

Allen read the document then asked, "Do I need a lawyer?"

Careful not to infringe upon his rights Frankie answered, "It's up to you. This is your opportunity to tell us your side of the story. If you want a lawyer, I'll take you back upstairs but if you want to talk I'll listen and tell the prosecutor what you said."

"What's this about anyway?"

"A woman has made some allegations against you."

"What kind of allegations?"

"Allen, if you want to talk, I need you to sign this document."

He looked from Frankie to Mia then back to the form. They watched his hands as he played with the pen, both remembering the victims saying his behavior would suddenly change. After a few moments, Allen stood up and said, "I'm ready to go back upstairs."

Frankie and Mia were on their feet the moment he stood up.

"Okay. Leave the pen on the table."

Dropping the pen, Allen stepped from around the table. Frankie grabbed his arm and led him back to the elevator. When the doors to the elevator closed, he looked down and said, "I told you I wasn't going to talk."

Frankie returned to the squad room, dropping onto her chair with a loud sigh.

"Are you really surprised?" Mia asked.

"No, but I *am* disappointed."

"Yeah. I'd liked for him to have confessed – even if it was a half-ass confession."

Frankie nodded, turned to her computer, and began typing her reports.

CHAPTER
TWENTY-SEVEN

FRANKIE AND MIA worked on their reports in relative silence. When she finished, Frankie stood up, twisted, and stretched then said, "Are you about done?"

"I think I've done about as much as I can do tonight. Is it really 2am?"

"Yeah. I'm glad the kids are with Sophie tonight."

"How's your little sister doing?"

"Sophie's just fine. I have a feeling Sophie's help is about to end though. She has a new man-friend." Laughing Frankie added, "Having the kids around might cramp her style a bit."

"Good for her! She needs a nice guy." Changing her tone Mia asked, "How are Bruce and Keith?"

The smile faded from Frankie's face. Involuntarily her thoughts flashed back to Bruce being brought into the Emergency Department. She relied on him, and his partner Keith and they were hurting because of her. She knew they didn't blame her, but she blamed herself.

"Frankie," nudged Mia.

Snapping from her memory Frankie answered, "Sorry. They are good. Bruce is restless and says he's tired of Keith babying him, but secretly I think he loves it. Soph has a work trip coming up and they are going to stay with the kids."

"It'll get back to normal, Frankie."

"Mmhmm." Frankie blinked her eyes, "If you'll put the info on the board, I'll go make another copy of the case file so the day squad can take it to the prosecutor's office in the morning."

"Are you going to let the day crew process the car?"

"Unless you feel like going out there tonight. Sawyer might be willing to sign consent."

"I'm game. Want me to go ask him?"

Frankie nodded and walked out the door to make copies. She was just finishing up when Mia returned. "No Bueno. In fact, he was kind of an ass." Frankie laughed.

"I guess the novelty of being in custody has worn off. Glad I drafted a search warrant! I'll have the other squad get the warrant signed and we can process it on Thursday." Mia yawned in response.

"I think we have a full squad Thursday night – maybe we can go find Tre's momma too."

TWENTY-EIGHT

FRANKIE WAS WIRED when she put the case file on the table for the day shift. With her kids and the dog with Sophie she really didn't want to go home. She picked up her phone to text Derek when, as if by design, her phone beeped with an incoming text.

"Saw lights on – working late?"

"Hmm awfully late text. Derek wanting a late-night visit?" teased Mia.

Looking at her phone she couldn't help but smile as she typed, *"Just about to wrap it up. What are you doing out so late? Hot date? ;)"*

"No, Derek's got an early docket in the morning. It's Jim. He saw our lights on."

Mia didn't immediately respond. Jim Craven was an FBI agent who helped them with a rape involving organized crime. The late nights and high stress situations they experienced had solidified a solid friendship. It was obvious to everyone but Frankie that Jim was interested in being more than just her friend.

"Got caught up doing surveillance. Up for a drink? Kelly's?"

"Sure. I'll be on my way in 5."

"Want to grab a drink on your way home? Jim suggested Kelly's?"

"Sure. Erik's working off duty. I'll see if he wants to swing by after."

The drive to Kelly's Pub took about fifteen minutes and Frankie's mind raced the entire drive. She felt something akin to guilt. She and Derek had never defined their relationship, and some would argue they didn't really have one. He had never met her kids and she had never met any of his family. They had never talked about not seeing other people and meeting Jim for a drink was not a date. Since the night of the shooting Frankie had been fighting a nagging feeling that Derek was hiding something about his relationship with his co-counsel. She'd only said the words aloud to one person, but she'd thought them plenty over the past month.

Frankie parked her Jeep next to Mia's Echo in the lot across from Kelly's Pub. She waited at the back of the car while Mia said good-bye to her husband Erik.

"Is Erik coming?"

"No. He's worn out. They served a couple of warrants today and then he worked off-duty so he's going home to sleep."

"Frankie!" a booming voice called from inside the pub.

As she and Mia approached Jim, she thought she saw a glimmer of disappointment in his face. Jim enveloped the women in a hug. After saying their hellos, they found seats towards the back of the bar.

"What are you ladies drinking tonight?"

"Bud Light for me," said Frankie. "The colder, the better."

"Girl after my own heart."

"Boulevard Show and Tell for me," said Mia.

"You got it."

"Frankie, what are you doing?" Mia asked when Jim got to the bar.

"Having a drink, same as you."

"Seems like you might be playing with fire. What about Derek?"

"What about him? Jim and I are just friends." Frankie paused before saying, "Can I ask you something?"

Mia nodded.

Frankie was hesitant to speak her fears aloud. "What do you think about Derek and Jessica Moon leaving together the night they were shot?"

"What did he say they were doing?" Mia knew Frankie and Derek had a strange relationship, but it seemed to work for them, so she had never said anything.

"He didn't. He basically said they were walking to their cars when they were shot but I don't buy it. The first officers on the scene told me how they were found. They were crumpled on the ground beside the passenger side door of *his* car. I mean, we never said…"

Sitting the drinks down Jim said, "Looks like I am interrupting a serious conversation here."

"Perfect timing," was Frankie's response.

Jim kept the women entertained for the time it took to drink a couple of beers. He had grown up in a fishing village in North Carolina before becoming a police officer in Chicago. His stories ranged from night fishing and bonfires on the beach to car chases in a busy city. Jim regaled them with images that left them holding their sides in laughter.

"Am I losing my touch?" Jim asked as Mia yawned.

"Not at all. It's just been a long day. Besides, I think it's time to go wake the hubs up." She winked at Frankie then said, "We will finish our talk later."

"Drive safe Mia. See you Thursday."

Jim and Mia said their good-byes, leaving him and Frankie at the table by themselves.

"What's that all about?" asked Jim.

"Hmm? What's what all about?"

Jim wasn't going to let her off that easy, "Let me guess, Mia's worried about you and I hanging out because of the counselor."

"Something like that."

Reading her mind, Jim asked, "Did Derek ever tell you where they were going that night?"

Although Frankie hadn't seen Jim since their case ended, they had talked on the phone and texted. She had shared her concerns with him. Jim suggested she ask Derek directly but knew Frankie was afraid of what his answer would be.

Frankie told Jim the same thing she had told Mia. Jim sucked his lips in and looked away from her briefly.

"You don't believe his story."

Jim took a long drink of his beer and stood up, "Want another one?"

Frankie put her hand on his arm, "Tell me the truth."

"To be honest, no. It may have been innocent. You and I are sitting here having a drink and nothing is going to happen between us. Maybe that is all they were going to do. Have a drink. But if it's so innocent, why did he lie to you?"

The same question had been plaguing Frankie since Mac told her how he'd found them.

CHAPTER
TWENTY-NINE

"MOM! WE'RE HOME!"

"Let her sleep Ty," yelled Dani.

"You're not the boss of me! I want to show her what we did with Aunt Sophie last night!"

Frankie had forgotten the kids were out of school for teacher in-service. She was just getting up when Tyler burst into her bedroom.

"Look mom!" In his hands was a canvas painting of a little boy building a sandcastle by the ocean. Thrusting the canvas towards Frankie, he exclaimed, "I painted it myself!"

"Aunt Sophie helped you," interjected Dani.

"So! I still did most of it myself. What do you think mom? I made it for you!"

Smiling Frankie answered, "I love it, Ty. I know just where I'm going to hang it. Thanks, bud."

"Dani made one too. But she left hers in the living room."

"I'll come out and look at it, just let me get dressed first. Then I will whip up some breakfast."

Gruffly Dani said, "Aunt Sophie already got us food."

Frankie smiled at her insolent teenage daughter, "Where is Sophie?"

"She said to tell you she'd call you later. She had a lunch thing," answered Tyler. "She was all dressed up and smelled *really* good."

Ruffling his short hair Frankie said, "She did, huh?"

"Yeah. Mom, you should get some of her perfume."

Frankie laughed, "Hmmm, why's that bud?"

"Because then you might have a lunch-thing too." Frankie grabbed her son and squeezed, "May-be bay-be."

"Stop it," he giggled.

The day flew by with few interruptions from work. Frankie had just fixed lunch and was lacing up her running shoes when her cellphone rang. Stepping out of the living room she answered, "Thomas."

"Hey Frankie, it's Sergeant Baker. Got a minute?"

"Yeah. Go ahead."

Frankie hoped Baker had some good news on her case.

"They let Sawyer go. The prosecutor said there just wasn't enough to charge him. The other squad processed his car for you. Can we release it to him?"

"Ye…no. I want to get photographs of the car in different lighting. Tell him he can pick it up when I come back on Thursday."

"Is that all you need? I can send Coleman out to do it."

"Yeah. Ask him to get photos in low lights. The victims we've talked to have given conflicting reports on the color. I'm thinking it might have been the way it looked in different lights."

"Got it. See you Thursday."

"Thanks, Sarge."

Frankie hung up the phone and paced the room. She couldn't understand why the prosecutor didn't file charges.

Operating on a hunch she sent Baker a text, *"Who was the prosecutor?"*

Several minutes passed before Baker responded, *"Jessica Moon."*

With that Frankie punched the pillow on her bed. Was the case really bad or did Moon refuse to charge him because it was Frankie's case?

FRANKIE SPENT the rest of the day playing games with Tyler and helping Dani study for a test. When the kids were in bed, she grabbed a beer and settled into her chair to read a book. She and Baker exchanged a few text messages but as she flipped the pages in her novel the phone was quiet. Frankie contemplated texting Derek but didn't know if she could resist saying something about Moon, so she didn't.

Just as she was preparing to go to bed, she heard her phone sound with an incoming text.

"Can I get a ride tomorrow?"

The text was from Carl, one of the teens involved in V.I.S.I.O.N. They had their monthly meeting at the University athletic center the following evening.

"Sure. I'll get you at 5."

She sent Brooklyn a text and confirmed she needed a ride as well. Frankie enjoyed working with the group of teenagers she mentored. Her goal was to give the kids a more positive view of law enforcement and a safe place to dream. She had teamed up with the local university's basketball team who provided space for the meetings, mentors for the kids, and tickets to home games. It was a small, but enthusiastic group. Frankie fell asleep thinking about the teens and their unique personalities that seemed to blend so well. She was glad she could expose her kids to positive role models.

The alarm clock jolted Frankie out of a dream-filled sleep. She could hear Dani in the shower, but Tyler was still snoring in his bed. A text from Derek awaited her when she reached for her phone.

"Want to come by tonight?"

"Can't. Have a VISION meeting. Maybe this weekend?"

Frankie knew better than to invite Derek to the meeting. He hadn't even met her children so there was no reason to believe he would want to meet the kids she mentored. But his text gave her an idea.

"Hey Jim – are you busy tonight?"

"What do you have in mind sunshine?"

Frankie couldn't help but smile at Jim's response.

"I have a meeting with the kids I am mentoring. Would you want to come talk to them? We are starting our vision notebooks tonight."

"Sounds fun. When and where is the meeting?"

Frankie smiled as she sent him all the information. It was going to be fun having a friend join her for the meeting. Plus, the kids could hear from someone besides her for a change. She was still smiling when she dropped the kids off at school and went for her run.

THE DAY PASSED QUICKLY. Frankie did her household chores and gathered the supplies for the VISION notebooks. She had magazines, blank paper, scissors, glue, and any other craft item she could think of, including notebooks for each teen to fill.

Frankie picked up Brooklyn and Carl, then pizza for the group. The kids helped her unload the Jeep and set up the room before the rest of the teens and mentors arrived. At exactly six o'clock Sam, Laura, and Ross barreled into the room. The scene was chaotic with everyone talking at once while they fixed their plates and grabbed a drink.

Laura found her seat first and asked, "Miss Frankie, what are the notebooks for? Are you going to make us do homework or something?"

"Hey everybody, let's find a seat…"

Before Frankie could finish her sentence, Jim walked in the door.

Frankie waved him in and continued, "Find a seat and I'll explain what we are going to do. We also have a special guest tonight."

Slowly the group quieted down and turned to face Frankie.

"This is Special Agent Jim Craven with the Federal Bureau of Investigations. He is assigned to the Kansas City field office."

"Y'all can just call me Jim if you want. How's everyone doin' tonight?" Jim's southern brogue was distinct as he greeted the group.

"Crav…Jim, if you would, can you tell the group a little about your-self and how you became an FBI agent?"

Clearing his throat, he said, "Sure enough. I grew up in a small fishin' village on the coast of North Carolina."

Jim went on to tell the group of captivated listeners about his child-hood on the coast working on a shrimp boat. He talked about making the decision that he wanted more out of life. He worked two jobs to pay his way through college and when he graduated, he set his sights on the big city and started applying at police departments. With a lot of hard work and determination he ended up in Chicago.

Carl asked, "What was it like in Chicago?"

"Crazy. Busy. Fun. I became a detective and almost turned down the chance to go to the FBI. I was having so much fun and wasn't sure it would be worth it to leave."

"What made you change your mind?" Brooklyn asked.

Jim paused, giving the question serious thought, before answering. "I just needed a change I suppose. And if I wouldn't have taken the oppor-tunity, I wouldn't be here with you all tonight."

Jim winked at Frankie.

She looked at Jim and said, "Thank you for sharing your story with us." Turning back towards the kids she said, "Okay tonight we're going to start working on a dream notebook. How many of you have heard of something called a vision board?"

Frankie looked into a sea of blank faces.

"A vision board is a place to put what you want out of life. You find photographs of things that represent your goals and dreams. You can add quotes, motivational phrases, Bible verses, or anything else that will motivate you to pursue your dreams. But I thought instead of making a board we would make a notebook. Something you can build on. I've brought a bunch of different magazines, glue, markers, scissors, and other craft supplies for you to use. We'll be working on a different page for the notebooks each time we come together. Tonight, we will start with jobs. If you could do any job in the world, what would it be? Let's start with you Ty."

Tyler looked up from his book and said, "A policeman."

Frankie smiled and said, "Alright! Who's next?"

Carl looked around the room and said, "I want to be an architect."

Brooklyn meekly said, "I want to be a teacher."

Sam, the newest member of the group, said, "I want to be a soldier like my dad was."

"I want to be a nurse like my auntie. She's loaded," said Laura.

"I want to edit films," said Dani. "Like for Hollywood."

Ross was the last to answer. At first Frankie thought she was going to have to prod him to talk but just as she started to say something he said, "I think I'd like to play basketball."

Sam and Laura started to tease him, but Frankie quickly said, "Enough. Maybe we need to set some ground rules. In this group, we don't laugh at one another's dreams. In this group, anything is possible if you are willing to work hard enough. With that in mind, Ross let's talk about how you can make that happen."

A smile crossed his face. Ross said, "I play basketball at the park every single day. I practice my free throw, layups, and footwork. And I've applied to go to camp this summer."

"That's great," affirmed Frankie. "Maybe we can talk to Coach Q about letting you work out with the team here at the university sometime."

Ross beamed, "You really think they'd let me do that?"

"Maybe. We won't know until we ask."

One by one Frankie went around the room and asked each teen how they were going to make their dream job happen. As they brainstormed, she helped them to realize it was okay to dream big if they were willing to work hard to make it happen. After they had each had a chance to share their plan she said, "Now we need to put it on paper."

Frankie and Jim worked the room, guiding each of them through the process of creating their page. The time went quickly and before she knew it Frankie was telling everyone to start cleaning up. The kids started carrying things out to the Jeep while Frankie put the tables back in order.

"I didn't realize how tired I was," yawned Frankie.

"Are you on tomorrow night?" Jim asked.

"Yeah, but I don't go in 'til 3."

"I'm working a late wire, want to go for a run in the mornin'?"

"Sure. The park?"

"Let's go to the river so we can grab breakfast after!"

"Sounds good. See you there!"

On the drive back to her house Brooklyn asked, "Miss Frankie is Agent Jim your boyfriend?"

Frankie was taking a drink of her diet Coke and choked on Brooklyn's question, spewing soda across the steering wheel. "No, we're just friends."

"Hmmm. If you say so."

THIRTY-TWO

FRANKIE WOKE to a text message from Jim.

"Called back in on the wire. Raincheck on the run?"

"Sure. Stay safe!"

Frankie's day went by quickly and before she knew it, she was in her Jeep and on her way to the office. She could hear Mia and the rest of the squad talking when she got off the elevator.

"What's going on guys?"

"Getting ready to walk an in-custody through for the day shift," answered Detective Rich Coleman.

"He's hoping that new prosecutor, Jessica-something or other, will be the one to review it," teased Detective Brett Wheeler.

Frankie just smiled and dropped her stuff at her desk. She immediately started working on trying to identify "Tre."

Mia waited for Coleman and Wheeler to leave then asked,

"How late did you and Jim stay out the other night?"

"Maybe ten minutes after you left."

"You know he's into you right?"

"No," Frankie looked up from her computer and her voice faltered. "We're just friends."

"Did you tell Derek you were hanging out with him?"

"You mean like he told me about hanging out with Jessica? Besides, there's nothing to tell, Mia. We're just friends and, to be honest, I'm not even sure what Derek and I are. I mean after all this time I think I'd like to have something more than an occasional roll in the hay. When we're together it's great but I sense he has no intention of making any type of commitment to me. He's never even expressed an interest in meeting my kids. Shouldn't that tell me something?"

Mia paused before saying anything. It was hard for Frankie to say what she had just said. She didn't want to make things more confusing.

Softly she said, "Maybe you should tell him what you just told me."

"Yeah, maybe." Frankie turned her focus back to her computer. She didn't initially find anything for Tre Stockton, but when she searched for Aurelia Stockton, she found an address. "I think I've found him!"

"Tre?" Mia asked.

"Yep. I looked up the address listed for his mother and found a Treyvon Stockton. I'm pulling him up now."

Mia moved around to stand behind Frankie. "He *is* a big guy."

"Yeah, no wonder she was scared." Frankie started looking through his criminal history. "Looks like he has quite the history. Three assault charges – all against females. White females."

"What's his deal?"

"I don't know – but there is a definite bias. He also has a couple of warrants. Looks like a Jackson County failure to appear and a Kansas City bench warrant."

"Why don't you call Sarah while I put together a line-up to show her."

Mia nodded as Frankie dialed Sarah's number.

After Frankie was off the phone Mia asked, "Do you think it's possible this is a hate crime?"

"Maybe. I'm not sure what to think yet. You ready?"

Mia nodded.

On the ride to Sarah's house Mia asked, "How was the VISION meeting?"

"Not bad. We had five kids show up, not counting mine. Jim came and talked about his life in a small town and how he worked hard to make something of himself. It was the perfect segue into the project. When Jim was finished all the kids told what they want to do when they get out of school, and we brainstormed how to make it happen. We even started working on their dream books."

"Jim came to the meeting?"

"Yeah, I thought it would be good for them to hear from someone besides me and Coach Q. I wish I could get Derek to come in. He would be a great role model. He grew up poor and made something of himself. Did you know Jim almost didn't go to the FBI?"

"No, why not?"

"I don't know for sure. Brooklyn asked him and he said he just needed a change. Something about the way he said it makes me think there is more to the story than what he said."

Mia said, "I bet it was a girl."

"It wouldn't surprise me." Pointing at a brick ranch house Frankie added, "I think that's Sarah's house."

Mia put the car in park just as Sarah walked out the front door. Her shoulders were hunched forward and her skin sallow. Her cream-colored sweater hung from her body and her eyes were bloodshot from a lack of sleep.

"Thanks for meeting with us Sarah." After making small talk, Frankie turned on her audio recorder and said, "I'm going to show you a series of photographs. If you see anyone you recognize I would like you to point him out, sign the photograph, and indicate how you know him. Since this is an audio recording, I need you to say the number of the photo. If you do not recognize anyone, please say so and we will continue trying to identify the man that attacked you. Do you understand?"

"Yes," said Sarah.

Flipping through the photographs she suddenly said, "That's him! That guy! He's the one that raped me! Number four."

Turning the recording device off Frankie thanked Sarah.

"How did you find him?"

"The clerk from the store helped us."

"I was so mad at her. I thought she'd help me, but she just stood there and acted like they were friends."

"She came through. We're going to put out a pick-up order for his arrest. I'll call you when he gets picked up."

Tears fell from Sarah's eyes as she said, "Thank you. Maybe I can sleep now."

Frankie gently touched her hand and said, "I hope so."

Inside the car, Frankie turned to Mia and asked, "What do you think about doing a residence check for this asshole?"

THIRTY-THREE

FRANKIE WAS glad they were driving towards the city during the evening rush hour. Traffic heading out of the city was bumper to bumper and moving at a slow crawl.

A half hour later they were parked down the street from the address Frankie located for Treyvon. A 'for rent' sign was posted in the yard of the small saltbox house.

"What are the chances this is the right address?" Mia asked.

"I'd say fifty-fifty. Cheyenne said Tre's mom moved, but it's worth a shot. Maybe we'll get lucky and someone will know their new address."

"It doesn't look like anyone's living there."

There were no blinds or curtains on the front picture window, allowing them to see through to the kitchen. There didn't appear to be any furniture in the house and the mailbox was full. Frankie picked up mail that had fallen onto the small front porch. It appeared to be junk mail but was addressed to "Aurelia Stockton or current resident."

"Looks like they have moved but didn't put a forward in at the post office."

Walking back to the car, Mia asked, "You think his momma knows about his warrants?"

"Maybe."

They had just gotten into the car when the unit phone started to ring.

"Sex Crimes Detective Boden. Slow down. Did you see where he went?" Mia scribbled on her notepad. "Okay. We'll be there in about 10 minutes…. I'm going to get a patrol car to check the area."

Frankie asked, "What's up?"

"Cheyenne, the girl from the gas station? She said Tre was just in the store and he was pissed. He told her he was going to kill her."

Frankie grabbed her phone and dialed while asking, "Is he on foot or in a car?"

"Foot," replied Mia.

"Hey Mac. Are you working? Where are you now?" Frankie gave him a description of Tre and his last location. "We're on our way there now."

Mia pulled the car away from the curb.

"242 to 1061 on private."

"Go ahead 242," Frankie answered.

"Frankie, I think we have him. Want us to stop him?"

"Where are you?"

"73rd and Woodland, heading east."

"Okay, just keep an eye on him for a minute. We're getting close."

Mia drove faster, "Want me to turn on the lights and sirens?"

"No. Mac's got eyes on him."

The drive seemed endless, even though it was only a few blocks. Frankie tapped the door repeatedly with her fingers. She didn't want the man Mac was following to run. But was he even the man they were looking for?

Frankie grabbed the car radio about three blocks out,

"1061 to 242 on private."

"Go ahead 1061."

"Do you still have eyes on the suspect?"

"Affirmative. You ready for us to stop him?"

"Yea. We're almost there."

Frankie returned the police radio to the hook just in time to hear, *"242 copy a ped check."*

"Go ahead 242," answered dispatch.

"Gregory and Paseo. Black Male. Red t-shirt and blue jeans."

"242 on a ped check 1833."

Jumping out of the car, Frankie walked up just as Mac pulled the wallet from the man's pocket.

"What are you stopping me for man? I was just walking. Didn't do a fuckin' thing wrong."

"Someone said a man matching your description was threatening to harm them. Where've you been today?"

"Just walkin' man. Waitin' for my momma to get home."

"Where does your momma live?"

"Just up there," nodding his head northward. "Like, three or four houses up on the other side of the street."

Mac handed Frankie the wallet as she approached. From it she retrieved a Missouri Identification card. Treyvon T. Stockton. He towered over her small frame.

"Who's she?"

"Detective Thomas," turning towards Mac she asked, "Have you ran him in the computer yet?"

"Nope," answered Mac.

Frankie looked at Mac and tapped her wrist. Mac recognized the signal they used when they were partners.

"Put your hands behind your back," Mac said as he put his hand on Tre's arm.

Once he was handcuffed, Frankie said, "Stockton has a failure to appear for Jackson County and a bench warrant out of Kansas City."

Mac keyed up his microphone, *"242 to dispatch. Start me a wagon."*

The patrol wagon driver piped in, *"249's en route."*

"Thanks 249. 1840 hours," answered dispatch.

"Treyvon it looks like you'll be heading downtown," stated Mac.

"Whatever," Stockton's light eyes bored through Mac. "Can I call my momma? She's expecting me to be there when she gets home."

"You can call her when we get downtown."

Once the patrol wagon arrived Frankie told Mac she and Mia were going to go follow up with the clerk about the threats.

"Let me know what you find out."

"You got it."

"Thanks Mac. Stay safe!" Frankie and Mia yelled in unison.

In the car Mia asked, "Do you think it's the same guy that threatened Cheyenne?"

"Yep. Sarah identified him and he matches the description she gave us."

"Still want to go by the Fast Stop to be sure?"

"Yep. We need the surveillance from the other night anyway and I want to know exactly what he said to her."

They parked in front of the building and saw Cheyenne was busy helping customers. They waited until the last person walked out the door before walking inside to take her report.

"Did you get him?"

"We stopped a man matching his description. What was he wearing?" asked Mia.

"Red shirt and jeans."

"That fits. What exactly did he say to you today?"

Frankie pulled out her recorder and laid it onto the counter.

"He came in pissed off. He said he saw cops here the other day and wanted to know what I told them. I told him the cops were here for something else. I told him somebody did a pump and run and the owner makes us call the police every time and make a report. But I don't think he believed me. He said I better not tell anyone I saw him here the other night. And if I did tell he was going to come back while I was working and spray the building."

"Have you ever known him to carry a gun?" Frankie asked.

Giving her a look like she was the dumbest woman on the planet Cheyenne said, "I know I've seen a bulge in his pants and it sure as hell wasn't his junk."

Mia and Frankie coughed in unison trying to not laugh.

Frankie pulled Tre's photo from her bag and showed Cheyenne, "Is this him?"

"Yeah, that's Tre. You got him locked up?"

"He's in police custody. Turns out he had a couple of warrants so he's going to spend the night downtown."

"His momma will just bail him out. Then he's going to come here and find me."

"Not tonight she won't. His warrants require a court appearance," assured Frankie.

"Will you let me know if he gets out?"

"Yea. We'll give you a call," Mia grabbed her notepad and gathered her contact information.

As they left Cheyenne called out, "He's crazy, you know? Seriously crazy."

Nodding, the pair left the business.

THIRTY-FOUR

"MR. STOCKTON, I am Detective Thomas and this is Detective Boden. We want to talk to you about some allegations that have been made against you."

Tre leaned back in the seat with his legs stretched out in front of him.

"By who?"

Evading his question Frankie asked, "Where were you Saturday night?"

"Out."

"Can you be a little more specific? Where were you around midnight?"

"Probably at my uncle's. Or maybe my girl's house."

"Did you go anywhere else?"

"Naw."

Pulling a photograph from the file, she laid it on the table and asked, "Do you recognize this woman?"

Scooting back into the seat and sitting up straight, he leaned over the table and looked down at the photograph. Tre picked it up, stared for a moment, then let it drop from his fingers onto the table.

"I don't know her."

"Have you ever seen her before?"

"I don't go around with *her* type."

"What do you mean, *her* type?" Frankie asked curiously.

"White girls."

Mia put her pen down and asked, "Why not?"

Tre didn't initially respond. He pulled his lips in, sucked his teeth, then curled his lips in a semi-snarl. Mia and Frankie leaned back in their chairs and waited.

He twisted in his seat without speaking. Finally, he said, "My people don't associate with no white chicks."

"There has to be a reason," pushed Mia.

Leaning back in his chair he put his hands across his flat stomach and looked from Frankie to Mia. He crossed his legs at the ankle then said, "Two fucking white bitches killed my uncle last year. Therefore, I don't associate with *your* kind."

Frankie thought she saw an opportunity to build rapport and said, "I'm sorry to hear that Tre. What happened?"

Tre appeared to be sizing her up; deciding if she was being sincere or playing him. Frankie didn't move. She laid her pen down, put her folded hands onto the table and waited.

"They robbed him. Shot him."

Softly Frankie said, "Damn. That's awful. Where'd it happen?"

"Westport. Fucking bitches left him there to die in the street like he was some kind of animal." Shoving the photograph back across the table he said, "Like I said, I don't know the bitch."

"Were you in Westport Saturday night?"

"I told you I was with my uncle or at my girl's house."

"Where does your uncle live?"

"In those apartments off of 63rd out by Blue Parkway."

"Your girl?"

"53rd and Michigan."

Frankie asked Tre to give her the names and addresses for his uncle and his girlfriend. When she had what she needed she asked him, "Is there any reason your DNA would show up in that girl's rape kit?"

His eyes bored into hers, his gaze unwavering. Frankie didn't flinch. Tre's foot began to tap the floor and his hands brushed at invisible lint on his pants.

With a crack in his voice Tre answered, "No."

"Any reason you might be on surveillance video in Westport? Maybe near Kelly's."

Sitting up Tre brushed the invisible lint again then said, "Maybe. I mean, I might have gone down to see who was hanging out. I might be on there."

"Okay, so earlier you said you didn't go to Westport. You were at your uncle's and your girl's house. Now you're saying you went to Westport to see who was hanging out?"

"Yeah, I mean after I left my girl's I went by there on my way to my uncle's."

"Got it." Westport wasn't on the way from 53rd and Michigan to the apartments on 63rd Street, but Frankie wasn't ready to confront Tre yet. He was putting himself at the scene, so she was going to let it go. For now. "Did you talk to anyone while you were there?"

Tre hesitated before answering, "I may have talked to some girls, but it wasn't *that* girl. I mean, she's lookin' rough."

Frankie looked over her notes and waited.

"Even if I talked to her *kind*, that chick doesn't look like anyone I'd talk to. Her hair's a mess and what's up with her clothes?"

"She had a rough night," interrupted Frankie. "Tre do you ever go to a gas station at 75th and Holmes?"

"I used to. My momma used to live by there and she'd send me there for milk sometimes. Why?"

"Any reason you'd be on video there Saturday?"

"Naw, I mean, I don't know. Maybe. My momma still lives near there. I might have gone there to get her some milk or something."

"No other reason?"

"Naw. Not that I remember."

Frankie and Mia continued the line of questioning and when they were satisfied they had locked him into his lies they ended the interrogation.

"How long am I gonna be in here?"

"It's up to the judge Tre. Both of your warrants require a court appearance. You'll probably be able to see a city judge tomorrow for the bench warrant. I don't know about the Jackson County failure to appear warrant."

"Alright."

CHAPTER
THIRTY-FIVE

"YOU THINK the prosecutor will charge him?" asked Mia.

"They should, but who knows. She had a forensic exam which will hopefully give us his DNA. Plus, he denied knowing her. He said he was never with her, but we have surveillance video that contradicts that. At the very least we've established he's a liar. Of course, we'll go out and talk to his uncle and his girlfriend and see what they say, but I doubt they'll be of any help to him."

"You want to go tonight?"

The clock on the wall read 730pm – still early enough to make a few house calls. "Let's do it," Frankie said.

Mia drove to the address Stockton had given for his girlfriend first. "Are you sure this is the right address," she asked Frankie.

The windows of the house were covered in plywood. Shingles were missing from the roof and the ones remaining were broken and scorched. Soot fanned out from behind the plywood covering the doors and windows and blanketed the siding.

Reviewing her notepad Frankie said, "It's the address he gave. He said her name is Mona Andrews." She typed the address into the car's computer. "Looks like a Mona Andrews did live at this address at one time. When I run her name no other addresses come up. I'd say it's safe to say she doesn't live here now – and Tre wasn't here visiting her on Saturday."

"Did the computer say when the fire was?"

Mia typed in a new search and said, "Fire was dispatched three weeks ago. Notes say they called the Bomb and Arson Unit out. I'll pull the report when we get back to the unit."

"Okay. Let's check out the uncle's place. Maybe he can tell us something."

After the short drive Frankie led the way to the apartment where Tre said his uncle lived. Her raps on the door were met with a gruff, "Just a minute."

Both women stepped to the side as they waited for the door to open. The frail man who answered the door was sitting in a wheelchair.

"Are you Kenneth Stockton?"

"Who wants to know?"

"I'm Detective Thomas and this is Detective Boden. We are looking for Kenneth Stockton."

"That's me. What do you want?"

"Is Treyvon Stockton your nephew?"

"Harrumph," Kenneth broke into a fit of coughing.

Frankie waited until he stopped coughing then asked, "Was that a yes?"

"TT is my sister Aurelia's boy. What do you want with him?"

"Did he come over here Saturday night?"

"He comes over 'bout every day. Brings me food and stuff I need."

"What time was he here on Saturday?"

"Same time as he always is. Why are you asking me these questions?"

Sensing Kenneth's impatience she said, "He's been accused of some stuff and when we asked him about it, he said he was here. We're just following up. What time does he normally come by?"

"Right around dinner time. 7, I think. He didn't come by today though. Aurelia brought me some food on her way from work. Who's accusing him?"

"A woman he encountered in Westport." Frankie gave Kenneth little information before asking, "How long was he here?"

"He was here about thirty minutes."

"What kind of car does he drive?"

Kenneth rubbed his chin before saying, "It's an old beater. A Buick, I think. Damn thing barely ran. One of the doors wouldn't even open from the inside."

Frankie jotted the information onto her notepad.

"Who's the girl? And what's she accusing him of? He ain't got no girlfriend."

"A white female about his age. She's accusing him of rape."

"Hmpf, it wasn't TT. He wouldn't be with no white girl."

Frankie and Mia looked at one another. They had heard this before.

"No kidding?" asked Mia. "Why is that?"

"We don't associate with *those* types."

"Hmm, you mean white women?" Frankie innocently asked. "Why?"

"Two white girls killed my little brother so me and my people don't associate with *those* types."

"I'm sorry for your loss. What was your brother's name?"

"Terrence Stockton. He was killed 'bout a year ago in Westport," tears welled in Kenneth's eyes. "They left him lying in the street like he was nothin' but a piece of trash."

"Did they find the girls who did it?"

"Mmhmm. They're in jail."

"That's good. Thank you, Mr. Stockton. We appreciate your time," said Frankie.

Walking back to the car Mia asked, "You think there's more to that story?"

"Definitely. I'll check and see what I can find in the computer."

CHAPTER
THIRTY-SIX

FRANKIE HAD JUST PULLED up the file on Terrence Stockton's murder on the in-car computer when her phone began to ring.

"Hi Brooklyn, what's up?"

"Hey Miss Frankie. My momma stopped by the house today. She said that guy that attacked her has been grabbing other girls. She said she's ready to talk to you now."

"Where's she at Brooklyn?"

Mia pulled into an empty parking lot and waited. She suspected they were going to go hunt for Brooklyn's mother, Asia.

"Thanks Brook. I'll message you when I'm done." Frankie disconnected the phone and turned to Mia, "Asia is at the laundromat on Independence Avenue. She said she'd give us a statement."

Mia drove while Frankie created a photo line-up of Sawyer on the in-car computer. As she worked, she updated Mia on the Stockton murder.

"Treyvon and his uncle made it sound like Terrence was murdered for no good reason by two crazy white women. According to the reports I found, he *was* found dead in the street near the Pub. The women were identified and arrested quickly – in *his* car. Police found a baggie with a couple of rocks and a 9mm handgun on his body. When they searched his car, they found two eight balls of crack, two more handguns, a pound of weed, and a baggie of sheetrock crumbs."

"Sheetrock crumbs?"

"Yeah, apparently, he tried to sell the sheetrock crumbs as crack to the girls. They took the baggie and once they realized it wasn't real crack, they confronted him. He got mouthy so they shot him. They claim they didn't know the dope was in the car, but they were charged with possession as well as murder. A security guard was watching the cameras and saw the whole damn thing. He called 9-1-1 but it was too late to save Terrence. The girls were apprehended a couple blocks away."

"Damn."

Frankie finished the line-up just as Mia was parking the car in front of the laundromat. She grabbed her notepad and recorder and the two walked inside. Asia was sitting at the same folding table she had been sitting at when Frankie and Mia picked her up and transported her to the hospital a few weeks before.

"Miss Asia, do you remember us?"

Mia and Frankie sat at the table across from Brooklyn's mother. Asia's gold eyes bored into Frankie's.

"Yeah, you're Brooklyn's friend. You didn't get him off the street yet."

Exasperated Frankie answered, "No ma'am. We haven't." She reached across the table and touched Asia's dark, espresso-colored hands, and with a softer voice said, "But with your help we might be able to."

Asia looked from Mia to Frankie and said, "What do you want to know."

"Can you tell us what happened the night you were attacked?"

"And I won't get in any trouble?"

"No ma'am. We don't care if you were trying to make a date or score dope. We care about what happened to you."

Asia took a deep breath and slowly exhaled. She looked around the laundromat to see if anyone else was in the store.

Mia noticed her hesitation and asked, "Miss Asia, do you want to go somewhere else and talk?"

"No, here's as good a place as any. Floyd is the only one here and he's listening to the T.V."

Frankie pulled out the recorder and explained the process to Asia.

Once she was certain Asia understood Frankie said, "Tell us what you remember. How you remember it."

"It was November. I don't remember the exact date, but it was the day before you came and found me. I was using again. I promise I didn't lie to Brooklyn. I was clean for almost three months, but then I went to a party. One of my friends gave me a hit from a pipe and it was downhill from there.

"That night I was hurting and looking for a fix. I was walking down Prospect when this guy in a little silver car pulled up and asked me if I was working. I told him I wasn't. I wasn't planning to turn any tricks that night. I had a friend who said he'd hook me up on credit, so I was walking to his place. The guy called me a stupid whore and pulled away. I didn't really pay attention to where he went." With a crack in her voice she said, "I should have."

Asia removed a tissue from her bag and blew her nose. Tears glistened in her eyes but never fell down her cheeks.

"I was only about a block away from my friend's house when the dude came back. But this time when he pulled up next to me, he pulled a gun out and told me to get in the car. I started to say something but then I heard the gun cock. He was serious. He was going to shoot me if I didn't get in the car. I pulled the car door open and got in…I didn't want to die.

"He drove down a couple of side streets then pulled down an alley and parked. He told me to get in the backseat, but I didn't move. He started yelling at me, calling me names. I didn't care. I wasn't getting into that back seat. He got out and opened the back door, grabbed me by the hair, and yanked me into the back of his car. I fought him, but eventually he got me back there. That's when he started punching me. I don't know how many times he hit me, but I'm pretty sure I passed out. When he was done doing what he wanted to do to me he grabbed me by the feet and pulled me out of the car. He left me in a pile, half naked, in the alley. As he drove away, I saw my bag and some clothes fly out the window."

"Do you think you'd be able to take us to the alley?"

Asia didn't immediately answer. She fumbled with the tissue in her hands then said, "I can try."

Mia and Frankie looked at one another and nodded.

Frankie said, "Let's go for a ride."

THIRTY-SEVEN

"BEFORE WE START DRIVING, I want to show you a few pictures and see if you recognize the man that hurt you." Frankie had left the recorder on while they sat in the front seat of the car.

Asia looked at the photographs on the computer carefully before saying, "I'm not sure. I don't want to pick the wrong guy."

Frankie looked at Mia who was watching from the back seat. "Take your time Miss Asia. Does one look more like him than the other?"

Asia touched the computer screen before saying, "Maybe number four, but I'm not for sure. It was dark and these pictures are just too small."

"That's okay. Let's see if we can find the alley."

Frankie was disappointed Asia didn't give a positive I.D. but was glad she picked Sawyer as the one who looked most like the guy that attacked her. Asia directed Frankie to Prospect and ultimately to where she was forced into the car. Once they got onto side streets Asia was less confident giving directions. After about ten minutes she scooted forward in the seat and started tapping the dash. Before Frankie could point out another alley, Asia screeched, "That's it. That's the alley."

Frankie stopped, but before she could put the car in park Asia jumped out and started racing down the dark alley. She stopped about midway down the alley and exclaimed, "He parked right about here."

Frankie and Mia rushed to Asia's location.

"He pulled me out of the car here," she pointed to an area about three feet from where she stood. "Over there – shine your flashlight over there!"

Frankie shone her light in the area Asia was pointing. On the ground was a pair of panties and a sock. Was it possible after all this time they were Asia's?

"Those are mine!" Asia shouted.

She moved towards the items when Mia shouted, "Wait, don't touch those!"

Asia gave her a puzzled look.

"We want to take some photographs and collect them as evidence," Frankie explained. "Are you certain these are yours?"

Asia's shoulders slumped forward. She nodded in understanding. She stood next to Frankie and said, "Shine your light."

Frankie did as Asia asked.

"See that?" She pointed at a black mark near the waistband, "If you pick them up you'll see they have an A on them. I sometimes do laundry at the Shower House on 12th Street and have to mark my clothes, so no one steals them."

Frankie nodded, put her hand on Asia's shoulder and said, "That's great Miss Asia. This is really going to help."

Asia released a deep sigh and smiled.

"Let's see if Crime Scene can come out and get some good photos…I don't think our camera will give us what we need in this lighting."

"I'll go make the call," Mia said.

"WHERE CAN we take you Miss Asia?"

The Crime Scene Unit had just finished, and Frankie didn't want to leave Asia out on the streets in the cold.

"I'll be fine. I have some friends I can crash with."

"We can take you there if you want."

"You can drop me back at the laundromat. Floyd said he would stay open 'til I got back. I'll meet up with my friends later."

Frankie suspected Asia didn't have anywhere to go, or any friends to stay with, but she couldn't force her to go to a shelter.

Frankie and Mia dropped Asia at the laundromat. Looking at the clock on the car radio Mia asked, "It's almost 10, still want to try and find Tre's mother?"

Tapping her fingers on the steering wheel Frankie said, "Yeah, let's close the loop on this."

The drive to Aurelia Stockton's house was brief. They were surprised to see a porch and living room light illuminated. It was almost as though she were expecting them. The door was answered on the first knock. A broad woman, wearing a pale blue robe, filled the doorway.

"What took you so long," was the gruff greeting.

"Um, are you Miss Stockton? Treyvon Stockton's mother?"

"Yeah. What do y'all want?"

Frankie took a step closer and asked, "It's a bit chilly, may we come inside?"

Aurelia stepped aside and led the women to her living room. "You can have a seat here," pointing towards the plastic-covered sofa.

"Did your brother call you today?" Mia asked.

"No, but my son did. Said you all locked him up for nothin'."

Mia opened her notepad and said, "Ma'am, we didn't lock him up for nothing. He was arrested on a Jackson County failure to appear warrant and a Kansas City bench warrant. He didn't go to court or pay his fines, so the judge issued warrants."

Slightly mollified, Aurelia said, "I thought he took care of those. But they don't send detectives for that. What do y'all want with him?"

Frankie looked around the tidy living room, stopping on the photo of Aurelia with two men she assumed were her brothers. Flanking the photograph were images of Treyvon at various ages. He looked like a sweet boy.

"*What made him change?*" Frankie wondered to herself. Aloud she asked, "Miss Stockton, do you know Cheyenne Connor?"

"Cheyenne who? Oh wait, you mean that girl from the Fast Stop over on 75th?"

"Yes ma'am."

"She's a good girl. Why are you asking about her?"

"She said Treyvon came into the store tonight and threatened her. Said he told her he was going to kill her."

Aurelia smoothed the robe covering her legs, then folded her hands in her lap. She looked up and said, "I don't think my boy would do that. He always liked Cheyenne. In fact, I think he kind of has a crush on her."

"Miss Stockton, do you remember seeing Tre on Saturday?"

Aurelia didn't hesitate, "I was with my cousin Latisha in Topeka this weekend. I left before breakfast and didn't get back until Sunday afternoon."

"Did Tre stay here while you were out of town?"

"I don't like him to stay here while I'm gone."

"Is there anywhere you can think of he might have stayed? Another relative's house?"

Aurelia took the strap of her robe and began running it through her fingers. She sat quietly for a few moments then said, "His daddy's sister. He might have stayed at her house."

Frankie and Mia looked at one another then back to Aurelia. Mia asked, "What is her name and where does she live?"

"Georgia Williams. Her brother, Von, is Treyvon's daddy. But he's been dead since Tre was a baby. She lives down by Grandview. Off Bannister Road. Why do you ask14?"

"Miss Stockton, another woman made some allegations against Tre. She said he kidnapped her in Westport. He drove her around and took her to a house and raped her."

Aurelia sucked in her breath and put her hand to her chest, "My baby ain't no rapist. He ain't even got no girlfriend. Who's this girl?"

"We can't give you her name ma'am."

"That girl's probably just upset he didn't call her after they had sex."

"We showed Tre a photograph of her, and he claims he'd never seen her before. In fact, he said he didn't associate with *her* kind."

Looking up, she asked, "Is that girl white?"

"Yes, ma'am," answered Frankie.

"Then she's wrong. My boy didn't have nothing to do with it. He doesn't associate with white girls. *We* don't associate with them."

"That's what he said," said Frankie. As she started to put her notepad back inside her bag she asked, "You said he didn't have a girlfriend, but he said he was at his girlfriend Mona's house Saturday night."

Aurelia stuttered, "That's not possible. Mona...um...she's gone to be with the angels."

"What happened to her?" Frankie asked.

"There was a fire at the house while she was babysitting. Tre was there. He got the little girl out, but he couldn't get back inside to get Mona."

"How scary. How long ago was that?"

"I'm not sure. A month or two."

"Did they ever figure out what caused the fire?"

Aurelia was beginning to get irritated, "Why you so interested in a fire?"

"No reason, just curious. We best be going ma'am. Thank you for your time." Once the door was closed and they were out of earshot

Frankie said, "Damn I wish it wasn't so late. I'd love to pay Miss Williams a visit."

Mia looked at her watch, "Yeah, 1030 is probably a bit too late for a knock and talk. Let's do it tomorrow. What do you think about the fire?"

"I think we need to talk to Bomb and Arson and make sure it wasn't homicide."

THIRTY-NINE

"YOU NEED A RIDE?"

Ciara looked at the gold Honda and the man sitting in the driver's seat. With a smile she said, "I don't talk to strangers."

"Then let's not be strangers," was the man's easy response.

Ciara shook her head, laughed, and continued to walk.

The Honda continued to creep forward while he talked, "I just thought you might need a ride. You don't want to be late."

Ciara looked at her watch. She was going to miss first period and would end up in detention if she didn't hurry up.

And the man looked harmless. He had to be her dad's age.

"My school's just down the street."

The man nodded. Once she was inside the car, he mumbled, "If you think I'm driving you to school you're stupid."

"Let me out of the car," screamed Ciara. She reached inside her sweatshirt pocket for her cellphone. When she realized she didn't have it she started to cry.

At the sight of her tears, he backhanded her and yelled, "Shut the fuck up."

After about ten minutes, the car pulled into an apartment complex. It was still early. There were people walking around on their way to school and work. Ciara looked around the parking lot and thought, "Maybe I can yell for help."

As if he could read her mind, the man turned to her and said, "If you make a sound, or try to run, I'll shoot you."

The man stepped out of the car and walked around the front to the passenger side. Ciara saw the grip of a handgun sticking out of the back of his pants. He opened the door and drug Ciara out of the car. He half-pulled, half-drug her to the entrance of the apartment. At the door, he used a key and pushed Ciara inside.

Ciara scanned the living room and tidy kitchen. The couch had decorative pillows, but she didn't see a television. She eyed the telephone hanging on the wall. If she could get to it and call 9-1-1 the police would come.

Shoving Ciara down the hall he said, "Don't even think about it bitch."

The man pushed her into the bedroom and shoved her face down onto the bed. Ciara's face and nose were pressed into the bedspread. She pressed her hands into the bed and tried to push herself back up.

Shoving her back down he said, "Don't move."

He pulled on her clothes, exposing her young body. Ciara twisted and pushed against him. She tried to yell for help, but he shoved her face into a pillow.

"I. Can't. Breathe." Her voice was muffled.

Grabbing her by the hair he pulled her up off the pillow and said, "Shut the fuck up!"

He flipped her body over and covered her mouth with his hand. Ciara watched him pull the gun from his waistband and lay it next to her head. She moved her hand slightly towards the gun. He grabbed her hands and held onto them with one of his. With his free hand, he pulled her pants off and tried to penetrate her. Ciara twisted her body and opened her mouth to scream. Before any sounds escaped, he grabbed a pillow and said, "If you yell, I'm going to shove this in your mouth!"

Ciara looked at his face. His steely gaze bore into hers. She laid there in silence. When he finished, he let go of her hands, stood up, and grabbed his gun.

"Put your clothes on."

Ciara just laid there and watched him put his pants back on, returning the gun to his waistband. He grabbed Ciara by the hair and made her sit up.

Throwing her clothes at her he said, "I said get your clothes on. And don't even think about leaving anything behind."

Ciara stared at him with wild eyes. Her hands trembled in fear. When she was finished getting dressed, he pushed her out of the apartment and back to his car. He drove a few blocks, made a series of turns, before finally coming to a stop in an alley. When he got out of the car to get Ciara she noticed the nametag hanging from the mirror.

"Allen," whispered Ciara.

Reaching the passenger door, he opened it and pulled her from the car by the hood of her sweatshirt. "If you say anything to anyone, I'll find you and kill you." With those words, Allen got back into the car and drove away.

Ciara watched the car turn and drive out of sight. She slowly walked up the alley but hesitated at the street. She looked both ways, scanning for a payphone. As she started to walk towards a phone in a store parking lot, she noticed the Honda parked across the street. Ciara made eye contact with Allen. He held up a finger and simulated a gun before pulling the car out of the lot.

Ciara walked up and down the street, unsure where to go or what to do. She gravitated towards the phone, but each time she got close she thought she saw the Honda and kept walking. After the third time seeing the car, she stopped walking and sat on the bench at the bus stop. Ciara kept her hands buried in the pockets of her sweatshirt, shivering in the cold.

The bus stop was on the outskirts of the grocery store parking lot. Ciara's face burned and her hands ached from the cold. She hadn't seen the gold Honda in more than an hour, so she decided to go inside the store to get warm. She wandered up and down the aisles of the store, not really looking at anything. When she started her third path around the store, she noticed she was being followed by a security guard.

"Do you need help finding something?" The security guard asked.

Tears welled in Ciara's eyes as she asked, "Will you help me?"

CHAPTER
FORTY

FRANKIE HAD JUST GOTTEN to work and dropped her bag on the chair when the phone began to ring.

"Sex Crimes Detective Thomas." Frankie grabbed her notepad and began writing. "Are you freaking kidding me? Okay, give us fifteen. Boden and I'll be out."

"What do we have?"

"Sawyer is at it again." Frankie slammed her hand down onto her desk, "Fuck! This time it's a seventeen-year-old. Rhodes is with her up on the Avenue. She's pretty shaken up but says she thinks she can identify the guy. Rhodes is taking her to County. We'll meet them there."

Frankie's cellphone dinged.

"Derek or Jim?" teased Mia.

"Hmm…" Frankie was reading the message and didn't hear what Mia asked.

"Hey beautiful. How's your day going? Want to come by after your shift? I miss you. D"

"Hey yourself. Just caught a case. Probably going to be a long night. This weekend?"

"Sure. Stay safe. XO"

"Frankie!" Mia said jarring Frankie from her thoughts.

"Yeah. Sorry, it's Derek. He wanted me to come by after work. I told him we just caught a case and will be late. I'll put together a line up and then we can head to the hospital."

"Mmhmm. Maybe you can put a big R on his forehead, so she'll pick him out," laughed Mia.

"Seriously! Hopefully she can pick him out of the lineup."

On the way to the hospital Mia turned on the car radio and the sound of, "I Gotta Feeling" by the Black-Eyed Peas filled the car.

Mia started to laugh, "It's an omen!"

Joining in the laughter, Frankie replied, "I sure hope so!"

CHAPTER
FORTY-ONE

FRANKIE ENTERED the doors of the Emergency Department with confidence, not slowing down as the waves of memories hit her. She pushed through, determined not to let them stop her from doing her job. The forensic nurse on-call exited the SANE room just as Frankie lifted her hand to knock.

"Detective Thomas," said Angela. "Ciara is talking to Meghan and Officer Rhodes. Her mom's filling out some paperwork out front. I'm going to go talk to her mom and then I'll be back."

"Thanks."

Frankie waited outside the door for a moment before knocking lightly.

"Come in," was the soft response.

Closing the door, Frankie looked around the room and tried to see it through Ciara's eyes. The walls of the small room felt like they were closing in around her. The exam bed was in the center of the room with diagnostic equipment flanking it. Officer Rhodes hulked over the table, looking down at the girl. The victim advocate, Meghan, sat next to her with a bag containing a change of clothes and a book on recovering from the trauma of being raped. The room was quiet compared to normal examination rooms in the ED, but it was just as sterile.

"Detective, this is Ciara Edens," said Officer Rhodes.

Frankie introduced herself to the doe-eyed girl lying on the examination bed. "Thanks Rhodes. Do you have what you need for your report?"

"Yeah, I think so, but can I talk to you guys outside for a minute?"

Frankie and Mia looked at one another then back to Ciara. Frankie nodded and said, "Sure. Ciara, we'll be right back, okay?"

Frankie walked out the door preparing for the onslaught of victim-blaming statements she had heard from officers over the years. The girl was lying. The girl is a prostitute who didn't get paid. Frankie was tired and not in the mood for any of it. Shoulders pressed back, she folded her arms across her chest and waited.

"This is legit man. This poor girl was grabbed right off the street. Forced into a car. Raped in an apartment and kept all night at gunpoint. Then this morning he dumped her in an alley. I'm telling you she's been through some bad stuff," rattled Rhodes.

Slightly taken aback Frankie uncrossed her arms and said, "Slow down. Do you know where it happened?"

"No. She said he took her to an apartment. I think she could identify it if we drove her by, but I figured it was more important to get her to the hospital. Did you see her face? He hit her pretty hard."

"I noticed," Frankie said.

Rhodes was worked up and needed to help do something. Frankie could either enlist his help or risk him unintentionally interfering.

"Do you know if they had surveillance cameras at the store by where he picked her up or where you found her?"

"I don't know, maybe," Rhodes said. Eagerly he added, "Want me to go get it for you?"

"That would be great – see what they have. If they have footage see if they will burn a disk. If they can't, or won't, give them my number and tell them I'll be by tomorrow with a warrant, a disk, or both. Also, canvas the area for us. Talk to local business and people hanging out to see if anyone saw anything. Be sure to write a report on whatever you find out."

"You got it. I'll call you if I find anything major."

"Thanks Rhodes – be safe!"

Once Rhodes was out of earshot Mia said, "Man, he was fired up!"

"I know! I was preparing for him to say some shit about this girl, but instead he actually wants to go out and try to find the guy that hurt her."

Frankie and Mia went back into the examination room and began the interview. After gathering all Ciara's biographical data Frankie asked, "Can you tell us what happened?"

FORTY-TWO

CIARA TOOK A DEEP BREATH, clenched and unclenched her fists, then exhaled. She did this a couple of times before saying, "My brother and I got into it yesterday morning, so I decided to take the Metro to school, but I got off at the wrong stop and had to walk farther than I thought. This old guy pulled up and tried to talk to me."

Frankie and Mia listened as Ciara told them about her experience.

"Do you remember the name of the apartment complex he took you to?"

"I don't remember the name of the place, but it was around Truman and Brooklyn. I know someone that lives near there so when he pulled in, I thought maybe I could run to her place. Before he got me out of the car, he told me he'd kill me if I tried anything."

"Was it his apartment?" Mia asked.

"I thought it was at first, but when we got inside it looked more like an old lady's place."

"What happened after he raped you?"

"He made me lay there. He kept an arm on me and said if I moved, he'd shoot me. He wouldn't let me get up. The one time he let me go to the bathroom he followed me and stood there while I peed. He made me sleep on the floor right next to the bed. When he woke up, he forced me to go back to his car. He drove around for a while then dumped me in an alley."

"Ciara did the man ever tell you his name? Or did you see anything in the apartment or car that had his name on it?" Frankie asked.

"He didn't tell me his name and I don't remember seeing anything in the car." Ciara hesitated before saying, "Wait, there was a plastic ID card. Like for work. I think the name on it was Alex or something like that. It was definitely an A name. And there was a big S hanging on the door of the apartment."

Frankie looked at Mia. A big S. Maybe for Sawyer?

"Do you think you'd recognize him if you saw him again?"

"Yea, I think so." Ciara's voice cracked, "Do I have to see him again?" She pulled her knees up to her chest and wrapped her arms around her legs.

"We have some photographs for you to look at. Would you be willing to take a look and see if you recognize any of the men in the photos? And if you do, we need to know where you know them from."

Frankie pulled out a manila folder with six 8X10 photographs.

Ciara took her time, looking at each photograph carefully. After a few moments, she took the photograph marked as #4 and said, "That's him. That's the guy that raped me."

Frankie asked, "Are you sure?"

"Yes. I'd recognize that face anywhere."

Frankie smiled at her, "Thank you Ciara. Detective Boden and I are going to go see if we can find this guy. Do you think you'd be able to take us to the apartment later?"

"Would I have to go inside?"

"No. We just want to have you show us where it is then we'll take you home."

"Okay. Yeah, I can do that."

Frankie and Mia thanked her and asked Meghan to call them when they were finishing up.

CHAPTER
FORTY-THREE

FRANKIE AND MIA got in the car just as the unit cellphone began to ring.

"Sex Crimes Boden. Yeah, hold on. Let me put you on speaker."

"It's Rhodes. I'm up on the Avenue. I haven't gotten any surveillance video yet, but apparently her mother has been doing her own investigation."

"What do you mean?"

"She went to a few stores and asked around. People are saying Ciara was getting in and out of cars."

"Shit. Did they say her specifically? Was she showing Ciara's picture?"

"No, they were saying a young, pretty, black girl was getting in and out of cars."

"Well, hell that could be anyone."

"I know. Do you want me to show her picture around?"

Mia looked at Frankie and asked, "What could it hurt?"

Frankie nodded. Aloud she said, "Yeah. Mia will send you a photo to your phone. Be sure to write all this in your report."

"Copy that. Did she identify the guy?"

"Yes. Given this new information I'm going to have her parents bring her to HQ when she finishes up at the hospital."

"Let me know. I'll have my reports done before I leave tonight."

"Thanks Rhodes. Stay safe."

Disconnecting the phone, she hit the steering wheel and said, "Shit."

"Do you think she was working?" Mia asked.

"Honestly? No, but her mother has planted doubt so we're going to have to ask her about it. It did seem odd to me that he kept her there all night. I think she's hiding something."

"A boy?"

"Maybe."

FORTY-FOUR

TWO HOURS later Ciara was sitting in the interview room with Meghan, waiting on Frankie and Mia to come in.

"Why did they want me to come in?" Ciara asked. "I thought they had everything they needed."

Meghan had been a victim advocate for a long time and knew it was not uncommon for detectives to have follow-up questions. She was surprised it was this quick but didn't think it would do any good to tell Ciara that. Instead, she said, "Sometimes they have follow-up questions. Is there anything you forgot to tell them? Or anything you left out?"

Ciara fidgeted with the straps on her purse. Ciara held her stomach and bent forward.

Meghan touched her shoulder and said, "Ciara, if there's anything you forgot or weren't completely honest about, this is your chance to set it straight. I've worked with Detectives Boden and Thomas for a long time. They are both very understanding. Just tell them the truth."

Ciara lifted her head and nodded slightly just as the door opened.

Frankie laid her notepad and case file on the table and said, "Thanks for coming in. I'm sure you are exhausted, so hopefully this won't take too long."

Softly Ciara asked, "Why did you need to see me again?"

Frankie's voice was calm, but firm, "I need to verify some things you told us earlier. It's really important that you tell me the truth. Do you understand?"

Ciara nodded.

"We have some reports of a young black woman getting in and out of cars on Independence Avenue. Is there any reason anyone would identify you as that woman?" Ciara shook her head, "It wasn't me."

"Okay. You said you were held at the apartment overnight. Did he give you anything to eat or drink?"

Ciara played with the lid on her bottle of water. She kept her gaze down, refusing to meet Frankie's eyes.

"He really did rape me."

"Ciara, we believe he raped you. We just want to make sure we have all the facts right before we arrest him."

Ciara sat in silence. Tears trickled down her toffee-colored cheeks.

"Ci..."

At the same moment Ciara mumbled, "He didn't keep me at the apartment all night."

Frankie inhaled deeply before asking, "Were you with him voluntarily?"

"No."

"Can you tell us what really happened?"

"I got into it with my brother yesterday, just like I said. I was upset when I got to school and one of my friends was leaving to go hang with her cousin and his friend. The dudes had a motel room out off Blue Parkway and they were going to hang out, watch television, and maybe play some video games. Nothing major. I was already in a bad mood because of my brother so I decided to ditch school and go with her."

"What's your friend's name?"

"Latonya Briggs."

"Do you know her cousin's name or his friend?"

"Her cousin is Demarco, and his friend is William."

"What happened next?"

"Demarco drove us to the motel and that was it. We ate pizza, played games, and watched television. I didn't mean to stay all night, but I fell asleep and next thing I knew it was like 6 AM. Demarco was getting up to go to work so I asked him to take me to school. He told me he couldn't, but he dropped me off at the Metro Stop. I took the bus to Independence Avenue just like I said before. Everything else happened the same... except...."

Frankie waited for Ciara to finish her sentence. After a long silence Frankie nudged, "Except what?"

"Except he didn't force me into the car. I noticed what time it was and realized I was going to be late. If I'm late again they're going to put me in detention. And the guy seemed harmless. He was old - like my dad's age - so I got into the car. When he pulled out of the parking lot, he told me I was stupid if I thought he was going to take me to school."

"What happened next?"

Ciara told Frankie the same story she had shared at the hospital. When she finished Frankie asked, "Ciara, did you have consensual sex with anyone at the motel?"

"No, it wasn't like that."

"Why did you tell us the man kept you in the apartment all night?"

Ciara looked from Meghan to Frankie, "I was scared. I knew I was in trouble for being out all night and thought if I said he kept me I might not get grounded."

"Is there anything else you need to tell us? Any other part of your statement you need to change?"

"No," Ciara said emphatically. "Everything else happened just like I said."

CHAPTER
FORTY-FIVE

"WHAT DO you mean you don't want us to arrest him?"

Frankie asked, her voice rising.

"I just don't think you have enough Detective. None of the cases you have told me about are solid by themselves. You must see the problems," replied Jessica Moon, the on-call prosecutor.

All Frankie could see was red. Her pulse was racing, and her head felt like it was going to explode. Through clenched teeth she said, "We have a positive identification, injuries, and potential DNA evidence."

"You have three likely prostitutes and one teenager who admitted to lying. Her own mother thinks she was working the streets, how can I expect a jury to believe she wasn't?"

"We have three women who were targeted because of their vulnerability. We have a scared teenager who lied about events leading up to the rape but didn't change her story about the rape itself."

Frankie was furious with Moon and her laziness. In the back of her mind, Frankie wondered if her relationship with Derek was influencing Moon. For weeks she had wondered why they were leaving the courthouse together. Was it possible she and Derek…

Moon interrupted her thoughts, "I'm not going to issue an arrest warrant based on what you've told me."

"Surely *you* see that he's a danger to the community, and if he rapes someone else tonight, it's on us."

"Detective Thomas, I think you're being overly dramatic."

Overly dramatic? Was Moon serious?

"I am not authorizing you to arrest him and if you do, I'm letting you know now he'll most likely be released. I don't intend to issue a warrant."

"I'll be in touch." Frankie disconnected the call and yelled, "Bitch!"

Mia looked at her and asked, "What the hell is her deal?"

"She says we don't have enough. That I'm being 'overly dramatic.' What the fuck else does she want?!" Frankie's face was beet red. "I swear this is personal."

Baker stepped out of his office at the sound of the raised voices.

Frankie told him what Moon had told her adding, "What the hell else do we need to do here? This is ridiculous."

"Give me her number. We're on the hook if he hurts someone else. I'll see if I can talk some sense into her," responded Baker.

About ten minutes passed before the phone rang.

"Sex Crimes. Detective Thomas."

"Detective Thomas, it's Jessica Moon. I still don't agree with you arresting Sawyer tonight, however Sergeant Baker said he was going to direct you to pick him up. With that in mind, if you get him into police custody, I expect all the completed case files on my desk by 8am. I won't decide without all of them being presented together."

"Okay." Frankie disconnected the phone and said, "She doesn't think we can do it."

"I guess she doesn't know who she's dealing with," laughed Mia. "Let's go get him."

Minutes later Frankie and Mia were on the highway heading south towards Sawyer's house. She picked up the mic and said, *"1061 on Metro."*

"Go ahead 1061."

"Do you have a 2-person crew that can meet myself and 1064 on a residence check in the area of Gregory and Wabash?"

"244. We can respond."

"Copy, 244 is out with 1061 and 1064 on a residence check at 2243."

Frankie looked at the clock on the radio and questioned the wisdom of starting this so late. Chances are he would lawyer-up again, but it was still going to be an all-nighter trying to get their reports done. It was the right thing to do, but she was going to pay for it in the morning.

CHAPTER
FORTY-SIX

FRANKIE PARKED the unmarked car on the side of the road about a block from Sawyer's house. The house was situated on the corner of 73rd and Wabash. His 4-door Honda was parked on the side street.

"Do you think he'll talk?"

"No, but I could be wrong. Maybe he'll want to confess his sins," Frankie laughed.

"Something tells me he doesn't think he's committing any."

Before Frankie could respond, a patrol car pulled up behind them. She and Mia stepped out and met Officers Shane and Stickler at the rear of their car.

"Hey, if it isn't the dynamic duo!" Frankie exclaimed.

Reaching his arm around her shoulders Shane asked, "How ya doin' kid?"

He and Frankie had worked together when she was on patrol.

"Hey Shane. Stick. How are you guys doing?"

"Good. What's the scoop on this one?"

Frankie and Mia explained the history to the officers and said, "If you guys will watch the back, we'll attempt to make contact at the front."

"Copy that. Do you have a radio?"

"No, I forgot to grab one when we left."

"Let's split up then. I'll go to the front door with you. Boden, you and

Stick can go to the back. That way at least one of us has a radio in case shit goes south."

"Good idea. Let's go."

Frankie and Shane crept their cars forward with their lights out. As they prepared to get out of the car the front door of the house opened. Sawyer was looking down as he exited the house and didn't notice their cars.

"1061 to 244. Stand by."

They watched as Sawyer got into the driver's seat of his car and pulled away.

"I'm going to follow him. Will you guys run parallel?"

"Copy."

"Where do you think he's going?" Mia asked.

"I don't know. Maybe to find another girl? Or maybe just to the store. I guess we'll find out," Frankie said.

Frankie stayed a couple of car lengths away and watched as Sawyer made his way to the highway then turned north towards the Avenue. Frankie hung back even more and watched his taillights. At 39th Street he exited the highway and turned back to the east.

"1061 to 244 on private."

"Go ahead 1061."

"He's heading east on 39th Street. Probably going over to Prospect. You guys can stay in Metro. We're just going to follow him a bit."

"Are you sure you don't want some help?"

"Naw, we've got him."

"Copy. Let us know what happens."

"You got it."

Just as Frankie predicted Sawyer turned north on Prospect. She watched as he slowed down at the corner looking, she assumed, for a woman who'd get into his car. There were women standing at the storefronts near 39th Street but he didn't stare for long. He continued to drive north on Prospect. Frankie kept her distance so she wouldn't spook him. He sped up as the businesses became houses. When he got to the 2900 block, he slowed down again. Sawyer approached the Green Duck slowly and pulled into the parking lot. Frankie parked far enough away as not to be seen, but close enough she could see what *he* was doing.

Sawyer pulled through the lot slowly. It didn't take long for him to be approached. A young man leaned into the passenger window and rested his elbows on the window frame. Frankie couldn't hear what they were saying but watched them talk for several minutes. The man stood up, looked around and then gestured for a woman to come to the car. She walked slowly, her gait unstable. She was a few feet from the car when she stopped. The man, Frankie assumed her pimp, grabbed her by the arm and pulled her closer. He put something in her hand, opened the car door, and shoved her inside.

CHAPTER
FORTY-SEVEN

"YOU THINK he gave her crack or a condom?" Mia asked.

"Both. Do you have a good description on him? I'm not convinced she got into the car willingly."

"Yeah, it's already written down. Me either."

Sawyer pulled out of the parking lot and continued north. Frankie hung back, hoping he didn't take too many side streets. It would be hard to follow him unseen if he pulled back into the neighborhoods. Much to her surprise Sawyer stayed on Prospect until he got to 18th Street. He turned back west and after a few blocks pulled into an apartment complex.

"What are the chances," asked Frankie.

"You think this is where he brought Ciara?"

"I'd bet money on it. We can't let him get this girl inside."

Frankie grabbed the mic to contact the dispatcher, *"1061 on East Zone. Copy a car check. Truman and Brooklyn, in the Brooklyn Apartment Complex. Gold 4-door Honda, Missouri plates 7 Boy Henry Young 8 Boy. Occupied twice. 1064 is with me but start us a second."*

"1061 and 1064 are out at 2348. Any car in the area?"

"142, we'll respond to their location."

"Copy. 142 with 1061 at 2348."

Frankie grabbed her flashlight and prepared to exit the vehicle. The door was open, and her left foot was out when she heard Mia yell, "Gun!"

Sawyer was out of the car, pointing his gun towards her.

CHAPTER
FORTY-EIGHT

FRANKIE'S WEAPON DRAWN, she ordered, "Drop the gun!"

Sawyer didn't move.

Frankie and Mia yelled in unison, "Drop the gun!"

Sawyer hesitated, then laid the gun on the roof of the car.

"Back away from the car with your hands in the air."

Mia kept her weapon trained on Sawyer. Frankie holstered hers as she approached and put handcuffs on his meaty wrists.

"Guess you'll get a second chance to talk to us," said Frankie.

"Don't hold your breath bitch."

A mere wisp of a woman sat trembling in the passenger seat of the Honda; her knees pulled close to her chest. The pallor of her skin was punctuated by the purple bruising already radiating from her left eye. One hand cupped her leg and the other traced the red marks circling her neck.

Frankie thought to herself, *"Are those from Sawyer or her pimp?"*

As if reading her mind, the woman said, "That guy grabbed my throat and choked the shit out of me when he saw your car behind him."

Frankie felt as though she had been punched. Would Sawyer have strangled her if he hadn't seen them?

"What's your name?" Mia asked.

"Stephanie. Blackwell."

"How'd you know the guy you were with?"

"I ain't never met him before," she stuttered.

Mia nodded then asked, "How did you end up in the car with him?"

Mia didn't want to let on that she and Frankie saw the guy shove her into the car.

"I was hanging out at the Green Duck. I wanted to score, and my boy Damien said he'd give me something if I went with this guy and did what he wanted. Now, man, I didn't want to go. You see Josie had done told me about the guy in the gold 4-door. I told Damien I had a bad feeling about it and didn't want to go. He said it don't matter what I 'feel like' that I had to go with him if I wanted the rock."

"Did the guy say anything when you got in?"

"Naw he was cool for a minute but then he started driving around and he got all weird and stuff. When he saw your car, that's when he grabbed my neck and said he was going to kill me."

CHAPTER
FORTY-NINE

AFTER TAKING STEPHANIE'S STATEMENT, Frankie went to pull Sawyer out of detention. Standing by the elevator, Sawyer looked down and said, "I want a lawyer."

Frankie looked at him and said, "If that's how you want it." Looking towards the detention officer she said, "You can put him back in a cell."

Frankie and Mia fell into a familiar rhythm organizing the case files. Mia drafted the report on the car check while Frankie drafted the probable cause statement. Sergeant Baker started making DVD copies of the interviews and 9-1-1 calls.

"How much longer do you think we'll be?" Mia asked.

Frankie looked up and yawned. She stood, stretched, and looked at the dry erase board of notes before responding, "An hour? Sarge, how many more discs do you have to copy?"

"Just finished. Are we ready to make paper copies yet?"

Another hour passed before Frankie said, "Done."

"Good job detectives. I've left a note for the dayshift. They'll deliver the files to the prosecutor first thing."

Frankie grabbed a post-it note and jotted her cellphone number on it. "Just in case," she said as she looked from Mia to Baker.

Frankie sat in her Jeep thinking about the night, contemplating what to do next. She was too keyed up to drive home. Glancing at the clock it read 5:00 – was it too early to wake Derek up? As she started to pick up the phone it began to ring. Picking it up she smiled at the face on the screen.

"Hey babe."

"Whatcha wearin'?" was the sultry response.

"A smile now."

"Want to come by?"

"You read my mind."

"How far out are you?"

"Crossing the Paseo Bridge."

"Want me to stay on the line while you drive?"

"No, it's okay. I'll see you in about fifteen."

Frankie disconnected the phone and turned up the music, the sounds of Daughtry filling the air. The Jeep seemed to be on autopilot as her mind raced. Her kids were in bed asleep, and she'd be home before they woke up. She could sleep while they were at school. Knowing all of this, why did she still feel guilty going to Derek's house instead of home?

Derek was glad Frankie had answered the phone. The nightmare was still fresh in his mind, and she was the perfect way to excise it. Nightmares were not new, but this time was different. In it he was standing by his car in the parking lot. Bullets were tearing his flesh and Jessica was falling into his arms, her eyes wide, and questioning. The last thing he heard before he awoke in a sweat was her asking, "Why?"

Fifteen minutes later Frankie was walking through Derek's back door. He stood in the dark at the kitchen window waiting for her. With the help of two fingers of Johnny Walker Black, his hands had stopped trembling and his pulse had returned to normal. She took her coat and weapon off, slid out of her shoes and fell into his arms. Her body melted into his, her mouth finding his in the dark. Frankie shivered as his cold hands slid under her sweater and touched her bare skin. Hungrily she pulled his shirt off and ran her hands across his taut chest. He began to lead her towards the bedroom, but she stopped and pointed at the couch.

Their clothing littered the floor and as their hands and mouth explored one another's. When they were both satisfied, she lay spent against his chest.

Chuckling Derek said, "Well that just happened."

Frankie lay silent for a moment then asked, "Why were you up? Did you have another dream?"

Derek stroked her hair but didn't immediately answer. He didn't want Frankie to worry. Eventually he sighed and said, "Yes."

Frankie grabbed a blanket and curled up next to him on the couch. She looked at Derek and noticed his hair had gotten grayer and his eyes looked sad.

"Want to talk about it?"

Derek looked into Frankie's blue eyes, pulled her in closer to his body, letting her head rest on his chest and said, "No, just let me hold you for a minute."

CHAPTER
FIFTY

FRANKIE GOT HOME JUST as the alarm clock was sounding in her daughter's room. She gently nudged Keith and told him she was home.

"You work all night?"

"Yeah. I left about an hour ago."

"How's the counselor?"

"Better every day."

Keith noticed Frankie's elusive response and was about to question her when Tyler came running into the room.

"Mom!" Tyler squeezed Frankie around the waist and said, "I'm so glad to see you!"

Hugging her son, she leaned down and kissed the top of his head, "I'm so glad to see you too bud. Why don't you go get ready for school and I'll make us some breakfast?"

"Kay. Toaster strudel?"

Frankie laughed and nodded. She watched a weary-eyed Dani walk from her bedroom to the bathroom. She thought she heard a grunt that sounded like hello, but she couldn't be sure.

"Are you working tonight?" Keith asked.

"No. I have tonight off."

"Okay. Want to have dinner with Bruce and I?" Keith asked. He and his partner Bruce met while working for the Kansas City Missouri Fire

Department. Keith was a firefighter and Bruce was a paramedic. Keith lived next door and Frankie watched as the friendship became a romance. Eventually Bruce moved in and became part of their extended family.

"That would be nice. Why don't I whip something up?"

"Sounds good…"

"Mom where are my shoes?" bellowed Dani.

Frankie rolled her eyes and said good-bye to Keith.

The rest of the morning went smoothly. After dropping the kids off at school, Frankie returned home to sleep. The ringing of the telephone woke her from a deep sleep. It took a moment for Frankie to realize it was her phone and not part of a dream.

"Thomas."

"Did I wake you?"

Smiling Frankie said, "Yeah, but I'm glad you called. How's your day going?"

"Better now. I won the hearing this morning. You must have brought me good luck."

"Good. Did Jessica come talk to you this morning?" Frankie sat up and waited to hear what Derek would say.

"I haven't seen her. Why would she?"

"She was the prosecutor I spoke with last night. She didn't want us to pick Sawyer up. Said we didn't have enough. Wanted our cases by 8am…"

Before Frankie could finish her sentence, the call waiting clicked in.

"Hold on a second." She clicked over and said, "Thomas."

"Detective Thomas this is Jessica Moon from the prosecutor's office. I have a couple of questions about the cases that were submitted on the in-custody."

"Can you hold for just a second?" Frankie told Derek she would call him back then returned to the call. After answering several questions, it became apparent Jessica not only had not read the files but had no intention of charging Sawyer in custody. "So, you plan to just let him go?"

"I'll revisit the cases once the kits have been processed and we have some DNA."

"What if he does it again? And he will. How many women does he have to rape before you decide to charge him?"

"I don't believe we can win the cases we have without DNA. Give me something more and I'll charge him."

"What about the fact that he had a gun, and the last victim was not with him willingly," pushed Frankie.

"I don't recall seeing that in the case files. Perhaps…"

Frankie bit her tongue. Inside she yelled, *"You didn't even read the fucking file!"* To Moon she asked, "What about Treyvon Stockton. What are you going to do with him?"

Moon shuffled some papers before saying, "Looks like Mr. Stockton has a failure to appear in another case so we will take a little more time to look at this one before making a decision."

Frankie disconnected the phone and yelled, "Bitch."

Giving herself a moment to calm down she grabbed her phone and called Sergeant Baker. She told him what Jessica had said in colorful terms.

"What if we put a tracker on Sawyer's car?" asked Baker.

"We should just keep his car," growled Frankie.

"I'll talk to Fitzmeyer in Intelligence and see if they can place a tracker before we release the car back to him."

Frankie was still angry but somewhat pacified with Baker's plan. With the details ironed out she called Derek back. Getting his voicemail, she decided she needed to get up and burn off some of her anger.

CHAPTER
FIFTY-ONE

FRANKIE AND ISABELLE started their jog slow, but steady. Once they were warmed up Frankie increased her pace. Step by step, breath by breath, Frankie felt her anger dissipate. She would get Sawyer.

The afternoon flew by and before she knew it the kids were rushing through the door.

"Stop it!" yelled Tyler. "Hi mom! I'm glad you're home!"

"Hey buddy. I told you I would be."

"I know." Softly Tyler added, "But sometimes you aren't."

Frankie felt a twinge of guilt. "Do you have any homework?"

"Spelling words. I have to read a story too."

"Let's fix a quick snack and talk about your day first."

Frankie smiled at the animated way Tyler talked about his day. Dani snuck in behind him and almost made it to her bedroom when Frankie said, "Danielle."

"Ugh." The sound was barely above a whisper. "What?"

"Come here. How was your day?"

"Fine."

"Do you have any homework?"

"Yes."

Frankie smiled at Dani's one-word answers.

"I was going to my room to work on it," was Dani's insolent response.

"Why don't you and Tyler do your homework at the table?"

"Yes," yelled Tyler.

"I want to listen to my music," whined Dani. "In my room."

"I'll turn the radio on. Come on. You guys can do homework while I cook dinner."

Slamming her books on the table she said, "Fine."

Frankie ignored the outburst and went about prepping for dinner. The trio fell into a rhythm of work. Tyler wrote his words and Dani completed a math worksheet. Tyler finished his work first and went to his room to play with his Legos. Frankie got dinner into the oven and sat down with Dani as she finished her worksheets.

"Anyone home?" hollered Bruce.

Frankie jumped up from her chair and grabbed Bruce in a bear hug. Keith was only a few steps behind. Coming through the door he said, "Hey, get your hands off my man." Laughter filled the room.

Dinner was lively and loud. Tyler regaled the group with recess and lunchroom tales. Dani updated everyone with the latest middle school gossip. Frankie relaxed as she watched the scene unfold at her dining table.

Once they were all finished eating, the kids cleared the table and put the food away while Bruce and Keith dished with Frankie on the latest scandals at the fire house. When her laughter turned to a yawn Bruce and Keith took their leave. Frankie read Tyler a story, kissed Dani on the head, and made her way to bed. Just as she was drifting off to sleep the sound of a text message alert caught her attention.

"Sweet dreams. XO D"

CHAPTER
FIFTY-TWO

DEREK AWOKE IN A COLD SWEAT. His hands trembled and his breathing was labored. Bear was whimpering and bumping Derek's elbow with his nose. He tried to ground himself by feeling the floor beneath his bare feet. He began to stroke Bear's fur, feeling the course hair run through his fingers. He looked around the room, taking note of the pictures hanging on the wall.

He couldn't remember the specifics of the dream, just the feeling of helplessness and terror. The one image that wouldn't go away was Jessica's face. Her eyes pleading with him and her voice asking, "Why."

He picked up his cell phone and dialed, hoping it wasn't too late.

"Derek, is everything okay?"

Derek felt a pang of guilt, "Hey Jess. Did I wake you?"

"No, I was actually working on a case." Jessica looked at the clock, "I didn't realize how late it was. What's wrong?"

"Do you ever have dreams about that night?"

"Why do you think I'm still working at 1 A.M.? It's easier not to sleep. Did you have one?"

"Mmhmm. It's not the first. Probably won't be the last."

"Have you talked to anyone about it?"

"No. Have you?"

Jessica hesitated before answering softly, "Yeah. It seems to be helping. Most nights at least. I finally stopped having panic attacks when I leave work after dark, and you've already left. Maybe you should – talk to someone, I mean. I can give you the name of the guy I'm seeing."

"Sure. That would be great. I'm sorry for bothering you tonight."

"You're fine. Let's grab a drink after work tomorrow. What do you say?"

"Yeah. Goodnight Jess."

Derek disconnected the phone, got out of bed, and walked to the kitchen. With a glass of scotch in his hand he started pacing the floors of the house. Bear rubbed against his leg and nudged his hand with his cold nose. Without thinking Derek began stroking the dog's thick fur as they walked. Gradually his heartrate slowed and the tension in his shoulders eased. As he made his way back to his bedroom, he grabbed his cellphone and typed a message.

"Sweet dreams. XO D"

Derek fell asleep before receiving a return message.

FIFTY-THREE

AFTER A LAZY MORNING, Frankie climbed into her Jeep and headed to the office. The skies were clear, but the air was cold. She was mentally planning her evening when her cell phone rang.

"Thomas."

"What's up buttercup?"

Frankie smiled at the sound of her little sister's voice. "What's up Soph?"

Sophie chattered on about her new man friend and their evening plans.

"Jake's birthday is Saturday. It's the big 3-0. You're coming to the farm for the party, right?"

Frankie slapped the steering wheel. She'd forgotten Jake's party was this weekend. "What do you want me to bring?"

"Beer and that cute FBI agent."

Frankie laughed, "I'll see what I can do."

Frankie grabbed her gym bag out of the back of the Jeep, leaned against the side, grabbed her cell phone and sent a text to Jim.

"What are you doing Saturday night?"

Not expecting a quick answer, she started to walk towards the garage entrance. Before she made it to the door her phone dinged with an incoming message.

"No plans. What do you have in mind?"

"Want to go down to the farm for a party?"

"Sounds good — ride together?"

"No, I'll meet you there. I have to drop my kids off. I'll text you details later."

"Okay."

Frankie smiled. The weekend was looking up. Before she could drop her bag by her desk her cellphone started to ring. Looking down, she stepped outside of the squad room to take the call.

"Hey Derek. How's your day going?"

"Better now." After a few minutes of small talk Derek asked, "What are you doing next weekend? Are you working?"

"Friday and Sunday night. Saturday's Jake's birthday. I'll be down at the farm." Frankie hesitated before asking, "Want to be my date for the party?"

Frankie's question was met with silence. After an awkward moment Derek answered, "Thanks for the invite. I'll let you know."

Derek's tone told Frankie he had no intention of going to the party.

CHAPTER
FIFTY-FOUR

FRANKIE HAD a message from Bank of America saying they had a disk of still shots from the ATM. Someone would be there until 5pm if she wanted to pick it up. After answering a few messages, she headed to the bank to pick up the disk of photos.

By the time she finished at the bank it was rush hour. With the disk in hand, she made the slow drive back to headquarters. As she approached downtown, she caught sight of the county courthouse in the distance.

Looking at the clock she said to herself, "5:30. *Maybe I can catch Derek leaving work and talk him into going to the party?*"

Frankie pulled into the back entrance of the parking lot. Before she made it to Derek's parking spot, she saw him walk out of the building. Her stomach dropped when she saw he wasn't alone. Frankie watched Derek put his hand on the small of Jessica Moon's back and lead her to his car. Frankie sat motionless as he opened the door and helped Moon inside, laughing at something she said. Without seeing Frankie, Derek walked around to the driver's side and got in. He drove out the front exit and never looked back.

Frankie debated on following him but decided against it. She was on the job, and she had no claim on him. Yet, she couldn't just let it go. She picked up her cellphone, entered the number she had memorized years before, and hit send. One ring. Two. The call was sent to voice mail. Frankie couldn't form words, so she disconnected the call without leaving a message.

FIFTY-FIVE

"YOU DID WHAT?" Mia exclaimed. She and Frankie were driving to the house of Treyvon Stockton's aunt, Georgia Williams.

"I invited Jim and Derek to the farm for Jake's party."

"Have you lost your damn mind?"

"Not at all. Jim said he would be there. Derek waited too long to answer then just said he'd let me know. So, he's definitely not going to go. And I'm not sending him the information unless he asks for it."

"Did you tell him Jim's going to be there? I bet he'd drive down then."

"Nope. I'm not playing his little games," Frankie parked the car and said, "There's the house."

Frankie's knock was met with the sounds of a barking dog. Instinctively she stepped back and waited. Frankie loved dogs but wasn't keen on the idea of one jumping at her.

"Who is it?"

The voice on the other side of the door was deep and raspy; undiscernible if it was a man or a woman.

"Detective Thomas and Detective Boden. Kansas City Missouri Police Department."

"Hold on. Let me put the dog up."

Frankie looked at Mia, smiled and said, "Thank goodness."

Before Mia could respond, the door flung open. Standing in the doorway was a mere sprite of a woman. Her bright blonde hair stood out in stark contrast to her dark skin. "Come on in before you let all the warm air out!" Georgia directed, standing there in her shorts and Kansas City Chief's sweatshirt.

Frankie smiled at the woman she guessed to be in her early 70's. The smile the woman returned showed teeth stained yellow from too many years of smoking and drinking caffeine.

"Is this about Tre? My sister-in-law told me you might be stopping by. Would you like a cup of coffee?"

"Yes ma'am and no thank you. We just had a few questions for you."

Georgia dropped into an oversized chair and invited the women to sit on the sofa across from her.

"When was the last time you saw Tre?"

"He was by here late Saturday night the weekend his momma was gone. Came in through the back door. He wasn't here long though. Said his car was acting up so he left it here and took my son's car. Told me he had a job to do. I think he brought it back on Sunday morning."

Frankie looked up from her notepad and asked, "Did he tell you what kind of job?"

"No. But then, I guess I didn't ask either. He's had a lot of piddly jobs. It's hard for me to keep track."

"Does he have a bedroom here?"

"Well, it's not *his* bedroom, but sometimes when his momma's gone, he stays in the room off the kitchen. She doesn't like him staying at her house by himself."

Looking around the tiny house, Frankie noticed not a thing was out of place. "Have you cleaned that room since then?"

"Sure did. I always wash the bedding after he's stayed over. I like it to be clean in case someone comes for a visit."

"Do you know if he had anyone with him when he stopped by?"

Georgia seemed to give that some thought. After a moment she said, "I can't be sure. I thought I heard an extra set of footsteps but when I asked him, he said he was alone. He knows I'm not okay with him bringing girls in and having pre-marital sex in *my* house."

Frankie stifled a smile. "Is Tre or your son's car here?"

Georgia stood up and walked towards the kitchen window. Looking outside she said, "Tre's car is back there. Doesn't look like my son's is. He lives next door. He's usually home after 7."

"Thank you, Miss Georgia. May we look around your house?"

Georgia hesitated before asking, "Whatcha lookin' for? I already told you what I know."

"Ma'am we have reason to believe Tre brought the girl he kidnapped here. We'd just like to see if it matches the description she gave. Maybe take a few pictures."

"You gonna take any of my things? I know how the police work. You don't ever give people their stuff back."

"No ma'am. Only things I'm going to take are photographs. Unless I find something that belongs to her. Can you show us your back door?"

GEORGIA LED Frankie and Mia through the kitchen to her back door. The floor looked like it had just been mopped. As she scanned the room, the light from the digital clock on the stove caught Frankie's eye. She wondered if Sarah had noticed it. A small hallway led to another bedroom with a closed door.

"Is that the room where Tre stays when his momma's gone?"

"Yes."

"When you cleaned the room, did you notice anything out of place. Anything that didn't belong to you or Tre?"

Georgia smoothed her hair back from her face before answering. She walked out of the small room, grabbed a glass from the cabinet, and turned to the sink to fill it with water. After taking a drink she said, "There was an earring. At first, I thought it was Tre's."

Frankie and Mia looked at one another. Sarah had not mentioned a missing earring, but it was possible she didn't think it was important or didn't remember.

"May we see it?" Frankie asked.

Georgia picked up a glass ring holder from the windowsill and removed a small hoop earring with fake stones embedded in the metal.

Frankie took a latex glove from her pocket and took the earring from Georgia. "What makes you sure this isn't Tre's?"

"Because he said it wasn't. He said he didn't know who it belonged to."

"Where did you find it?"

"It was on the bedspread in that room."

Frankie was about to respond when she heard the front door slam and a man's voice saying, "Momma? You home?"

"Detectives, this is my son Lamont. Lamont, these detectives are here about Tre."

Lamont extended a hand to Frankie and Mia. Shaking their hands he asked, "What did Tre do now?"

"A woman has made some allegations against him," answered Mia. "Did you happen to see him last Saturday? It would have been late?"

Lamont stroked the stubble on his chin. "Detective I can barely remember who I saw yesterday."

"This ain't no time to be cute Lamont. Tell 'em what you know," chastised Georgia.

Leaning against the counter, Lamont said, "I didn't see Tre here, but he did take my car. Damn boy didn't even ask if it was okay. He just took it. Hell, I didn't even know it was gone until he called me."

"Do you know what time he called?" Frankie asked.

"Must have been about 3 AM. He said the car broke down in Westport. He was giving someone a ride and it stalled out. I went outside and saw his car was in the drive, but it wouldn't start. I ended up taking Momma's car to go get him. Turns out he'd run my car out of gas."

Georgia's face scrunched up in anger, "Why didn't you tell me 'bout this Lamont?"

Looking down and away from his mother, Lamont answered, "Because you don't like me taking your car and I didn't want to hear it."

"Are both cars here now?" Frankie asked.

Lamont looked up. "Yeah. Tre's car still won't start. Mine's in the driveway next door."

"Will you give us permission to look inside your car and process it for any evidence?"

Before Lamont could answer Georgia said, "Of course he will."

"Thank you, ma'am. Lamont?"

He just nodded in agreement, not daring to contradict his mother.

Mia got the information from the car and Lamont's signature while Frankie called for the Crime Scene Unit and a tow truck.

"Lamont, I'm going to get a search warrant for Tre's car. We'll tow it to the garage for processing. I'll let him know when we are finished with it," Frankie said.

"I've got keys, why don't you get what you need now?" Georgia asked.

"Because the car belongs to him and he's not here to give us his permission. Thank you, though."

The house wasn't far from the crime lab, so the wait for the crime scene unit was not long.

"Hey Ash, good to see you! You by yourself tonight?"

"Hey Frankie. Mia. There was a shooting down on the Avenue, so Yang and Rhino are down there. Greg is back at the unit recovering some stuff from last night's shooting. I told him I could handle this one on my own."

Frankie gave Ashley all the information she needed for her reports then stood back while she took photographs of Lamont's car. When Ashley was certain she had taken enough photos, she got out the fingerprint kit and swabs to collect possible DNA samples.

Ashley was thorough. She lifted possible fingerprints, swabbed the seatbelt and door handle for DNA, and used the alternate light source to look for biological fluids on the seats. Frankie and Mia watched in silence as Ashley did her job.

When she was about finished Frankie asked, "Can you use luminal on the front seat?"

Mia looked at Frankie with question in her eyes as Ashley went to the Crime Scene van to retrieve the spray.

"She was pretty banged up when we saw her at the hospital. It's possible her blood is on the seat or somewhere else in the car."

"Good call!"

Ashley sprayed the luminal in the front seat and floorboards of the car. At first it did not look as if there would be any reaction. Frankie started to turn away, but Ashley stopped her, "Wait. I think I see something." She pointed towards the headrest of the passenger side of the car, "There."

A blue glow emanated from a small spot on the headrest. Ashley quickly marked the spot, careful not to contaminate any possible evidence. She grabbed her camera and took a photograph using the flashlight then collected a swab and processed the area.

"Nice catch Ashley. Hopefully it will be the victim's blood."

"Anything else you need me to do?" Ashley asked.

"No. I'm going to need to get a warrant for the other car so we're going to tow it to the garage."

"Sounds good. Let us know when you're ready to process it."

"Thanks Ash! It'll probably be tomorrow night." Frankie and Mia turned to go back inside Georgia's house. They handed Lamont his keys with the list of things seized from his car. "Is there anything else either of you can think of that might be helpful?"

"His momma said it was a white girl accusing Tre. Is that right?" Georgia asked.

"Yes…"

Lamont interjected, "Tre wouldn't have been with no white girl."

"So we've heard," said Mia.

CHAPTER
FIFTY-SEVEN

ON THE DRIVE back to the office, Frankie called Sarah and confirmed she had been wearing hoop earrings with stones embedded in the metal the night she was kidnapped.

"I assumed I lost it when I fell in the mud."

"We found one in the house we think Tre took you to. We would like to drive you by there when you have some time."

"How about Sunday? I've got a lot going on this week, but I'm off on Sunday."

Frankie set up the appointment time then emailed Ashley and asked her to send a photograph of the car they had just processed. Frankie would take some photographs of Tre's car after they got the search warrant and show them to Sarah when she came in on Sunday.

The phones were quiet the rest of the evening. The only call came from Gary Kinder from the local news station asking if they had any news.

"Got any sex?"

Laughing, Frankie said, "Hey Killer. We don't have anything new tonight."

"Do you have a court date on that case with the girls from Stevenson Auto?" Kinder was hoping Frankie would give him something on the case she and Jim worked together.

"Nothing official yet." Frankie knew a plea deal had been offered, but nothing was official so she couldn't release the information.

"Alright, call me if anything comes up."

"You got it Killer."

Frankie finished the search warrant for Tre's car and reports from the evening. She left a note on the warrant asking the day shift to get it signed. There was no rush, so no need to bother a judge at home this late.

As they walked to their cars Mia asked, "Did you ever hear from Derek?"

Frankie didn't immediately respond.

"Frankie?"

Stopping at Mia's car, Frankie turned to her and said,

"No, but I did see him."

"What? When?"

Adjusting the bag on her shoulder she said, "On my way back from Bank of America."

"Where was he?"

"Leaving the courthouse," Frankie looked down at her shoes then back up to Mia. "With Jessica Moon. He had his hand on the small of her back as they walked to his car. They seemed pretty cozy."

Mia stared at Frankie incredulously. "Did you say anything to him?"

"No. He didn't see me. I called him and he sent me to voice mail. I don't really have a claim on him…"

"But it kind of confirms what you already thought. What are you going to do?"

"I don't know. Wait 'til I see him and confront him I guess."

Mia reached out and touched Frankie's forearm. "Maybe he'll have a good explanation. Like you said, maybe they're just friends."

"Yeah, maybe." Changing the subject Frankie asked, "Are you and Erik going to drive down to Jake's this weekend?"

Mia shook her head, "Erik is working off-duty so I'm going to go see my family. Tell Jake I said happy birthday… and tell Jim I said hello." Mia winked as she put the key in her car door.

Frankie laughed, "I will. I'm kind of hoping he and Sophie hit it off. She deserves a nice guy."

"I thought she was seeing someone."

"She is, but it must not be too serious. He's not coming to the party."

Frankie and Mia said their good-byes. Before she could pull out of the parking lot her cellphone dinged with an incoming text message.

"Working tomorrow night? Want to swing by for a drink?"

"Can't. Getting up early Saturday to head to mom's. Need my beauty rest."

"Okay. Have fun at the farm. XO D"

Frankie wasn't surprised Derek wasn't coming but she was a little disappointed. She was tired of keeping her life compartmentalized.

CHAPTER
FIFTY-EIGHT

FRANKIE CALLED the office on her way into work on Friday. The day squad had been working a case all day and didn't get the search warrant signed for Tre's car. Although she was frustrated, she understood.

"It's still early," she said aloud to her empty Jeep. "I should be able to walk it through before everyone's gone."

It took Frankie about two hours to get the search warrant signed and a Crime Scene Unit en route to the garage.

"Mia, you want to come?"

"I can't. Baker just assigned me a new case. Call me if you need any help."

"Copy that. See you in a bit!"

While Frankie was waiting for Crime Scene, she snapped a few photographs of Tre's car to show Sarah. She had just finished when she heard Rhino's booming voice.

"Frank-eee!"

They exchanged small talk and then got down to business. Frankie told Rhino the case facts and gave him the information he would need for his report along with a copy of the signed search warrant. When he was finished photographing the outside of the car, they opened the doors to start working on the inside.

"Rhino, make sure you get a photograph of the inside of the passenger door, okay? She mentioned there not being a door handle. And this one is definitely missing."

Rhino finished with his camera then began dusting for fingerprints and swabbing the car for DNA. Last, he pulled out the alternate light source.

"You said one of the rapes occurred in a car, right?"

"Yeah. Pretty sure it was this one. The other one didn't light up and from what Sarah and Tre's cousin said, I think this was the first car they were in."

With glasses on and the overhead lights out, he scanned the car with the light source. The front seat illuminated on the passenger side. Rhino marked the areas of illumination and turned the overhead lights back on.

"Want me to cut it?"

"Do you think you can you get any evidence by swabbing?"

Rhino leaned on the roof of the car and said, "Honestly, probably not. If they were leather, I could probably swab and get what you need but since this is upholstery it needs to be done in the lab."

"Cut them."

After Rhino finished, Frankie started looking through the car with hopes of finding something that would put Sarah inside. She was about to give up when she noticed something underneath the passenger seat on the floorboard.

"Rhino, can you take a photo under the seat? I think there's something under there."

After snapping a few photographs Frankie reached under the seat and found two buttons.

"I wonder what the chances are that these are from Sarah's blouse?"

Rhino recovered the buttons and promised to email Frankie the photographs of Sarah's clothing so she could see if any buttons were missing.

Frankie was preparing to leave when she heard her phone beep with an incoming text message. She couldn't help but smile when she saw it was from Jim.

"What time's the party tomorrow night?"

"Probably eat about 6."

"See you then."

CHAPTER
FIFTY-NINE

FRANKIE DIDN'T NEED an alarm clock to wake her. Tyler yelling at Isabelle to quit chasing the cat jolted her from a fitful sleep. She rolled over and looked at the clock on the table next to her bed. 730 AM.

"Ugh. Guess at least I'll be able to get a run in before we go."

Frankie put on her cold weather gear, grabbed her sneakers, and headed to the kitchen. Tyler was putting cereal in a bowl and watching a Sponge Bob Square Pants cartoon on the television.

"Hey mom. Are you going for a run?"

"Yep. Want to join me?" Frankie tousled Tyler's unkempt hair, bent down, and kissed him on the top of the head. Occasionally she could get him to jog with her.

"Naw. I'm watching my show. You and Izzie can go."

Frankie laughed as she snapped the leash onto Isabelle's collar. "Let's go girl."

She returned forty-five minutes later to Danielle fixing herself breakfast and growling at her brother. Frankie fed the dog and was preparing to jump in the shower when it dawned on her she had not sent Jim directions to the farm. She grabbed her cell phone and texted him the details.

"Thanks. See you in a bit!"

"Both of you - pack an overnight bag. Ty, you are going to stay at grandma's house. Dani you are going to stay at your dad's."

"Why can't we go to the farm with you?" whined Danielle.

"Because it's a grown-up party. There won't be any kids there."

"I'm not a kid," Dani said as she stomped off mumbling down the hall.

Tyler looked up at Frankie, "But I want to tell Uncle Jake happy birthday too."

"You can give him a call while we are driving. Maybe you can make a birthday card for me to take to his party."

Tyler grabbed his crayons and construction paper from the cabinet. Frankie watched as he carefully picked out the paper, folded it in half, and started drawing on the front, taking special care with his artwork.

Two hours later the trio was on the road to Frankie's dad's house. The Jeep was quiet except for the sounds coming from the radio. Danielle had her earbuds in and was still pouting about not being able to go to the farm while Tyler was reading a book he had gotten for Christmas. Frankie watched in the rearview mirror, smiling at his intense facial expressions while he read.

Frankie dropped Dani off with her ex-husband then drove the short distance to her mom's house with Tyler and Isabelle. As they made their way down the lane towards her mother's home décor shop Frankie said, "Looks like grandma has a full shop today, Ty."

Not looking up from his book he said, "Mmhmm."

"Put your book in your bag so we can go inside."

Slamming the book shut Tyler said, "Fine."

"Tyler Nathaniel Thomas."

"Sorry mom," Tyler said, shoving his book into his backpack.

"You head on in, I'll walk Izzie."

Tyler grabbed his bag and jumped out of the Jeep. Frankie grabbed Isabelle's leash and watched Tyler bound through the shop door, shouting hello to his grandmother. Frankie laughed as she watched him through the windows entertaining the women in the shop.

Frankie finished walking Isabelle just when the last customer left. She visited with her mom until the next customer came, then took her leave. She hugged Tyler and told him she'd see him the next morning, climbed in her Jeep, and headed to the farm.

CHAPTER
SIXTY

FRANKIE DROVE the Jeep down the rough gravel road leading to the farm. The flat road was aptly named Moonglow Road and became a steep descent ending at a small stone bridge that crossed Shack Creek. She was glad it had not been raining or it may have been impassable. She slowed the Jeep to a crawl when she reached the bridge, stopping briefly to look down the waterway. The afternoon sun was beginning to fall behind the trees; rays of light floated through the trees in a soft glow.

Frankie looked forward as she crossed the bridge and felt her heart warm at the site of the land that had been in her family since before she was born. Over the years the farm had belonged to her uncle, her cousin, and finally her father. Frankie had grown up there riding the trails in the woods and splashing in the creek. When her dad decided to move off the farm about ten years earlier, Jake had stayed behind and made the old farmhouse on the property his home. Jake and her dad, Frank, had built a large barn and made subtle improvements to the property but it had maintained a rustic, yet warm, appeal. Countless hours had been spent there as a family, but it was Jake who would always call it home.

The barn door was standing open when Frankie parked the Jeep. Old-school country music blared from the speakers and a giant heater was warming the space. Jake was outside, standing by the smoker he and their dad built, checking the brisket he was cooking.

"Happy birthday little brother," exclaimed Frankie. Jake bent down and enveloped her in a bear hug.

"Thanks sis. Where are the munchkins?"

"Dani's at her dad's and Ty is with my mom. I'll pick them up tomorrow before I head to work. Assuming, that is, I can crash here tonight."

Ruffling her spiky hair, Jake said, "You know you don't have to ask."

Frankie laughed.

"Ty and Dani said to tell you happy birthday too. Dani was mad I wouldn't let her come but Ty made you a card."

Jake looked at the card and smiled. "Tell Ty I'll hang it on my beer fridge!"

Smiling, Frankie went about getting things ready for the party.

"Is your new girlfriend coming tonight?"

Sophie's booming voice masked Jake's answer. "Happy birthday big brother!" The trio laughed and raised a beer in celebration.

Jake's new girlfriend, Ann Marie, was the first guest to arrive. Frankie smiled as Jake kissed her chastely, keeping his arm around her while he tended to the smoker. Ann Marie laughed at anything Jake said that was remotely funny. It was obvious how much they cared for one another. Frankie said as much to Sophie when they went to the kitchen to finish cooking the side dishes.

"Oh yeah, I think he's going to pop the question this spring. I've never seen him like this with a girl before. I bet at the very least he asks her to move in with him."

Frankie smiled. She watched through the window at Ann Marie standing on her tiptoes to kiss a smiling Jake. Wistfully she said, "I hope so. He looks really happy."

Frankie was back in the barn, bending over the cooler, grabbing a beer when Jim arrived. He snuck up behind her, bent down, and whispered, "Got anything in there for me?"

She about jumped out of her skin, then broke into laughter. Flicking water from the melted ice into his face she said, "I've got something for you alright!"

Jim laughed and tried to duck the drops of cold water. Frankie handed him a cold beer and began the introductions.

"Jake. Sophie."

Jake, a man of few words, simply nodded. Sophie boisterously greeted Jim, slapping him on the back.

"And this is Jake's girlfriend, Ann Marie," finished Frankie.

Jim extended his hand, "Nice to meet you ma'am."

Sophie said, "You came to the hospital when dad…"

"Yep. How's Frank doing?"

"Much better. Thanks for asking," Frankie said.

Sophie turned at the sound of someone calling her name and bounced away.

"Squirrel," Frankie and Jim both laughed. "That's my sister."

"Where's the counselor tonight?" Jim asked, assuming Frankie had invited Derek.

Frankie started picking at the label on her beer and thought about how much she should tell him. "I invited him. He said he'd let me know, but then texted that he wasn't coming. I kind of knew he wouldn't."

"Has he ever met any of your family?"

"Nope. We keep our lives pretty separate. I've never met his family either."

"Are you all ready to eat?"

Jake's booming voice unwittingly changed the subject.

The partygoers lined up to pile food onto their plates. Frankie turned to Jim, "Jake spent all day smoking the brisket. It'll melt in your mouth." It was obvious how proud she was of her little brother. "Sophie made the baked beans, and I whipped up the potato salad. There'll be a bonfire after everyone's done eating."

"Smells great," said Jim as he piled the meat onto his plate.

The pair found a seat and chatted amicably while they ate their dinner.

"You've got a little something'…" Jim smiled as he pointed to Frankie's cheek.

Frankie blushed and used a napkin to wipe the bar-b-que sauce from her cheek.

"This is definitely not the kind of bar-b-que I'm used to," said Jim.

"You mean because it's good?"

"Don't misunderstand, this is really good. I mean, *really* good. But, come on you don't like pulled pork sandwiches with coleslaw on top?" Jim teased. "My mouth is waterin' just thinkin' about it."

Frankie scrunched her nose up in distaste. "Let's just say I stick to seafood when I go to North Carolina. I'm not a fan of vinegar-based bar-b-que."

"When are you goin' back out there?"

"The kids and I are planning to go for a couple weeks in August. Sophie's talking about riding along this year."

"That's usually about the time I go. I like to visit right at the end of the season. Maybe we can go out on the boat if we are there at the same time. Where are you all stayin' at?"

Frankie smiled at Jim. She and the kids had gone to Topsail Island the past five summers. She actually counted down the days between visits. When they started working together Frankie discovered Jim was from a fishing village near where they stayed. His mother owned a bookstore on the island that she and the kids loved to visit, and his father owned a commercial shrimp boat and a deep-sea excursion company.

"We've got a little house we stay at right on the beach. My friend, Nadine, lives out there. She comes to Missouri to visit her kids for the summer and rents the cottage to us pretty cheap. It's down by one of the old missile towers."

"It's not Miss Paceley's house, is it? I think it's called Dolphin's Delight or something like that."

"Is there anyone you don't know on the island?"

Jim shared in Frankie's laughter, "Miss Paceley worked at momma's bookstore for a couple seasons. Then after Hurricane Fran, Daddy and I spent a winter helping her repair all the damage done to her place. We got to know her pretty well. She's a doll. How'd you all meet?"

"I was looking at the Sunday paper and saw an ad for a place to rent on Topsail Island. The kids and I were planning to go back that summer, so I called her. She was in town for the holidays, so we met at Westport Flea Market for a burger. It was like we were destined to be friends. We still meet there for a burger from time to time. Now she makes a point of coming home early so we can have dinner on the island before the kids and I head back."

CHAPTER
SIXTY-ONE

OVER DINNER, and a few more beers, Jim regaled the group with stories. He talked about growing up on the Carolina coast, life as a detective in Chicago, and finally as an agent with the FBI. The men enjoyed hearing all his crazy escapades. The women enjoyed his southern charm and easygoing manner.

Sophie leaned over and whispered, "What's up with Jim?"

Innocently, Frankie replied, "What do you mean?"

"Is he dating anyone?" Sophie nudged Frankie's shoulder, "Or is he trying to date you? You could do worse you know."

Peeling the label from another beer bottle, Frankie said, "I don't think he's dating any one person. Want me to try and set you two up?"

"Mmhmm…maybe."

The rest of the evening went by quickly. Friends came and went, and the groups alternated between the bonfire and the barn. As the temperatures dropped the crowd thinned out and the bonfire was left with Jim, Ann Marie, Jake, his friend Bill, and his sisters.

Jake grabbed a cold beer and asked, "Who wants to go hill climbin'?"

Jim looked at Frankie and whispered, "What's he talkin' about?"

"I'm in!" Standing up, Frankie looked down at Jim, stuck her hand out and said, "Let's go and you'll find out."

Jake pulled his 4X4, king cab pick-up truck around from the side of the barn. Window down he shouted, "Climb in!"

Frankie, Jim, and Sophie climbed into the back while Ann Marie and Bill climbed into the front seat next to Jake. He drove down the hill and across the creek, then made a sharp turn into the woods instead of continuing up the steep hill. The ride through the woods was bumpy but laughter filled the cab as their bodies knocked into each other. The full moon lit the trail as they explored the dark hills around the house.

Satisfied they had explored the woods sufficiently Jake returned to the barn. Frankie looked out the back window at the moon as it hung suspended over Moonglow Road. The group huddled around the bonfire and talked about their lives while watching the constellations fill the sky. Bill left first, hugging Frankie and Sophie before climbing into his car. Jake and Ann Marie were next.

"Hey, make sure this fire's out before you two come inside. A'ight?"

"We know the drill Jake," Sophie answered.

Jim stood, "I guess I should make my way back home."

Frankie stood and said, "You don't have to rush off. Sophie and I wouldn't mind if you stayed and kept us company."

Jim leaned down and enveloped Frankie in a hug, holding on an extra moment, before placing a kiss on the top of her head.

Releasing her he looked at Sophie and said, "Bye Sophie-girl. Hope to see you again soon!"

"Absolutely Jim."

Frankie grabbed a couple of beers from the cooler, handed one to Sophie and said, "Scoot over sis and share that blanket with me."

CHAPTER
SIXTY-TWO

FRANKIE AND SOPHIE sat outside talking into the wee hours of the morning. They watched the fire die and the pre-dawn sky begin to lighten before they went inside to sleep. Morning came quickly and Frankie didn't have the luxury of sleeping in since she had to pick the kids up and be at work by three. Sophie heard her getting ready and said, "Why don't I grab Dani and Ty on my way home?"

"That would be amazing. I'll run and get Ty. Meet you after I pick up Dani?"

"Sure. Text me when you have Ty."

Frankie enjoyed a quick breakfast at her mom's before going to meet Sophie. With the exchange made and a change of clothes in the Jeep, she headed straight to her office. She relieved the day shift an hour early and started preparing for her appointment with Sarah.

Mia hadn't arrived yet and the phones were quiet. Frankie printed off the photographs she had gotten from the Crime Scene Unit. She placed the photos of the car on the table first, taking a label and placing it on the bottom right corner of each one. She would have Sarah sign the photographs if she recognized the cars, then mark which car was the first and which was the second on the label. She pulled the photographs of Sarah's blouse, the buttons, and the earring and placed them on the table.

Next, she grabbed the envelope from Bank of America.

Frankie was surprised to find the envelope contained actual prints instead of a disk. The first photos showed the side of the car. It was difficult to say for certain, but it looked like Lamont's car. The next photographs were of a man's profile. Tre's profile. That was unmistakable. The last were photos of Sarah. Her leaning over Tre. Her mouthing something to the camera. Then…

"What the hell?"

"Good afternoon to you too. I always seem to walk in at just the right moment."

"Shit. This looks like… shit."

Mia looked over Frankie's shoulder and repeated, "Shit."

"Is that the word of the day?" Baker asked as he walked in the door.

"Sorry Sarge. These pictures just surprised me, that's all."

"What do you think she's doing?" Mia asked.

"It looks like she's got her hand on his face while kissing him. It looks…intimate. I'm sure there's a good explanation but those photos won't look like a person in distress to the prosecutor." Frankie groused, "Especially if it's Moon."

Frankie picked up the photograph and stared. Sarah's hand cradled Tre's cheek while she kissed him on the other cheek. Frankie finished getting the photographs in order, put them in a stack, and finished preparing for Sarah's arrival. Almost as if on cue a clerk from the lobby called to say she was there. Frankie escorted Sarah to an interview room and after a few pleasantries pulled out the packet of photographs.

As Frankie expected, Sarah did not hesitate in identifying the cars. Tre's car was the one he used to abduct and rape her. Lamont's was the one that stalled, allowing her to get away. Frankie showed her photographs of her blouse.

"That's the blouse I was wearing."

"Were any buttons missing when you went out that night?"

"No."

Frankie pulled out the photograph of the buttons. "Do these buttons look like the ones on your blouse?"

Sarah picked up the photograph and looked at the buttons. "I think so."

"Here's a photograph of the earring we recovered. Do you recognize it?" Frankie asked.

Sarah surprised Frankie and pulled an earring from her purse. It was a perfect match to the one in the photograph. "Yeah, it's the match to this one."

Frankie took a deep breath and said, "Now I need to show you some photographs from the ATM. Since they are still photos, and there is no audio, I need you to explain to me what is happening in each one."

Frankie laid out the photographs of the side of the car.

"That's the second car he had me in. You can sort of see his reflection."

Frankie laid out the photographs of Tre.

"That's when he was asking me what my PIN was."

Frankie laid out the photographs of Sarah leaning over Tre inputting her PIN.

"That's me putting my PIN into the ATM and withdrawing cash. You can sort of see that I'm saying, 'help me' in that photo."

Frankie laid out the photographs of Sarah touching Tre's face and kissing him.

Sarah gasped and said, "Oh my gosh. That looks terrible."

"Can you explain what we're looking at?" Frankie gently prodded.

Sarah picked up the first photograph, then the second, and then the third. Softly she explained, "He was starting to act like he might let me go. He didn't seem as angry, so I was trying to appease him. After I couldn't get the money out the second time, I was afraid he was going to get mean again. I asked him what he wanted me to do. He jutted his chin out, tapped the side of his cheek, and said, 'you know what you have to do.' So, I kissed him on the cheek."

"Can you explain why you were touching his face?"

Sarah put the photographs back on the table, "No. I think it was just a reflex. Like I said, he acted like he was going to let me go. I was just trying to keep him from getting angry again."

Frankie nodded, satisfied with Sarah's answers. "Are you ready to go see if you can identify the house and at least one of the gas stations?" Sarah nodded.

CHAPTER
SIXTY-THREE

FRANKIE AND MIA drove Sarah back to the Westport area. She showed them where she had been standing when Tre approached her and the direction he took in his car. They drove around and tried to find the parking lot where she first tried to escape, but Sarah was unsure of her surroundings.

They chatted amiably on the drive to Georgia's neighborhood. As they got closer Frankie said, "I'm not going to stop at any houses. I'm going to drive around the block and if you recognize the house you were taken to, I want you to point it out."

Sarah nodded and carefully appraised the houses while they drove. When they approached Georgia's house she said, "I think that's it. That one over there. He pulled in the driveway and parked around back. I remember there being a small stoop at the back door."

"Great. Now we're going to drive around where one of the 9-1-1 calls originated from. If you recognize the gas station where Tre stopped, please point it out."

Before they could see the first car in the lot Sarah said, "That's the gas station. It's where that clerk was and where he tried to kick the bathroom door in."

"Good. Good."

Frankie continued to drive around, but Sarah wasn't able to identify the other gas station. Their last stop was in the area of the ATM. Sarah's gaze followed the highway, moving from side to side. As they approached an exit she said, "That's the exit he took to go to the ATM. I remember the Quick Trip sign."

Frankie turned and as they neared a stop light Sarah said, "Turn right. I think it's…there it is. There's the ATM."

"Excellent. I'm going to take some photographs while we're here, okay? You can stay in the car."

When Frankie was finished, they returned to police headquarters to drop Sarah back at her car.

CHAPTER
SIXTY-FOUR

GINA STOOD in the bus stop shelter, trying to stay out of the wind. She looked at her watch. The bus should be there soon. Distracted by the cold, Gina didn't notice the black car with tinted windows slowing down as it approached where she was standing.

The car came to a stop in front of Gina. The passenger window lowered about a third of the way and a man's voice asked, "Need a ride?"

Gina looked at the car and squinted her eyes, trying to see who was driving, "Sean?"

A grunt came from inside the car. Gina opened the door and sat down. The car was moving when she looked over and realized it wasn't her son's friend Sean in the driver's seat.

"Who are you?"

"How much?"

"How much for what?" Gina knew what he wanted but she wasn't a working girl.

"Pussy."

"Let me out. I ain't no whore."

"You aren't going nowhere." The man appeared to drive aimlessly, making a series of turns off the main streets.

"Let me out. I can find you what you want if you just let me out."

He pulled the car to a stop in an alley and said, "Shut up and get in the back."

"Let me out!"

Brandishing a handgun, the man growled, "I said get in the back."

With some difficulty Gina climbed over the seat into the back. She tried to open the door, but the automatic lock was engaged. The man got out and opened the back door, grabbed her feet, and pulled her down. She kicked and squirmed, but he was strong. His steely eyes bore into hers. Gina was terrified.

"What the…?" He recoiled from the warmth of where Gina urinated in the seat.

Gina used his surprise and pulled on the car door handle by her head a second time, but it still wouldn't open. The car was running so she pressed the button to open the window. With the window lowered Gina reached outside and pulled the door handle and the door flung open. Gina's legs were bent, with her knees pulled close to her chest. She extended her legs and pushed the man off her. She scooted backwards out of the car and ran. Gina heard the footsteps behind her but didn't look back.

"Bitch this ain't over," he shouted.

Gina felt a thick arm around her waist as they fell in a heap onto the ground. The fall knocked the air out of her, but Gina kept reaching forward, trying to get away. The man began to punch her body. Gina's hands flew to protect her face, but it was to no avail. He didn't stop hitting her until she lay there unconscious. Satisfied, he got back into the car, leaving her broken and battered body on the side of the road.

CHAPTER
SIXTY-FIVE

THE PHONE WAS RINGING when Frankie and Mia walked into the office. "I've got it Sarge. Sex Crimes Detective Thomas."

"It's Mac."

"What do you have Mac?"

"I'm pretty sure Sawyer is at it again. A lady was standing at the bus stop when this guy pulled up and offered her a ride. She said she thought he was a friend of her son, so she got into the car. When she got inside, he propositioned her. She told him to let her out because she 'ain't no whore,' then he flipped out. He took her to an alley and tried to rape her. When she tried to get out of the car the back door wouldn't open. She got so scared she pissed herself. Literally. Eventually she got the window down and opened the door from the outside and ran. He chased after her and beat her up pretty good Frankie. The ambulance is taking her to County."

"Do you have a scene?"

"Just where he beat her up. She said everything else happened in the car, but it's gone."

"What kind of car was it?"

"She thinks it was a black 4-door with tinted windows. She didn't get a plate. Doesn't he drive a silver or tan car?"

"Yeah, but we have his car at the garage. He may have a rental."

"Balls."

"Yeah. Mia and I'll be out soon."

Mia looked at Frankie and said, "I guess it's too much to hope for us to have a quiet night to catch up on reports."

"I guess so," Frankie said. "Mac has a scene and is pretty sure it's Sawyer."

"Are you freaking kidding me? Don't we still have his car?"

Frankie nodded and shared what she had learned from Mac.

"Let's run by his house and see what he's driving these days. Then, if this girl is up for it, we drive her by his house and see if she recognizes the car."

Mia grabbed her bag and asked, "Want me to drive?"

"Yeah, that would be great."

Frankie grabbed her coat and followed Mia to the car. Minutes later they were heading south on 71 Highway toward Sawyer's house. Mia parked about a block away while Frankie kept a look out for Sawyer.

"Check it out," yelled Frankie. "Do you see it?"

"Yep, I do," said Mia.

Parked next to his house on the side of the road was a black 4-door car.

"How much do you want to bet the inside of that car smells like urine?" asked Frankie.

"That's a fool's bet."

"1061 start a car to 73rd and Wabash."

"244, we'll head that way."

"Copy. 244 out with 1061 at 2115 hours."

Frankie grabbed her camera, opened the door and said, "I'll be right back."

Mia watched Frankie cautiously make her way to a tree across from Sawyer's house. From behind the tree, she snapped a couple of photographs then made her way back to the car.

"These aren't frame-worthy but hopefully they're good enough this gal can identify the car."

Moments later Shane and Stick were parked next to Frankie and Mia with lowered windows.

"Last time you guys went to this house you called us off. What's the plan this time?" teased Shane.

Frankie said, "Looks like he may have done it again, this time in a rental. The suspect car is parked on the street. We're going to go talk to the victim in the hospital and show her a picture of the car. We need you guys to watch the house and make sure he doesn't leave. Assuming she identifies him and the car, we'll tow it to be processed and snatch him up. Again."

SIXTY-SIX

TRE SAT in the parking lot across from the Fast Stop. Watching. Waiting. He didn't think he'd ever seen the store this busy. But he was patient. Cheyenne was working but Tre didn't want anyone to see him go inside. He didn't want any witnesses. That bitch wasn't going to get away with ratting him out.

Cheyenne looked up from the register when the door dinged signaling another customer. Startled she said, "Oh, hey Tre. How've you been?"

Tre walked around the store and made sure no one was inside. Once he was certain they were alone, he pulled his gun and pointed it at her.

"Get your traitor ass out from behind the counter."

"Tre, what's going on? I thought we were friends. You need money? It's been a good night. I can give you the money out of the drawer – whatever you want. Come on man, you don't want to do this."

Tre paused, his eyebrows knit together in question, "Grab what's in the drawer and the safe."

"I can't get into the safe, but I haven't made a drop tonight so there's a lot of money in the drawer. At least $500."

"Get it, then get your ass around the counter." Tre waved his gun while issuing directions.

Cheyenne opened the drawer to the register and hit the button that would send a silent alarm to the police department. She prayed silently the police would get there in time.

Tre watched her grab the money and put it into a paper liquor bag. Gesturing with the gun he ordered her out of the store.

"Where are you taking me Tre?"

"We're going for a ride."

"Why don't we go to my place. It's close. We can have a drink and talk."

"I'm done talking bitch. Get in the car. Now."

Cheyenne looked around. A police car was driving in their direction. She started to raise her hands to flag the car down but caught a glimpse of the gun out of the corner of her eye and lowered her hands. Cheyenne got into the passenger side of the car and started to pray. Tre tore out of the parking lot onto 75th street and drove east towards the highway.

Moments later lights were flashing, and sirens were wailing behind the car. Gun still in hand, Tre hit the steering wheel.

"What the fuck did you do?"

"I didn't do nothing Tre. I promise. Just pull over. I'll tell them I went with you on my own. I'll tell them I gave you the money. Whatever you want me to say I'll say."

Ignoring her pleas, Tre drove faster, turning north onto Prospect. The police car followed, shrinking the distance between them. Soon there were two cars, then a patrol wagon, behind them. Tre was familiar with the terrain and navigated the streets fearlessly. He approached Emmanuel Cleaver II Blvd and turned east but didn't take into account for the recent moisture on the streets when he accelerated. The rear of the car began to fishtail on a patch of black ice. Tre gripped the steering wheel, attempting to maintain control, but the car began to spin. Cheyenne wasn't wearing a seatbelt and her tiny body bounced inside the car, much like the silver ball inside a pinball machine. When the car came to a violent stop, wrapped around a light pole, Cheyenne's body lay crumpled on the passenger floorboard. Tre's face rested against the side of the steering wheel. A sharp object penetrated his eye socket.

CHAPTER
SIXTY-SEVEN

FRANKIE WALKED through the emergency department doors and marched into the room of Sawyer's latest victim. She stopped cold at the sight of the woman lying on the bed. Her eyes were swollen, and blood was caked around her mouth. Purple bruises were starting to form on her cheeks. Fingerlike red marks encircled her neck.

Frankie introduced herself and Mia then asked, "What's your name?"

With a hoarse voice she answered, "Gina. Gina Bradshaw."

"Gina, can you tell us what happened tonight?"

With a voice barely above a whisper, Gina said, "It was cold, and I thought he was my son's friend, so I got in the car."

"Were you working tonight?"

Gina looked at her hands then looked up and firmly said, "Detective, I used to work the block, but I gave up that life a long time ago. I got into the car because it was cold, and I thought he was a friend of my son's."

"I believe you Gina." Frankie pulled out a folder containing a series of photographs, but before pulling them out she asked, "Do you think you would recognize the man if you saw him again?"

"I think so."

"Would you look at some photographs for me?"

Gina nodded.

"Do you recognize anyone in these photos?"

Gina looked at each photograph carefully before identifying Sawyer. "That's him. He's the one. That's the man that tried to rape me."

"Thank you." Frankie grabbed the camera from her bag, "Can you take a look at this photo and tell me if you recognize this car?"

Gina looked at the photos Frankie had taken and said, "Those aren't good pictures. They're pretty dark, but it does look like the car he was driving."

"Thank you, ma'am. We'll let you know when we get him into police custody."

After exchanging contact information Mia and Frankie left the hospital.

"You think that bitch will hold him this time?" Frankie's face was red and contorted in anger as they drove to meet Stick and Shane.

"Maybe we'll get lucky, and she won't be the one on-call."

Frankie grunted her response. The drive passed quietly. Mia turned up the radio just as "I Gotta a Feeling" started to play.

"See Frankie, a good sign."

Frankie couldn't help but laugh, "Yeah, maybe this time!"

When they pulled in next to Stick and Shane Mia asked, "Any activity?"

"Not since you left, but I think someone is home. We can see lights turning off and on in rooms periodically, but no one has come outside," answered Stick.

"Okay, this is how we'll do it. Two to the front and two to the back. We bring him out and take him into custody. Nothing crazy," said Frankie.

The two cars kept their headlights off as they approached Sawyer's house. Mia and Stick went to the back of the house while Frankie and Shane went to the front. A firm knock brought a woman in her sixties to the door.

"May I help you?"

Surprised Frankie asked, "Um, is Allen here?"

"He's not here right now."

"Are you his..."

Before Frankie could finish the woman interjected, "I'm his wife."

Frankie was taken aback. She didn't realize Sawyer was married, much less to a woman who was old enough to be his mother. "Um, do you know when he'll be back ma'am?"

"I'm not sure. He said he was going to check on his momma. She hasn't been well. Can I give him a message?"

"That won't be necessary ma'am. Thank you."

Frankie and Shane began to walk back towards her car. When he was out of earshot Shane asked, "What now? Want me to tow the car?"

Frankie shook her head, "Not yet. Let's sit back and watch. I have a feeling he hasn't gone far."

They made a production of moving their cars, driving past the front of Sawyer's house, only to find a place to watch without being seen.

"You really think he's there," asked Mia.

"Yep."

"What's your play?"

"Wait and see if he comes out. If he doesn't show his face within the next hour or so, we'll go grab the car."

The wait wasn't long.

SIXTY-EIGHT

FRANKIE WATCHED the lights on the second floor extinguish. Shortly after, Sawyer opened the back door. He scanned the yard then continued to walk outside. He opened the driver's side door of the black 4-door, got inside and, despite the cold air, he rolled the windows down.

"1061 to 244 on private."

"Go ahead Frankie."

"Let's follow him and see where he goes."

Frankie hung back as Sawyer turned north onto Prospect.

"You think he's hunting?"

Frankie nodded.

"244 to 1061. We'll run parallel."

"Copy."

Sawyer slowed down to look at a group of women standing on the corner of 59th Street and Prospect. Just when Frankie thought he was going to stop, he pulled away and continued driving north. At Cleaver II he turned west and then turned back north on Troost Ave, stopping at a convenience store on the corner of 41st Street.

Frankie parked down the street and watched a woman approach the passenger side of the car. After a few moments, she saw the passenger door open, and the woman climb inside.

"Where do you think they're going," asked Mia.

Before Frankie could answer, Sawyer pulled out of the parking lot and back onto the street. They followed him to an apartment complex where he parked the car in front of the apartment door. Frankie stayed back and watched Sawyer motion for the woman to wait in the car while he walked to the door, knocked, then used a key to open the door.

"You think he's going to take her inside?" Frankie asked.

Before Mia could answer Sawyer walked back to the car, opened the door, and grabbed the woman sitting on the passenger side. He half-led, half-shoved the woman towards the door.

"We can't let him get her inside. It's obvious she doesn't want to go."

"1061 copy a residence check. 2212 E 17th Street, Brooklyn Street Apartment Complex. Black Kia. Missouri license 4 Zebra 8 Robert 9 Anthony. 1064's with me. Hold the air"

"Copy 1061. Holding the air at 2018 hours."

Frankie angled her car behind Sawyer's and turned on the emergency lights. She and Mia exited the car in unison.

Mia yelled "Gun!"

The first round flew past Frankie as she took cover in the doorframe of the patrol car. She returned fire, hitting Sawyer in his left shoulder, just above his heart. His body jerked back with the impact.

"Drop the gun," Frankie and Mia yelled in unison.

Sawyer fired a second shot towards Mia and Frankie. Mia inched forward, taking cover by the engine block and fired, hitting Sawyer in the abdomen. With the impact he dropped the gun, doubled over, and screamed out in pain. He fell backwards into the open doorway of the apartment. Frankie and Mia approached with caution, putting him in handcuffs.

"1064 start a bus. We have a party down."

"1064, ambulance en route."

"244 hold us out with 1061 and 1064."

Frankie applied pressure to the stomach wound and waited.

Mia got the woman out of the Kia and put her inside their police car. She grabbed the first aid kit and ran back to help Frankie. The paramedics arrived within minutes.

"What do we have Frankie?" asked Bruce.

"Two gunshot wounds. One to the stomach and one to the shoulder."

"Frankie, you have blood on your arm," said Bruce.

"It's his. We need to get him to the hospital."

"I don't think that's his blood. I think it's yours. We've got him, but you need to get to County."

"He's right Frankie," said Mia. "Come on, I'll take you."

Frankie conceded and headed to the car. The adrenaline that was coursing through her veins began to slow. Frankie leaned her head back against the seat, closed her eyes, took a deep breath, and exhaled. She opened her eyes and watched as Shane strung yellow tape around the scene. The red and blue rotating lights pulled her into a trance.

CHAPTER
SIXTY-NINE

TRE LAY against the steering wheel unable to move. He could hear the firefighters talking as they attempted to stabilize the object in his eye to prevent further damage. In the background he could hear paramedics working on Cheyenne outside the car.

"I can't find a pulse. Get the paddles."

"Serves the bitch right," thought Tre. *"She shouldn't have snitched. This wouldn't have happened if she had kept her mouth shut."*

"Charging. Clear." Her body thumped against the backboard as the electrical charge attempted to restart her heart.

"I better not be blind," he thought. Out loud he asked, "Is she dead?"

"Still no pulse, charge again."

The firefighter providing aid to Tre said, "They're working on her. Is she your girl?"

"Charging. Clear."

Tre gave a half-laugh, "Naw, but I was 'bout to teach the bitch a lesson."

Paddles were placed on Cheyenne's chest. Again, her body thumped against the backboard as the electrical charge was initiated.

"We have a pulse. It's weak, but it's there. Load her up."

A second ambulance arrived on the scene and, with his eye stabilized, Tre was loaded for transport.

The firefighter pulled one of the responding officers aside and said, "I don't know if this is important but when I asked that guy if the girl with him was his girlfriend he told me no but he was 'about to teach the bitch a lesson.' I don't know what he meant, but it seemed off to me."

The officer climbed into the ambulance and pulled the wallet from Tre's pocket and said, "You don't say."

CHAPTER
SEVENTY

"CHANGE the bandage tomorrow and follow up with the department's doc to make sure it's healing properly. Got it?"

Frankie nodded at her longtime friend, Dr. Michael Wilhelm. One of the bullets had grazed her, leaving a hole in her jacket, but just scraped her arm. The doctor was being overly cautious in her opinion, but he had saved her dad's life when he had his heart attack so she trusted he would not steer her wrong.

"What are you going to tell the kids," Mia asked.

Frankie looked at her and said slyly, "Who said I'm going to tell them anything?" Mia shook her head.

Sergeant Baker walked through the Emergency Department doors as Mia and Frankie were preparing to walk out.

"Where are you two going?" he demanded.

"Hey Sarge! We're heading back to the unit," answered Frankie.

"Did you get your wound treated?"

Frankie nodded.

"Have you talked to IA or the shooting team?"

"No. They're going to give me a day. I'll call my union rep in the morning and set up an interview."

"Have you received an update on Sawyer?"

"He's in surgery. Officer Garrett is sitting on him. He said he'd call me if there were any updates," answered Frankie.

"What the hell happened out there Frankie?"

Frankie and Mia began explaining, each sharing tidbits of the story. Frankie's easygoing demeanor turned quiet with the realization that the evening could have ended so differently. The scrape on her arm could have been a hole in her body.

Or worse, in Mia's.

"When do you think we'll be able to talk to him?"

Sergeant Baker shrugged his shoulders. "I suppose it depends on how long it takes before they release him from here. We'll keep a uniform on his room. He'll go straight from here to the jail."

Frankie nodded in understanding.

"Do we have anyone processing the cars? Or the apartment?" Frankie asked knowing she and Mia would not be allowed near the scene while the internal investigation was ongoing.

"We have both covered," answered Baker.

"Mia, are you ready to go?" Frankie stuffed her hands inside her jacket pockets to hide the trembling. "We need to put this case together."

Mia nodded and started to walk towards the door.

Turning back, she asked, "Are you coming Sarge?"

Sergeant Baker nodded and said, "I'm going out to the apartment, then I'll head back and help you all get everything together."

Frankie and Mia walked to the car in silence. Frankie's blood was boiling. There could have been – would have been - another victim if she and Mia had not stopped him.

Once they were inside the car Frankie said through clenched teeth, "She has no choice but to hold him now."

CHAPTER
SEVENTY-ONE

JUST AS THEY walked into the squad room Mia's phone began to ring.

"Hey babe," Mia said.

"Hey yourself," said Erik. "We just got into a car chase with a suspect I thought you and Frankie might be interested in. Does the name Treyvon Stockton mean anything to you?"

"Seriously? I thought he was still in custody. I'm going to put you on speaker." Mia motioned for Frankie to listen.

"Looks like he got released from Jackson County yesterday. He had a girl with him. Cheyenne something."

The color drained from Frankie's face. The clerk from the Fast Stop was with him. Was it willingly? Cheyenne said he was crazy, but surely, he wasn't that crazy. "Really? Where is she? And why were you all chasing him?"

Erik explained the situation to Mia and Frankie. There was no question that Cheyenne wasn't in the car voluntarily.

"Where are they now?"

"Headed to County. He's going to need surgery. He had a foreign object embedded in his eye. I'm not sure about her. They were trying to revive her right before they left."

"Okay. Thanks Erik. We've got to get this case file together, but we'll come to County when we're done. Love you," Mia said.

"Love you too."

Frankie looked at Mia, "You two are so cute. Look…I'm sorry."

Mia turned to face Frankie, "For what?"

"I should have let patrol stop him. I would never have forgiven myself if something happened to you."

"Stop it. We did our job tonight. That girl is safe because of *us*. Now let's get this case file put together so the prosecutor will hold him."

Frankie nodded and gave her a slim smile.

Changing the subject Mia asked, "Why did Jackson County release Stockton? What the heck is happening over there?"

"That's a very good question."

"Did they give a reason?"

Shaking her head, Frankie said, "I haven't seen the release sheet yet. I lay you odds it's the same prosecutor that let Sawyer go. Tre was at County for a failure to appear so maybe the prosecutor's office thought they had time to issue a warrant on him."

"You really think that's the case?"

Looking out the window towards the dark courthouse, Frankie replied, "No."

BAKER ARRIVED at the apartment just in time to make entry with Sergeant Scott Millsap of the Assault Squad. Baker donned gloves and followed Millsap through the door. He didn't plan to assist in collecting evidence but didn't want to risk contaminating anything.

"Does this look like a man's apartment to you?" Millsap asked, picking a peach throw pillow off the chair. "No television. The furniture is covered with blankets and there's nothing on the counter."

"My bet is on a relative. What does the mail say?" Baker asked, gesturing to the envelopes sticking out of the wire box hanging on the wall by the telephone.

"Eugenia Sawyer. Wonder what their relationship is? My bet is she's old. Maybe his mother or grandmother. I mean, the phone isn't even cordless." Millsap chuckled.

Baker laughed, walking past Millsap to the one bedroom. "Scott, you need to see this!"

"What's u...." Millsap stopped and stared. The bed was covered with plastic sheeting. Ropes hung from the bedposts. "What the hell?"

"I'd say he was either planning to rape the girl and didn't want to leave any evidence or he was going to rape and murder her and not leave any mess. Whatever he was going to do, it was planned. That girl should be glad Frankie and Mia found her when they did."

Crime Scene took photographs of everything and packaged up the plastic and the ropes. It was unlikely Sawyer wore gloves when he spread the plastic across the bed so they hoped his fingerprints and DNA would be on it. Baker looked through the closet, dresser and nightstand in the tiny room, looking for anything that would link it to Sawyer, but all he found were clothes that obviously belonged to a woman. Most likely an older woman.

"Hey Ash, can you come photograph this?" Baker pointed to the floor where the bed and nightstand met.

"Sure, what do you have?"

Baker pointed, "Looks like a Taser or stun gun of some sort."

"You think he was going to use it on the girl he picked up?" Millsap asked.

"I don't know. He hasn't done anything like that to the other women that have come forward. His weapon of choice has always been fists and threat of a gun. My bet is it belongs to Eug…"

Before Baker could finish his sentence, he heard a husky female voice yell, "What the hell are you people doing in *my* house?"

The uniformed patrol officer stood in the doorway of the apartment and said, "Ma'am, you can't go in there."

"Like hell I can't. This is *my* house. Who are you to tell me I can't go in there."

Baker removed his gloves, picked up the search warrant from the counter and walked towards the door. "It's okay Maguire. She can come in. Ma'am, I will need you to stay in the living room though. Just until we are finished. Are you Miss Sawyer?"

"Harrumph. I am Eugenia Sawyer. Who the hell are you?"

Baker handed her a copy of the search warrant and calmly said, "I'm Sergeant Myles Baker with the Kansas City Missouri Police Department and we have a warrant to search your apartment."

"What in the world for? I haven't done a damn thing illegal for you to be in my apartment." The vein in Eugenia's forehead was pulsating in anger as she read the search warrant.

"Yes ma'am. I mean no ma'am. It isn't you we are investigating. Do you have a son?"

"I have two sons. Charles and Allen. They are grown ass men with jobs. They don't live here and they ain't done nothing illegal neither."

"Do either of them have a key to your apartment?"

"Both my boys do. I'm not a young woman. They need to be able to come in if something happens to me."

"I noticed you have a bag. Have you been away?"

Looking down at the bag she had sat by her feet Eugenia said, "Not that it's any of your damn business, but yes. I was out of town visiting my sister. She had surgery a few days ago and needed my help until her daughter could get there."

"Did you happen to leave plastic on your bed? Or keep, um, ropes attached to the headboard?

"What the hell kind of depraved nonsense are you talking about? No, I didn't put plastic or ropes on my bed."

"Do you own a Taser?"

"I am a single woman who lives alone Sergeant and, in case you didn't notice, I don't live in the safest neighborhood. So, yes, I own a Taser. It's not illegal. Now, will you please tell me what the hell is going on? Why are you all in my bedroom?"

"Miss Sawyer, we are investigating Allen for the kidnap and rape of several women: most recently a seventeen-year-old girl. She said he brought her here."

"Now you just wait a minute. My Allen would never do anything like that. He has a seventeen-year-old daughter himself. There's no way he would hurt a girl like that."

"Ma'am my detectives tried to stop him tonight and he had another woman with him. It appears he was bringing her here. He parked in front of your apartment and unlocked the door. He was bringing her inside when my detectives stopped him."

Eugenia's breathing became labored, and the color began to drain from her face.

"Ma'am, there's more, and you may need to sit down."

Fanning her face, she began to sit in the armchair and asked, "Oh my lawd, how can there be more?"

Taking a deep breath, and bracing for her response, Baker said,

"When my detectives tried to approach Allen, he pulled a gun and fired on them. He hit one of my detectives in the arm. They shot back…"

"Oh my God, where's my baby? Is he dead?" Eugenia began to wail, putting her face in her hands.

"Miss Sawyer." Baker raised his voice to be heard, "Miss Sawyer. Eugenia."

At the sound of her first name, she looked up from her hands, tears streaming down her face.

"Allen is at County Hospital. He was in surgery when I left. I don't believe his injuries are life threatening. I have every reason to believe he's going to live."

Eugenia continued to sob and said, "I need to get to him."

"Yes ma'am. I'll take you there."

"You should have told me when I got here." Eugenia stood from the chair and grabbed her handbag. "Take me there now. Please."

"Yes ma'am." Baker escorted her to his car. Once inside the car, the wailing stopped. He listened as she sniffled and occasional whimpers escaped her closed lips. He could only imagine the pain she was feeling.

Before Baker pulled into the parking garage Eugenia asked, "Did you say that girl was seventeen?"

Turning towards her Baker said, "Yes ma'am. Seventeen. She said he grabbed her off the street."

She fiddled with the straps of the purse in her lap. "That don't sound like my boy. He wouldn't hurt a fly."

Parking the car, Baker asked, "Is there someone I can call to be here with you?"

"No. You've done enough. Make sure they lock my apartment up. Y'ear?"

Baker nodded, "Yes ma'am."

CHAPTER
SEVENTY-THREE

SEARCH WARRANTS IN HAND, Frankie and Mia headed out to the garage where the vehicles would be processed. A tech from Crime Scene met them at the garage and began photographing the Honda at varying angles, in different light. Detective Billows from Internal Affairs walked in just as Frankie was grabbing gloves from the box hanging on the wall.

"Did you notice how the car seems to change color?" Frankie asked. "In one light it's tan, then it's gold. It can even almost pass for silver or white."

"You think he bought that color on purpose?"

Frankie shrugged, "Nothing would surprise me."

"Detectives, you know you can't be here while this vehicle is being processed," Billows said.

"We know Craig, but can we watch and take notes for our case?" Mia asked.

"As long as you look and don't touch."

Once they finished taking photographs, Frankie watched as Billows opened the car door and stood back so they could look inside. The interior of the Honda was clean. A lanyard hung from the rearview mirror, but the name tag had been removed. There was a bit of change in the ashtray and a jacket, too small for Sawyer, crumpled in the backseat.

"Billows can you grab that jacket?"

Billows pulled the jacket out of the car. Frankie noticed a patch with Northeast High School's mascot.

"Well, what do you know?" Frankie said.

"What do you have?" Mia asked.

"I think this might be Ciara's jacket."

Billows used his flashlight and looked under the car seats. He reached underneath the passenger seat and pulled out a non-driver's identification card. The name on the ID was Allie Wheaton.

"Does this mean anything to you all?" Billows asked, showing Frankie and Mia the identification card.

Frankie said, "I don't know how we missed this before."

"We didn't," Mia said. "Someone else did, but this does put Allie in the car."

"Can we use the alternate light source on the car?" Frankie asked.

"Sure," replied Yang.

Yang had the ALS in hand, threw the detectives glasses, and waited at the front of the car. Frankie turned the lights off in the garage, creating a dark space. If there were any bodily fluids inside the car they would show up with this light.

Yang used a black Sharpie marker to circle the spots that illuminated on the front seat. "Want me to cut these leather seats?"

Frankie smiled smugly, "Personally, I'd love to see that, but if we can get the evidence by swabbing then we should."

Moving to the backseat Yang said, "Holy crap!"

"What?" Frankie opened the other back door and looked inside. Laughing she said, "Mia, you have to see this!"

The backseat glowed. There were spots on the seats, door frames, backs of the front seats, on the ceiling, and floorboards.

"What the hell?" responded Mia.

Yang started marking the areas of illumination as Frankie and Mia talked about the number of samples the lab would have. Once he finished, Yang turned the garage lights back on and began collecting the samples. One sample per tube. Frankie turned to the back doors. The women had all told them they couldn't open the back door. Operating on a hunch Frankie looked at the door frame and noticed the doors had the child safety locks engaged. The doors could be opened from the outside but not from the inside. Just like a police car. The car was small, and Sawyer was large, so it was reasonable to think he left his side open while he raped the women.

"Yang, be sure to photograph the doors, okay?" Frankie pointed to the door frame.

He nodded in agreement while continuing to collect swabs from the interior of the car.

"What are we on?" asked Mia.

"QQ," replied Yang.

"Seriously? That's a lot of swabs!"

"There's a spot on the carpet that I can't swab. I'm going to have to cut it out."

"He should be glad that's all you are cutting," Frankie said.

While Yang was finishing with the Honda, Frankie and Mia moved to the Kia. The exterior of the black compact was clean, however when they opened the door the smell of urine overtook them.

"Damn, I guess she did urinate in the seat!" Mia said.

"For the love of…" Frankie caught her breath and backed away from the door. "I think we'll wait for you on you this one Yang."

Frankie heard a deep voice yell her name. She broke into a smile when she saw Scott Fitzmeyer from the Intelligence Unit walking her way. Fitzmeyer and Frankie had worked an investigation involving organized crime. Fitz was how she had met Jim.

Fitz sauntered over to Frankie and Mia, flashing his trademark smile. He reached out to shake their hands them pulled each one in for a half-hug. "What kind of mischief are you two up to now?"

"Do you remember the guy that was picking women up off the Avenue?"

"He the guy that hit while we were working the Reitzell/Kemp case?"

"Yeah, that's him. He's hit a few more times – the latest being earlier tonight. He popped off a couple shots at Mia and me. Last I heard he was in the O.R. getting his belly stitched up."

"No shit?" Fitz's dark green eyes bore into theirs, "Are you two okay?"

"One of the bullets grazed Frankie's arm, but I'm good," answered Mia.

"What? Why are you here?"

"I'm fine. It's just a scrape."

"Do you still want to put a tracker on his car?"

Frankie looked at Mia with question, "What do you think?"

"Given the luck, or lack thereof, with this damn prosecutor I say let's place it," said Mia.

"Yeah, unfortunately I think you might be right on this one." Frankie described to Fitz their most recent run-ins with Moon.

"Consider it done. We don't have the manpower to sit on his house 24/7 but we will have the tracker programmed to send an alert if he leaves his house. A second alert will sound if he goes within a specific geographical radius. If the second alert sounds one of us will be on him."

CHAPTER
SEVENTY-FOUR

PULLING ALL-NIGHTERS was nothing new to Frankie or Mia. The late hour and adrenaline dump had both laughing and acting silly when they returned to the office after processing the cars. They took turns telling jokes about the evidence found inside and how it may have gotten there. They giggled at the look Fitzmeyer gave them when they told him about Sawyer taking shots at them.

Baker walked in amidst their laughter and said, "You two are having too much fun."

"I don't know what you're talking about Sarge," Mia teased.

"How are the case files coming along?"

"We're almost done. Mine is ready to be copied and Frankie's finishing up the last report on hers." As an afterthought she asked, "Find anything good at the apartment?"

Baker sat down in one of the empty office chairs and sighed. After telling them what they found in the bedroom he said, "And his mother showed up."

Frankie sat up a little straighter in her chair, "What was she like?"

"A real peach," Baker went on to tell them about their interaction.

"Sorry you had to be the bearer of bad news Sarge," Frankie said.

"Just another day. Get your reports done. I'm going to go write mine so we can get the hell out of here."

Frankie nodded, "Before you do, did you hear about Treyvon Stockton and the car chase?"

"I heard there was a chase but didn't realize it was Stockton. Wasn't there a woman in the car with him?"

"Yeah. Cheyenne – the clerk from the Fast Stop. I'm going to run by County when we are done here and try to get an update."

Baker shook his head as he walked into his office. Frankie heard his heavy sigh as he dropped into his seat. The job weighed heavily on all of them. Just as Frankie was finishing her last report her phone dinged with an incoming text message.

"What the hell Frankie? Are you okay??"

"I guess you talked to Fitz. I'm fine. It's nothing but a scrape."

"Good. Do you think you'll be up for a run tomorrow?"

"Sure. I'll text you when I get up."

Mia noticed Frankie texting and asked, "Derek?"

"No. Jim. Fitz must have talked to him. He just wanted to make sure we were okay."

"Hmm. Have you told Derek?"

Frankie looked up from her phone and said, "No. No need to worry him. He has enough on his plate."

CHAPTER
SEVENTY-FIVE

THE SKY WAS JUST BEGINNING to lighten when Frankie and Mia walked into County Hospital.

Seeing Dr. Wilhelm, Frankie yelled, "Michael."

Turning he answered, "Hey Frankie. I'm surprised to see you back here so soon. Is everything okay? Need me to take another look at your arm?"

"Yeah. I mean, no we are good. We're checking in on the accident victims that were brought in earlier tonight. Treyvon Stockton and Chey..."

"Step over here," he interrupted.

Frankie and Mia exchanged a questioning look then fell into step behind the doctor.

Once they were out of earshot Michael said, "Stockton is going to lose his eye, but should live. The girl is another story. They revived her at the scene then lost her again in the ambulance. We have her on a vent now. I'll be honest, it's not looking good Frankie."

"Thanks Michael. Can we see Cheyenne?"

Nodding he said, "We are waiting on transport to take her upstairs for surgery. She's still in a trauma room. Make it brief."

Frankie and Mia walked the short distance in silence. Michael led the detectives into the trauma room filled with loud machines designed to keep this frail woman alive. Lying against the bloodstained sheets, Cheyenne's face was barely recognizable. Her closed eyes were swollen shut. Her hair was crusted against her head and caked with blood.

"Has her family been contacted?"

"I'm not sure, but I think her father was called."

"Do you think she can hear us?"

"You can talk to her. She can probably hear you but it's unlikely she'll respond."

Mia looked at Frankie then back at Cheyenne's ashen face and said, "You didn't know he'd been released Frankie."

"I know, but that doesn't matter to her." Frankie touched the young girl's warm, slender hand. With tear-filled eyes she said, "Cheyenne, we're going to make this right."

Mia touched Cheyenne's shoulder gently and said, "Fight girl."

The trio walked out of the trauma room together. Michael touched Frankie on the shoulder, "I'll call you if her status changes."

"Thanks Mike. We'll have an officer stay outside of Stockton's room once he's out of surgery."

Walking out of the Emergency Department Mia put her arm across Frankie's shoulders and squeezed, "It's not your fault. You weren't given a chance to warn her."

CHAPTER
SEVENTY-SIX

FRANKIE WAS EXHAUSTED and her head was spinning. The sun was beginning to rise when she got into her Jeep to head home. She looked at the clock on the car radio and thought, "*6:30. I bet dad's driving to work.*"

Frankie dialed her dad's cellphone and was met with a cheery hello after one ring, "Francesca!"

With a yawn she said, "Hey dad."

"Is everything okay Frankie?"

"Yea. I had a late night and thought I'd catch you on your way in to work."

Frankie and her dad made small talk while each drove to their destination. Frankie never mentioned the shooting, instead they talked about the kids, her siblings, and Jake's party. Frankie was pulling into her driveway just as her dad told her he needed to get into the shop.

"Have a good day today dad." Frankie turned off the Jeep and grabbed her bag. "And dad?"

"Yeah?"

"I love you."

"I love you too, Francesca."

Frankie opened the door to the sounds of a normal school day morning. Keith was directing the kids while getting his lunch together. At the sight of Frankie, he stopped talking and gave her a hug.

"I take it Bruce called. Please tell me you didn't say anything to the kids."

"He did and are you crazy? Of course, I didn't. They worry enough as it is."

"Thanks Keith. Do you mind dropping them at school? I'm dead on my feet."

Keith gave her a one-arm hug and said, "I was planning to. Go get some rest."

Nodding her thanks Frankie walked down the hall and gave both kids a hug before falling, fully clothed, onto her bed. After what seemed like minutes, she was jolted awake by the sound of her alarm. Looking at the clock she realized it was 130. Time to get up and get ready for work. She rolled over and looked at her phone, seeing a text message from Baker.

"You, Mia, and I are taking tonight off. Brett and Rich can handle it. See you tomorrow."

Frankie smiled. Baker was always watching out for their team. She quickly replied, *"Thanks Sarge. See you tomorrow."*

She was about to roll over and go back to sleep when her phone dinged again. This time the message was from Jim.

"Are you up for a run in the park?"

"When?"

"2?"

"See you there."

"Well Isabelle, so much for sleep. Want to go for a run?" With those words, the dog that had been sprawled on the bed next to her jumped up and ran towards the door. Laughing Frankie said, "I'll take that as a yes."

Frankie got to the park before Jim and used the time to stretch her tired muscles. It was an unseasonably warm winter day, which allowed her to run with gloves and a heavy sweatshirt.

Isabelle barked a hello as Jim approached the table. Her tail wagged with furor when he rubbed her head. Frankie and Jim started off walking to warm up and about a quarter mile in they started their run. It didn't take long for Jim and Frankie to find their rhythm; their feet pounding the pavement in unison. They chatted playfully while they jogged and talked about everything under the sun.

Taking a few minutes to stretch when they finished Jim asked, "Want to grab a diet Coke before heading home?"

Frankie looked at her watch, "As much as I'd love to, I think I'm going to go surprise my kids. They don't know I'm off tonight. In fact, I forgot to tell Sophie. I guess I'll surprise all of them," Frankie laughed.

With a hint of disappointment, Jim smiled and said, "Okay. Well, enjoy your night off."

Frankie hesitated then turned to him and said, "Would you like to join us for dinner? It'll probably just be pizza, but the kids are sure to provide entertainment."

"Are you sure?"

"Yeah. Let's say 6 o'clock?"

"Okay. I'll bring some beer to go with the pizza."

"Sounds good." With that Frankie and Isabelle climbed into her Jeep and headed home.

Jim stood up from the picnic table he had been resting on and watched Frankie pull away.

CHAPTER
SEVENTY-SEVEN

FRANKIE WAS PUTTING clothes in the dryer when Tyler burst through the back door. He and Dani were bickering and almost missed her standing in the kitchen. Dani nearly jumped out of her skin.

"I thought you were working tonight."

"Sarge gave me the night off, so I thought I'd surprise you."

Tyler dropped his bag on the kitchen table and said, "I'm always glad when he gives you a night off. What's for dinner?"

"How about pizza? And your bag doesn't go there."

"I'm going to do my homework here."

"Mmhmm, okay. By the way, a friend of mine is going to join us for dinner if that's okay."

"Whatever. I'm going to go do my homework." With that Dani stomped down the hall to her bedroom and slammed the door.

"She's pissed off because some boy at school was being an ass."

"Tyler Nathanial Thomas, watch your mouth," Frankie admonished while trying to hide her amusement.

"I'm just saying what she told Brittany."

Ruffling the hair on his head Frankie said, "I'll speak to her. You don't use words like pissed and ass. Okay?"

Tyler mumbled as he read his book and munched on the apple slices he had taken from the refrigerator.

"Tyler."

Swallowing his bite, he responded, "Yes ma'am."

The afternoon passed quickly with Dani holed up in her room and Tyler doing his homework at the table. Frankie picked up the clutter in the kitchen and wiped down the counters while answering Ty's math questions.

Frankie picked up the phone to order pizza and jumped at the back door opening. "Shit girl, I'm sorry. I forgot to text you! Want to stay for dinner? I was just about to order pizza."

"Yeah, and mom's friend is going to join us," Tyler said.

Sophie raised her eyebrow at Frankie, "Friend?"

"Jim and I went for a run today and I invited him to join us for pizza. I was thinking about calling Keith to see if he wanted to join us too."

"Hmm, maybe I *will* stay for dinner."

SEVENTY-EIGHT

"MY MOM IS A CRAZY DRIVER," Tyler said.

"Ty…"

"Really. Why is she a crazy driver?" Jim asked.

"She yells at people when they don't get out of her way. She always says move over you freakin' jack…"

"Tyler Nathaniel."

"Well, you do. Do your mom and dad live on the ocean?"

"No, but they do live on the river."

"Ty, do you remember where we sometimes go to get shrimp?" Frankie asked.

"Where all the boats are?"

Jim nodded, "That's the place. That's where I grew up."

Danielle had been quiet throughout most of the evening, but that got her attention. "Really?"

"Yeah, I was working on a shrimp boat before I even went to school."

"Your mom and dad made you *work* when you were a little kid?" Tyler asked.

"Yes sir. I plucked shrimp heads, scrubbed the boat decks, and worked in my momma's store too."

Frankie looked at Danielle, "You remember Miss Lolly's bookstore?"

Both kids nodded.

"Miss Lolly is Jim's mother."

Jim's phone rang before he could add to what Frankie's said.

"Excuse me." Stepping away from the table he said, "Craven."

Frankie cleared the table and Sophie loaded the dishwasher while Keith took the empty pizza boxes outside. They were just finishing up when Jim returned to the kitchen.

"I'm sorry guys, but I have to go. Something came up on one of my cases. Frankie, you got a minute?"

Frankie nodded, "Dani, would you please finish wiping the table off. Ty go jump in the shower." Following Jim into the living room she asked, "What's up?"

"You remember that homicide down in the bottoms? Katarina Schlovik? She was found in the trunk with two of Finnegan's soldiers?"

"Yeah."

"I just got a call from Fitz. They got the lab results back on Katarina's forensic kit. The report said there were signs of trauma consistent with rape. Two male DNA profiles were identified from vaginal and anal swabs. They uploaded them into CODIS, and we think we have at least one match."

"Are you going to help Fitz work on this one?"

"Looks that way."

"Mom! Will you get me a towel?" yelled Tyler.

"That's my cue to go. Nice to meet you, Keith. See you later Sophie!"

Keith and Sophie both yelled their good-byes.

"Thank you for dinner Frankie. I really enjoyed spending time with you all." Jim gave Frankie a clumsy hug.

"Anytime."

While they finished cleaning up Keith asked, "What's going on with you two?"

"Yeah sis, what's going on?" echoed Sophie.

"What do you mean? We're friends. That's all."

"If that's what you want to believe." Keith said.

"It's not about what I want to believe. It's what is." Frankie's phone began to buzz. She looked at the caller-id and laid it back on the table.

"Do you need to get that?" Sophie asked.

"Nope." Frankie pursed her lips, twisting them slightly with irritation. "Definitely not."

"Derek?"

"Yep."

"Talk to me, sis."

Frankie sat down at the kitchen table and told Keith and Sophie everything. How Mac found Derek and Jessica when they were shot. Seeing the two of them leaving the courthouse together the day before. The way Jessica had been refusing to charge her cases.

"I mean it could be nothing. They may just be friends like Jim and I are...."

Keith interjected, "Jim definitely doesn't want to just be friends with you. Have you talked to Derek?"

"No. I'm not even sure what I'm supposed to say. 'Hey Derek, I know we never said we were exclusive but why were you leaving with Jessica the other night?' Is it even fair for me to say anything?" Frankie wiped the tears from her eyes.

"If you're sleeping with him, then yes. Do you want to be exclusive? Has that ever even come up?" Sophie prodded.

Frankie's phone started buzzing again. After checking the caller-id she laid it back on the table.

"Looks like he really wants to talk to you."

"I'll call him later."

"You didn't answer my questions," Sophie said.

"Yes. No. I don't know. It was so much easier before..."

"Before you and Jim became friends," Keith finished.

"Yeah."

SEVENTY-NINE

DEREK LAY in his bed watching the blur of the rotating ceiling fan. A glance at the clock by his bed told him it was after midnight. He'd called Frankie twice, but she didn't answer. She always answered or called back. Tonight, she did neither.

Derek closed his eyes but found sleep elusive. Again. He thought having dinner with Jessica would help but the allure of her was quickly fading. She didn't want to talk about anything but work and all she did was complain. She complained about defense attorneys. Paralegals. Judges. Detectives. She spent thirty minutes complaining about a series of cases involving sex workers and the stupid detective that wouldn't let it go. The case facts sounded familiar to Derek, but he wasn't sure why. He planned to ask Frankie about it. If she ever called him back.

To make matters worse, Jessica had it in her head they were dating. Sure, he'd flirted with her. He'd even slept with her a few times, but he wasn't thinking about dating her. Tonight, she started asking him about spending the weekend together. Having dinner with her parents. Going out with some friends from college. Derek had no interest in any of that. No interest at all.

He glanced at the clock again. 2 AM. Too late to call Frankie. Derek got out of bed and walked to the kitchen. He pulled a glass down from the cabinet, poured a stiff drink, stood at the kitchen sink, and looked out the window at the moonlight reflecting on the pond. He finished the first glass and poured another. As the scotch warmed his body, he felt the tension leave his shoulders. By the third glass he felt like he could sleep, and if he was lucky, not dream.

CHAPTER
EIGHTY

FRANKIE RETURNED to work to find Sawyer was still in the hospital but had not been charged with the rapes.

"What the fuck do you mean she didn't charge him with the rapes?"

"Don't shoot the messenger, Frankie." Richard Coleman, said as he relayed the message from the prosecutor's office.

"Did she at least give a good reason?"

"She wants to wait on DNA."

"Great. Let's see how many other women he rapes. Or better yet, let's see if he escalates to murder. Did you see what he did to Gina Bradshaw?"

"I did. Do you want the good news?"

"There's good news?"

"He *is* being charged with two counts of aggravated assault on a law enforcement officer for shooting at you and Mia. His bail is set at $75,000."

"Well, that's something. Hopefully he won't be able to bond out." Frankie was slightly mollified. "What about Treyvon Stockton?"

"He's still in the hospital. He's being charged with kidnapping that girl from the Fast Stop…"

"Cheyenne Connor."

"Yeah. But the prosecutor said she wants the DNA results before she charges him in the other case," Coleman said.

"Let me guess. The prosecutor on both cases is Jessica Moon," snarled Frankie.

"Yeah. Was she the one you were talking too?"

Frankie was seeing red. She grabbed her case files, marched into Sergeant Baker's office, and slammed the door. She laid out the facts on both cases, using very colorful language, as though Baker hadn't been working them with her the entire time.

After Frankie's twenty-minute rant, Baker calmly said, "Both men are in the hospital. Both are being charged with felonies and will have to bond out. Is there any reason to believe either will be able to make bond?"

Frankie shook her head, then said, "Actually Sawyer might be able to. His wife is considerably older. When I ran financials on them it looked like she might own her house outright. If she's willing to use it as collateral she might be able to get him out."

"Did Fitz put the tracker on his car?" Frankie nodded.

"Then we'll just have to make sure it's released to her before he gets out. That way if he starts up again, we can catch him in the act."

"Mia is working with PIC to see if there are any old reports on him. He said he was in the Army. I'll check with the Veteran's Administration and see if they will send me his records. We've subpoenaed his cell phone records too. I'll write up a search warrant and see if we can get cell tower information on his phone. Maybe we can put him in the locations on the dates and times of the abductions." Frankie took a deep breath and exhaled slowly. Standing to leave she turned and said, "Thanks, Sarge."

Baker nodded. "We'll get him."

When Frankie returned to her desk, she noticed a missed call from Dr. Wilhelm. The day before he told her Cheyenne was still on the vent, but stable. Her hands trembled as she dialed the number, afraid the news was not going to be good.

"Dr. Wilhelm."

"Hey Michael. It's Frankie. I saw you called?"

"Yep. I wanted to let you know Cheyenne has been taken off the vent. She's still groggy but I think she's going to make it."

"Thank you, Mike. I'll stop in and see her tonight." Frankie released a heavy sigh. When she hung up the phone she uttered, "Thank God."

Mia looked up from the report she was working on and asked, "Cheyenne?"

"She's going to make it."

CHAPTER
EIGHTY-ONE

FRANKIE BUSIED herself with drafting search warrants and subpoenas. She had talked to the Veteran's Administration who told her she would have to put her request in writing. If the records didn't burn up in the fire of '73 she would receive them within thirty days. In the meantime, Frankie set out to dig up everything she could find on Sawyer. She did every type of computer check she could think of, looking for reports filed, registered vehicles, and every address he was ever associated with.

"We're going to Chipotle, want to go?" Coleman asked.

Frankie looked up from the computer screen just in time to see the rest of her squad grabbing their coats. Rubbing her eyes, she said, "Yeah. I could use a break from the computer."

An hour later they were back in front of the headquarters building. Frankie's phone began to buzz as she was getting out of the car. "Hey Sarge, I'm going to run to County to see Cheyenne. Call me if you need anything."

"I'm going to tag along," added Mia.

Baker nodded and said, "Don't stir anything up, ladies. I want to go home on time tonight."

Laughing Mia said, "No promises."

When it was just the two of them Frankie said, "I need to call Derek back. Do you mind?"

"No. I'll drive so you can chat on the way."

"Thanks."

Derek answered on the first ring, "Hey stranger. Are you working tonight?"

"Yeah. Mia and I are on the way to County now."

"Another case?"

"No. What's up?" Frankie realized she hadn't talked to Derek since they got into the shoot-out with Sawyer. Had they really grown that far apart? There was a time he would have been her first call.

"Nothing's up. I just miss you. Can we spend some time together this weekend?"

Frankie didn't immediately answer. She wanted to say yes. And she wanted to say no.

"Frankie?"

"Yeah. I mean, maybe. I'm working Friday and Saturday."

"Are the kids staying home?" Derek asked.

Softening, Frankie said, "No. Dani's going to her dad's and Ty is going to mom's. She's picking them up after school for me Friday."

"Why don't you spend the weekend at my house?"

Frankie considered Derek's offer. It was not lost on her that a month prior she wouldn't have hesitated at saying yes. Yet tonight she did.

"Fr…"

"I'll call you when I get off on Friday."

"Okay. I'm looking forward to it."

Softly Frankie said, "Me too."

When she hung up Mia said, "You hesitated."

"Only for a second."

CHAPTER
EIGHTY-TWO

FRANKIE AND MIA found Cheyenne's room in the Intensive Care Unit quickly. They stood looking through the gap the curtains made on the glass wall. Tubes and wires led from Cheyenne's body to monitors next to the bed and oxygen cannulas breathed air into her body. The once purple bruises on her face had changed to shades of yellow, green, and brown. A man not much older than Frankie sat next to the bed. His face was worn and haggard, but his clothes were neatly pressed. He was holding a worn book in his rough hands that he appeared to be reading aloud to her sleeping body.

Frankie tapped on the doorframe, apologizing when the man started. She and Mia introduced themselves then immediately asked how Cheyenne was doing.

"She could be better. Could be worse. She's opened her eyes some but has been really groggy. I'm her daddy, by the way." Extending his hand, he said, "Jerome Connor."

Frankie offered her hand in return, "It's nice to meet you Mr. Connor. May I ask what you are reading to her?"

Sheepishly Jerome said, "*A Secret Garden*. It was one of her favorite books growing up. She used to beg for one more chapter every night. I thought she might like it if I read it to her now."

"I'm sure she does sir." Frankie smiled at Jerome. "They issued a warrant for Treyvon for kidnapping Cheyenne. His bond is high, so I don't think he's going to get out anytime soon. I have another case I'm going to get a warrant for too. I think Cheyenne's safe from him now."

"Thank you, Detective. I'll let her know when she wakes up."

"Okay. We're going to head back to our office. I'll come back by and see her again this weekend if that's okay."

Jerome nodded and sat back down and wrapped Cheyenne's hand in his.

Standing near the elevator Frankie asked, "Want to see how Stockton and Sawyer are holding up?"

"Might as well make the rounds," replied Mia.

The charge nurse provided Frankie the room numbers for Stockton and Sawyer. Frankie glanced into Stockton's room while Mia made small talk with the officer sitting guard outside. The man on the bed looked less hardened and more like the boy in the pictures they had seen at his mother's house. A cast adorned his left arm, handcuffs his right, and a bandage covered his right eye. His left eye was closed so he didn't see Frankie staring from the doorway. When he started to stir, she quickly exited.

Sawyer was down the hall from Stockton with a different officer sitting guard outside his room. He could be heard before he could be seen.

"Get these damn things off me. Why can't I see my wife?" The rant continued. The door to the room was slightly ajar allowing Frankie to glance into the room unseen.

Sawyer was hooked up to an IV and one arm was handcuffed to the bed. Other than a bandage on his shoulder, he looked no worse for the wear. A blanket covered his bandaged abdomen and a pillow lay on his lap, but he was sitting up, spewing profanities and complaints at the officer sitting outside.

"He's been like this all night," said the officer. "He goes off about the handcuffs and not being able to see his wife for a while then changes it up and starts complaining about the police department and how we are all out to get him."

"Oh geesh. That will make for a long night," said Frankie.

"It's all good," said the officer. With a smile he added, "It's my Friday. As long as I'm sitting here, I'm guaranteed to go home on time."

Smiling Frankie said, "That's true."

"HEY FRANKIE, come take a look at this."

"Whatcha got Mia?"

"PIC sent me the list of reports from the last four years with unknown suspects matching Sawyer's description. There are at least thirty."

"Is anyone working down there tonight?" Frankie asked.

"Tony is working. He sent me this about five minutes ago. Why?"

"Let's go see if he can plot this list on a map. Give us a visual." Grabbing her notepad Frankie said, "Sarge we'll be downstairs."

The Perpetrator Information Center was located on the first floor of Police Headquarters. They were able to search databases detectives didn't have access to as well as run queries to detect patterns. Frankie opened the door to a room full of empty desks.

"Hello?"

"Back here."

Frankie looked at Mia and raised her eyebrow in question as they walked towards the sound of the voice.

With a gravelly voice Tony asked, "What can I do for you?"

Mia said, "We're from the Sex Crimes Unit. We…"

"You emailed me about the unsolved rape cases."

Mia nodded.

"Do you think you could plot the list you gave us on a map?" Frankie asked.

"How big you want it?"

Frankie touched her chin and bit her lower lip. "Seriously? How about big enough to put on a wall for reference? With case numbers identifying the plots or at least a legend."

"Easy enough. Give me about thirty minutes and I'll print something out and bring it up to you."

"Thank you." Frankie looked at Mia as they walked out the door. "Quick Trip?"

While she drove, Frankie filled Mia in on her dinner with Jim. "Keith seems to think Jim wants to be more than friends."

"Duh."

"Hmpf. Oh my gosh, I forgot to tell you. While he was at my house, he got a call from Fitz. Remember Katarina Schlovik? The girl that was found in the trunk of the car with those two dudes?"

"Yeah, what about her?"

"They got the results back from the forensic kit. Two male DNA profiles were identified. They uploaded them into CODIS and think they have at least one match."

"Maybe they'll get lucky, and the other profile will be in the system," Mia said.

"Hopefully."

The map from PIC was sitting on Mia's chair when they got back from Quick Trip. She and Frankie spread the map out on the table and surveyed the results. They used sticky notes to indicate where victims had positively identified Sawyer. Then they pulled case files for the others PIC plotted out. After two hours, they had identified ten possible cases to add to the ones they already knew about.

"I wonder how many victims didn't report?" mumbled Frankie.

Before Mia could comment, Baker walked out of his office and said, "You all ready to call it a night?"

The squad started to gather their things, but Frankie kept staring at the map.

"Frankie?" Baker asked.

"Huh? Oh, you guys go ahead. I'm going to finish plotting this out."

"Don't stay too late."

"Mmhmm."

In the quiet of the squad room Frankie continued to label the map. She found an empty wall and, using thumbtacks, hung it up. Standing back, she looked at the labels and looked at what could be a pattern.

All the women were picked up in areas known for prostitution, but not all the women were sex workers. Most of the women were raped inside the car and discarded like rubbish in an alley. All the alleys were within a half-mile radius. A couple of the women were taken to an apartment. The ages varied, but Ciara was by far the youngest. In fact, she was the only girl under eighteen identified. All the women were abducted at night, except for Ciara.

"What made her different?" Frankie asked aloud.

Looking through the files, Frankie made notes on which ones to pull from the archives. She'd go through them over the weekend and see if she could find any more victims that could identify Sawyer. Frankie took one more look at the map then closed the file and headed home.

"WHAT ARE you doing after work? Want to grab a drink?" Jessica stood in the doorway of Derek's office with her arms folded, making sure he would notice her ample breasts. It was Friday night, and they were the last two in the office.

Distracted he looked up and said, "I'm going to be awhile. I need to go over this case file again."

Licking her lips, she asked, "Want some help?"

Derek hesitated.

"Come on, let me help you go through this, then we can grab a drink."

"Alright, I *could* use some help, but no promises on a drink."

Jessica grabbed a report and a legal pad before slipping off her heels and plopping down in the chair across from his desk. "What case are you working on, anyway?"

"An unsolved homicide."

With eyebrows raised she asked, "Unsolved? If it's unsolved, why do *you* have it?"

"Detective Fitzmeyer brought the case file over. They apparently identified two DNA profiles in the forensic kit collected on the female. They are waiting for confirmation on one possible match and are hoping CODIS will give them the other. He wanted me to be up to speed on the case when they started to bring me search warrants to sign."

"What do you know so far?"

"This girl," Derek handed Jessica a photograph, "Katarina Schlovik was last seen leaving the Shady Lady on 12thStreet. She was accompanied by these two men." Derek handed Jessica two more photographs. "The Shady Lady is underwritten by the Marzullo family. It is commonly known that the Marzullo family is connected. The men she was seen leaving with are part of the Finnegan family – arch enemies of the Marzullo family. All three were found dead, in the trunk of a car, down in the west bottoms."

"Was she a dancer, prostitute or both?"

"We know she was a dancer but have no evidence of her being a sex worker. Based on what I've seen so far, it doesn't appear that much was left behind in the way of evidence."

Jessica looked at the photo of the woman on the slab at the morgue. An involuntary shiver ran down her spine. "Did you notice this?"

"What?"

"She has a rose tattoo on her wrist."

"Hmm. So?"

"It's kind of unique. Sex Crimes brought me a rape case not long ago where the girl had the same tattoo on her wrist. We're waiting on DNA before we charge the case. She was a dancer too. I'll have to pull the file to see if she worked at the Shady Lady or a different club."

"Are you thinking they might be connected?" Derek inquired. "The women might be but I don't know about the cases." Derek almost missed the text vibrating his phone.

"We are working an in-custody from the day shift. Not sure what time I'll be done."

Derek looked at Jessica then back at his phone.

"Okay. Maybe tomorrow?"

"K"

Putting the phone back in his pocket he said, "I'm starving. Want to go grab a bite?"

Jessica put the report she was reading on his desk and said, "Is it really almost 8? No wonder I'm so hungry."

Derek grabbed all the reports and put them back in the file folder. Satisfied his desk was in order he asked, "What are you hungry for?"

A chuckle escaped, "Mmhmm first things first. I need food."

Derek followed Jessica into the elevator and when the doors closed, he grabbed her and pressed her against the wall. His mouth found hers quickly as she lifted her leg to wrap around his waist. He ran his hand up her thigh, letting his fingertips brush against the back of her panties. A guttural moan escaped her lips. She ran her hands up his back as the elevator shuddered to a stop. Jessica stepped back, smoothed her skirt, and wiped the lipstick from Derek's mouth.

"How about we order in?" Jessica asked with a wink.

"I'll be right behind you." He followed her to the parking lot, climbed into his car, and waited until Jessica pulled out.

Derek followed her to her condo. They barely made it in the front door before their clothes were discarded. When they were finished, they collapsed, satiated, onto her bed.

After a few minutes Jessica asked, "Want me to order a pizza?"

"Sure. Do you have any beer?"

"In the fridge." Jessica sat up in the bed, grabbed her phone, and called for dinner.

Derek grabbed his shorts and walked out of the bedroom. He looked around the tiny condo as he made his way to the refrigerator and grabbed two cold bottles of beer. He blinked when the light came on.

Jessica was standing in the doorway with his dress shirt wrapped around her body. She took the beer from his extended hand and swallowed a long drink. She walked back to the living room and flipped on the television. Derek followed, plopping down onto the sofa next to her.

The pair chatted amiably about work over pizza and beer. After cleaning up Jessica said, "I think I need a shower."

Looking back at Derek she asked, "Want to join me?" Derek smiled and followed her to the bathroom.

Sleep was elusive for Derek. He hadn't intended to stay the night but didn't think it would be right to leave now. With the sound muted he turned the television on, flipped channels, and watched Jessica's chest rise and fall while she slept next to him. He looked at his cellphone. 2 AM and still no word from Frankie. Not that he was surprised.

Depending on how complicated the case was it could still be hours before she left work.

Jessica stirred when Derek twisted his body to get out of bed. She asked, "Where are you going?"

"To get a drink." He gently brushed her hair back from her eyes. "I'll be back."

She closed her eyes and smiled.

EIGHTY-FIVE

"I'M FREAKING EXHAUSTED," yawned Frankie.

With a half-laugh, half-yawn Mia said, "Me too. Stop that, it's contagious! Are you going to Derek's tonight?"

"No. I didn't know what time we'd be off so…"

"Don't you have a key? Go wake his butt up!" Mia winked at Frankie.

"It's 2 AM… you know what, you're right. I'll drive up and surprise him!" Frankie was still laughing when she got into her Jeep. She picked up her cellphone and thought about calling first but decided it would be more fun to surprise him. The sounds of Daughtry filled the car as she drove north.

Frankie pulled into the driveway, but something felt off. The back-porch light was on, and Bear was sitting on the porch. There were no lights on in the house and Derek's car was not in the driveway. She pulled out her phone and dialed his number. Two rings and the call went to voice mail. Frankie disconnected without leaving a message. She threw her phone onto the seat and backed out of the driveway.

She was pulling into her driveway when a text came through from Derek.

"Sorry I missed your call. Are you okay? Miss you. XO"

Frankie looked at the message and debated on whether she should answer it. Once inside the house she grabbed a beer and started flipping channels on the television. She fell asleep without answering his message.

The ringing of her cellphone awoke Frankie with a start. She was stiff from falling asleep in the chair. Rubbing her neck, she looked at the caller id and smiled. "Hey Jim, what's up?"

"Dang girl, did I wake you? It's after 9 o'clock."

Frankie stretched her tired body and said, "Late night. Got a confession though, so it was worth it."

"Good job! Want to go for a run. Or maybe some breakfast?"

"How about both? We can meet down by the river, then go to the City Café for pancakes?"

"Thirty minutes?"

"See you there!"

After warming up, Frankie and Jim fell into a steady rhythm. They talked about work while they ran, but when they got seated at the café Jim said, "Enough small talk. You're not yourself. What's going on?"

Frankie told Jim about going to Derek's and calling him. "I still haven't answered his text."

"You think he was with her?"

"Yea, or some other woman."

"What are you going to do?"

Frankie fumbled with the napkin she had placed in her lap while looking down at the table. She didn't know what she was going to do. She didn't feel like she had a right to do anything.

"Frankie?"

Looking up with tear-filled eyes she said, "I don't know. I guess I'm going to have to confront him."

Jim reached across the table and put his hand over hers, "You deserve better Frankie."

Before Frankie could respond the waitress returned with their plates. "Thank you." Frankie busied herself with putting syrup on her pancakes. Changing the subject she asked, "What did you find out about Schlovik?"

"Nothing yet. They said it may be a few days before we get anything back in the CODIS search. I think Fitz gave the prosecutor the case file last week so he would be familiar with it when we started requesting warrants."

"Good idea. Do you know who the prosecutor is?"

Jim shook his head as he chewed his food. "I didn't ask."

FRANKIE WAS JUST GETTING into the shower when her phone rang. Looking at the caller ID she declined the call from Derek and sent a message saying she would call back. After showering and getting dressed she looked at the phone again. She was still angry and debating on whether to call back before work.

Inside her Jeep she picked up the phone and stared at the screen. Just before backing out, she hit the callback button.

Derek answered on the second ring, "Hey babe."

With an icy tone Frankie answered, "Hey."

"I tried to call earlier. Are you still coming over tonight?"

"Yeah, I was in the shower." Almost as an afterthought Frankie added, "I came by last night." Frankie's statement was met with silence.

Stuttering Derek said, "I…I…"

"Look, we never said we wouldn't see other people, but since you invited…"

"You said you were working late."

"So, since I was working late you decided to find someone else's bed to fill?"

Once again, her statement was met with silence. After a few minutes Derek pleaded, "Will you please come up tonight."

Frankie didn't immediately respond.

"Frankie?" Derek said softly.

"Let me see how the night goes."

"Okay." Derek paused before saying, "And Frankie."

"Yeah?"

"I really do miss you. Stay safe, okay?"

With tears in her eyes, Frankie said, "I know. Me too. And I will."

Frankie sat in the parking lot next to police headquarters and rested her head against the steering wheel. She nearly jumped out of her skin when Mia tapped on her window.

"Are you coming in?"

Opening the door Frankie said, "You scared the shit out of me."

"Everything okay?"

"Yeah. No. I don't know. It's Derek."

"I take it last night didn't go well?"

"It didn't 'go' at all. He wasn't home. When I called, he sent it to voicemail. He was at *her* place."

"Did he say that?"

"No, but he wasn't at home. So, if it wasn't her, it was some other girl."

"Does he know about the issues we've been having with Jessica?"

Frankie shook her head.

"We haven't really talked. He's been so distant since the shooting." She lowered her gaze to the ground, "At first I thought it was in my head but now…"

Mia put her hand on Frankie's shoulder and softly asked, "Are you sure it's all him?"

Frankie looked up and said, "No."

"Talk to him Frankie. You always said you were friends first. Maybe this has ran its course or maybe it's time to take it to the next level. Whatever it is, you have to talk about it."

"You're right." Brushing the tears from her cheeks, Frankie grabbed her bag from the ground and said, "Let's get this night over with."

CHAPTER
EIGHTY-SEVEN

FRANKIE AND MIA started pouring over the files from the unsolved cases they believed could be linked to Sawyer. One by one they reviewed patrol car dash cam videos and listened to 9-1-1 calls.

A couple of hours had passed when Mia exclaimed,

"Frankie you've got to see this!"

Removing her earbuds, and pausing the call she was listening to, Frankie asked, "Is it bad?"

"You're going to have kittens. The victim in this case is Latasha Green"

Mia restarted the dash cam video. Frankie watched the patrol car pull up to a young woman sitting on the curb. The male patrol officer walked over to Latasha and politely asked if she had called 9-1-1. A female officer sauntered over while Latasha was sharing her experience.

Holding her face, Latasha said, "I was standing on the corner of Independence Avenue and Prospect trying to make a date so I could score some crack. This guy pulled up and asked me how much for head. I told him $20. He told me to get in and when he pulled away, he got real...I don't know...real weird. He started laughing and calling me a stupid whore. He pulled into an alley and told me to get into the backseat of the car. But, instead of me giving him head he pulled a gun on me. He yanked my pants off and stuck it in me."

The female officer barely let her finish before she asked, "What makes this rape? How do you figure this is rape and not just a non-pay?"

"You can go now," the male officer said. "I've got this."

"I just don't see how this is a report. Sounds to me like a non-pay. Theft of services maybe, but not a rape."

The male officer moved in between the victim and female officer, "Like I said, you can go. I've got this."

Latasha started to cry and said, "She's right. It's my fault. I shouldn't have been…"

The male officer asked, "Did you consent to having sex with this man?"

Latasha hung her head, but you could see her head shaking in dissent. "I told him to stop but he wouldn't. Then I tried to open the door, but it wouldn't open. So, I just laid there. I gave up."

"Ma'am, that's rape. Do you want to go to the hospital for an exam?"

Latasha looked back up and meekly said, "I don't have any money or insurance."

"You don't have to have either. Can I give you a ride?"

Latasha nodded.

Mia stopped the video. "What do you think?"

Frankie's face was red, and her forehead crinkled. "I think I want to throat punch that female officer. Was Sex Crimes even called? Was a detective assigned?"

Mia opened the manila folder and scanned the reports. "It looks like the on-call detective was called but didn't respond to the scene. The case was assigned to a detective on 1050 squad. Report says they tried to call her a few times, but she never returned their calls. They inactivated it for lack of victim cooperation."

Frankie read over the report. The detective the case was originally assigned was no longer in the unit. Reading his name, she wasn't surprised. He never wanted to be in the unit and had a reputation of being a fast closer.

Frankie looked at her watch, "Do you want to go with me to try and talk to this girl?"

Mia nodded as she grabbed the case file and her coat.

Inside the car Frankie asked, "Do you know how bad I want to go find that female officer and give her a little education?"

"You might want to calm down a bit before you do that," teased Mia. "Actually, maybe you shouldn't calm down. I'd love to see you take her out to the woodshed."

Frankie chuckled.

"You know it was probably her training officer that taught her to be that way. I remember my training officer making statements like 'you can't rape a whore' and 'what'd she think would happen?' 'That's life on the streets.' Unfortunately, that female officer is not alone in her attitude."

Frankie nodded, "I know, but it's just so sad. Guys like Sawyer are looking for girls like her so they can get away with it."

EIGHTY-EIGHT

FRANKIE PARKED the car in front of a two-story apartment complex. She looked around, then called the dispatcher to tell her where they were. Looking at Mia she said, "Just in case."

They approached the second-floor apartment, noticing the window next to the door. Light could be seen behind the closed blinds.

Knocking, Frankie looked to Mia and said, "Someone's home."

After a few moments and no response, Frankie knocked again. Just as they were about to leave a card and walk away, they heard someone unlock the door. A burly man cracked the door, "What?"

"I'm Detective Thomas and this is Detective Boden. Is Latasha home?"

"What do you want with Tash?"

"We want to talk to her about a report she made."

"She doesn't want to talk to you."

The man started to close the door, but Frankie put her foot between the door and the jamb. "Sir, we want to help her. I know the female officer on the scene was a jerk to her, but Detective Boden and I won't be." Frankie removed a business card and asked, "Can you give her my card and ask her to call me?"

The man grunted before he snatched the card from her hand and slammed the door.

"I wonder if she'll even get the card?" Mia asked.

Frankie started walking away from the apartment, "Dammit!"

She started to walk down the stairs and almost did not hear a soft voice say, "Ma'am?"

Frankie turned to see the woman from the patrol video standing in the apartment doorway.

"Are you really here to help me?"

Walking towards Latasha she said, "Yes. If you'll let us."

Latasha opened the door and stepped aside, "Come on in."

Frankie followed Mia into the tiny apartment. The space was sparsely furnished but not a thing was out of place. Latasha gestured towards the table and invited them to sit down. The man who had answered the door sat on the couch, arms crossed, staring at a silent television.

"Why are you here?"

Pulling the folder from her bag, Frankie said, "We think we know who raped you." Frankie pulled two sets of photographs from the folder and placed them face down. She retrieved the digital recorder and asked, "Can you tell us what happened that night?"

Latasha attempted to hide her trembling hands by placing them underneath her legs. She looked from Mia to Frankie then down to the table. Frankie was about to re-ask the question when Latasha looked up and said, "William, would you please watch television in the bedroom?"

With a grunt, William got up from the couch and left the room.

Latasha looked at Frankie, "He's heard the story, but I would just feel less nervous if he wasn't sitting over there."

"We understand," said Mia.

"It was a few months ago, but it feels like yesterday." Latasha took a deep breath. "I was standing at the corner of Independence and Prospect trying to make a date so I could score. I had been clean for several months, but William and I had gotten into it, and I fell off the wagon. I'd been on a bender for a few days. It started with pills but then I ran out and hit the street.

"This guy pulled up in a car and asked me 'how much for head?' I told him $20 and got in. I was pretty strung out and didn't notice, but thinking back now, he was super weird acting. He drove around the side streets and was…laughing. He called me a stupid whore and backhanded me for no reason. That sobered me up pretty quick. He finally pulled into an alley, and I was about to jump out when I saw the gun. He put it in my face and told me to get into the backseat. I had my hand on the door, but he had this look in his eyes. I really think he would have shot me if I'd have opened it."

"Do you think you would recognize him if you saw him again?"

Latasha nodded.

"What about the car?"

Again, Latasha nodded.

Frankie grabbed the first set of photographs. "I have a series of photographs I'd like to show you. Take your time and look at each photograph and tell me if you recognize anyone. If you do, I need you to sign it and say where you know him from."

Latasha took each photograph and laid it face up on the table. She looked at each one carefully then went back and looked at the photograph of Sawyer a second time. She picked the photograph up and studied it. She carefully placed the photograph back onto the table.

"That's him. That's the man that raped me."

"I have a couple of photographs of a vehicle. Can you tell me if you recognize it?"

Latasha took the two photographs and laid them face up on the table. She looked at the photographs and asked, "Are both these pictures of the same car? It looks like they are different colors."

Before Frankie could respond, Latasha pointed at the photograph and said, "This one is the car he was driving. It looked more silver, like this one."

"Thank you. Can you finish telling us what happened?"

Latasha stood up and asked, "Would you like a glass of water?"

Mia and Frankie both declined. Latasha grabbed a glass, filled it with water, and took a long drink. She returned to the table and sighed.

"I got into the backseat. Like I said, he had this look in his eyes. I knew if I ran, he'd shoot me so I figured I'd just do what he wanted."

Frankie noticed the tremble in Latasha's hand when she lifted the glass for a drink.

"I waited 'til he got out of the car, but when he did, I tried to open the back door. I thought if he was focused on getting into the car it would give me time to run, but it wouldn't open. It was like a cop car. The back doors wouldn't open from the inside. Before I could try again, he got into the back of the car and started yanking on my clothes."

"Where was the gun?"

"He had it on the back dash."

"Can you tell me what was going through your mind when he got into the backseat?"

Latasha looked away from Frankie. She took a deep breath and when she looked back her eyes were filled with tears. "I really thought I was going to die. All I could think about was William and my momma. I wanted a chance to tell both of 'em that I loved them. I had said some pretty mean things to Will, and I didn't want them to be the last things I ever got to say to him."

"What happened next?"

"I started to cry, and he slapped the shit out of me again. He grabbed my pants and pulled them down and shoved it in me. I just laid there 'til he was done. After he was finished, he grabbed me by the feet and pulled me out of the car. He threw my bag at me and drove off."

"Can you tell me anything about him or his car? Did you see or smell anything?"

Latasha didn't immediately answer. After a few moments she said, "I'm not sure. There was a thing hanging from the mirror, but I don't know what it was."

"Describe it if you can."

"It was like a shoestring with a clip. A plastic card hung from it. I think there was a picture on it, but I couldn't really see it. There might have been a name too, but it was too dark for me to read it."

"What about smells?"

"He had a smell. It wasn't like B.O. or anything. It was more like he had smoked weed and was trying to cover it up with cheap cologne."

"Did you have a cellphone with you that night?" Mia asked.

"Yeah."

"Can you give me the phone number?"

Latasha gave Mia the number.

"Who is the service provider?"

"Sprint."

Frankie asked, "What did you do when he left?"

"I'm embarrassed to say, but I sat there for a few minutes wondering if I had any crack left in my pipe. All I could think about was getting high. Then I just started to cry. I had truly hit bottom. I don't know how long I sat there but eventually I called William, and he called the police."

"Did you ever go to the hospital for a forensic exam?" Mia asked.

Latasha tapped her fingers on the table. After a few moments she said, "Yes. William took me after the cops left."

"Good. Is there anything else you can think of that would help us in this case?"

Latasha shook her head.

CHAPTER
EIGHTY-NINE

"WHAT DO you mean he's out?"

Coleman held up his hands and said, "Don't shoot the messenger. The hospital released him to our custody, and he made bail. Didn't you put a tracker on his car?"

"Yeah."

Frankie couldn't believe Sawyer was able to make bail. She called Fitz and told him about Sawyer's release then begrudgingly started to work on her reports. The evening went by quickly. Coleman and Wheeler left first, leaving Mia and Frankie alone in the squad room.

"Are you going to Derek's tonight?"

"Yes."

"What are you going to do?"

Frankie started gathering her things to leave. She forwarded the phone, grabbed her coat, and slung her bag over her shoulder. "Honestly, I don't know."

Mia followed Frankie out of the squad room and onto the elevator. Once they were outside the building, Mia said, "Tell him how you feel."

"I wish it were that easy."

Mia placed her hand on Frankie's shoulder then walked to her car. Before opening the door, she said, "Call if you need anything."

"Thanks, Mee. I'll see you tomorrow."

Frankie sat in her Jeep and stared at her cell phone. Almost as if he could read her mind, it began to ring. Seeing

Derek's face, she couldn't help but smile. "Hey."

"Whatcha wearin'?"

"A smile now."

"Good. Are you on your way?"

"Yeah."

"Okay. See you in a few. And Frankie?"

"Yeah?"

"I'm glad you're coming."

"Me too."

Bear greeted Frankie with a bark. She rubbed the top of his head and opened the back door. Looking down she said, "Come on bud."

Frankie placed her holstered gun on the table in the dark kitchen like she'd done a hundred times before. She was surprised Derek didn't meet her at the door. After she dropped her bag and coat, she walked softly down the hall. The bedroom door was cracked, and a bluish light lit her path.

Derek half-laid, half-sat in the bed with a blanket pulled up to his waist. His well-defined chest and easy-going smile made Frankie's heart jump into her throat. He gestured for her to come to him. Powerless to resist, she sat on the bed next to him and laid against his chest.

Derek reached his arms around her, pulled her close and kissed the top of her head. She let her arms circle his waist and just sat there breathing in his natural scent. Years before she had asked him what cologne he wore, and he admitted to not wearing any. His scent was indescribable and had the power to make her go weak in the knees.

Derek knew not to push but gently caressed her back and held her body close. He waited for her to lift her head, then leaned down and kissed her lightly on the lips. He hesitantly followed with another kiss. When she didn't push him away, he pulled her closer and began kissing with a fervor fueled by the fear of losing her.

Frankie responded by helping Derek with her clothes.

Once she was undressed, they fell into the comfortable rhythm of two people who knew one another's bodies well. When they were both satisfied, they lay spent in one another's arms. Derek ran his fingers through Frankie's short hair while she traced the scars on his chest.

"I've missed you, Frankie."

"Me too." Frankie didn't lift her head. She was afraid to look into his dark eyes; afraid she wouldn't be able to say what she was thinking. Instead, she laid her hand on his chest and said, "We need to talk."

DEREK TIGHTENED his hold on Frankie but didn't say a word.

Quietly she said, "You mean…more to me…than I can say, but…"

"You mean the world to me…"

"But I need more than this. I *want* more than this." Frankie disengaged herself from Derek's embrace and sat up, covering herself with a sheet.

Derek spoke softly, "Where is this coming from? I thought you liked things the way they are."

Tears glistened in Frankie's eyes.

"Derek, you had to see this coming. The last few months have been crazy. My dad almost died. My daughter was kidnapped. My best friend's husband was shot. Then you almost died. These are all things we should have gone through together, but…"

"Is this because I didn't call you when your dad was in the hospital. I explained…"

"Explained what? That you thought I'd be in bed, and you didn't want to wake me. Seriously?! Yes, that's part of it but that's not all. I stood outside the trauma room while they brought you back to life and realized if something happened, I would be cold-calling your family. And that's if the doctors told me anything. Not to mention if Mac had not called me, I wouldn't have even known you were in the hospital or..."

"Frankie..."

"Don't! And I know we never said we would be exclusive, but I guess I always thought...always hoped I was enough."

"You are baby." Derek laid his hand against her cheek.

Frankie let her face rest on his hand and whispered, "Then why have you been screwing Jessica and God knows who else?"

Derek laid back against the headboard, stared at the muted television, and put his hands in his lap. He sat silently, lost in thought.

After several minutes Frankie said, "Derek. Talk to me."

"I don't know."

"Are you in love with her?"

"No. It just kind of happened. We were spending a lot of time prepping for the murder trial and she was constantly flirting..."

"Don't you put all of this on her."

Derek turned to face Frankie, "I'm not blaming her or saying I had nothing to do with it. I just want you to know it wasn't intentional. Then after the shooting we got...close. She needed me and I guess I needed her."

"Why? What could she give you that I couldn't." Frankie wanted to understand.

"I could talk to her about what happened...and about the nightmares that came back."

"Why couldn't you talk to me?"

"I don't know. I never wanted you to think of me as weak."

"I would never think of you that way." Frankie paused then said, "Did you know I got shot the other night?"

Derek sat up straight in the bed, "What?! Why didn't you tell me?"

"That's exactly what I've been trying to say – I didn't think I could. I didn't want to add to your worry. You've been so distant and I guess I'm tired of trying to make this more than what it is."

"What do you want this to be? Why can't the way it is be enough?"

"Because it isn't."

Frankie grabbed Derek's t-shirt and pulled it over her head. She started to get off the bed, but he grabbed her arm and held her in place.

Frankie turned to look at Derek and said, "Because this," she gestured around the bedroom, "isn't all my life. Do you realize in all these years you have never met my kids, much less any other member of my family? And I've never met yours. We don't go to friends' houses or even go on dates. We talk, text, and spend stolen moments together. Here. Don't get me wrong, I love the time that we have together, but I am not sure it's enough anymore."

Derek let go of Frankie's arm and laid back against the bed. He didn't immediately respond, but instead weighed his words carefully. After several minutes he said, "I don't know if I can do that. I don't know that I *want* to do that. Frankie, I do lo…"

Frankie reached over and touched Derek's leg and said, "I know."

CHAPTER
NINETY-ONE

THE SOUND of Frankie's cell phone ringing pierced the silence.

"What the hell?"

"I didn't think you were on call," Derek said.

"I'm not." Hitting the telephone she said, "Thomas."

"Hey Frankie, it's Fitz. Sorry to call so late, but I thought you'd be interested to know Sawyer is on the move."

She took her phone and went to the kitchen to grab a notepad and pen. "Where's he heading?"

"We had the GPS set up to notify us if he drove within three miles of the areas he's been targeting. The alarm just sounded. Looks like he's heading towards Prospect now."

"Are you going to get eyes on him?"

"I'm heading that way. The car has stopped. Right now, it's at 31st and Prospect. Are you going to be up for a while?"

"Yeah, something tells me I'm not going to sleep much tonight."

"Okay. I'll let you know what I find."

Frankie laid her cellphone on the counter and stood looking out the window into the dark night. She almost didn't notice Derek walk up behind her. Sliding his arms around her waist he rested his chin on her head. Involuntary tears filled her eyes.

"Where do we go from here?" Derek asked.

"I don't know. All I know for sure is I don't want to just be one of many women you screw."

"It's not like that, Frankie."

Turning around to face Derek she said, "Let me put it another way. I'm not sleeping with other men, and I don't want you to sleep with other women."

"Okay. I will…"

Before Derek could finish his sentence, Frankie's phone began to ring. "Thomas."

"I'm in the area where his car pinged, but it's not here."

"What do you mean it's not there?!" Frankie couldn't believe it. The whole reason they put a tracker on his car was so they would know where he was and could stop him before he hurt someone else.

"I mean, he's nowhere to be seen. I'm going drive around a bit and see if I can find him."

"Okay. Do you need me to come out?" Frankie's question was met with a laugh.

"Girl, stay inside where it's warm. I've got this. If something comes up, I'll text you. Why don't you try to catch some sleep?"

"Thanks Fitz."

Frankie noticed Derek had opened a bottle of wine. The cork and foil were still on the counter, but he was not in the kitchen. She returned to the bedroom to find it empty. She started to call his name, then heard the water running in the master bath.

"Hey."

"I thought we could finish our talk over wine in a bubble bath," Derek said.

Frankie sat on the edge of the tub and looked down at him. She tenderly reached over and brushed his hair aside with her fingers. Derek responded by flinging bubbles at her. He started to laugh as Frankie spit and brushed the bubbles from her face. Derek grabbed her and pulled her into the tub with him, shirt and all. She collapsed against him in laughter.

CHAPTER
NINETY-TWO

MAGGIE and the driver were the last two people on the bus. Normally she sat in the front and chatted with the driver, but she was exhausted from working a double shift at the hospital and just wanted to sit in silence.

"Here's your stop Maggie. Be careful walking home y'ear?"

"Thanks Milt. Enjoy what's left of your night."

"Heading back to the barn. Time to call it quits."

Maggie smiled and waved as she exited the bus. It was barely out of sight when a car pulled up with the passenger side window rolled down.

"Get in the car."

Maggie huffed at the man driving, "I think you've got it wrong."

This wasn't the first time she'd been propositioned. She knew some of the women in her neighborhood sold themselves for money or drugs, but she wasn't one of them.

"I don't work the streets."

"I said get in the car."

"What is your problem dude? I said I'm not selling what you're looking to buy." Maggie continued to walk towards her house.

The man yelled, "Bitch!" as he drove away.

Maggie flipped him the bird and kept walking. *"Who the hell does he think he is?"* she thought. It had a been a long night and she was ready to go to bed. Maggie didn't notice the car parked across the street from her house as she walked up to the front door. She put the key into the lock and started to push the door open. A thick arm encircled her waist, and a hand covered her mouth to stifle any screams. There was no time for her to react as the man pushed her inside and slammed the door.

Once inside the house Maggie kicked and squirmed but she was no match for the man's size and strength. He threw her onto the couch and began to punch her body. With each hit, he cursed and called her names. Maggie tried to fight back, scratching and kicking at her assailant, but her feeble attempts were met with harder hits in quicker succession. She lost consciousness as he began to rip the scrubs from her body.

When Maggie awoke the assailant was gone and the remnants of her clothing were strewn across the floor. Stabbing pains permeated every part of her body. Fear consumed her as she looked around the dark room hoping the man was gone. The front door was slightly ajar, and her purse lay on the floor by the door. She crawled to the bag, praying her rent money was still inside. Slowly she unzipped the bag and pulled out her wallet. Tears streamed down her face at the sight of the cash.

NINETY-THREE

FRANKIE WAS JUST STARTING to doze off when she heard her cellphone chime with an incoming text message.

"Call me if you're still up. F"

Frankie carefully slid out from under Derek's arm, grabbed a dry t-shirt and went to the living room. Her call was answered on the first ring. Frankie could hear Fitz's laughter as he answered.

"What are you still doing awake? Don't you ever sleep?"

"I was about to, but your message interrupted me. What's up?"

"I never did find your boy, but the GPS came back online about five minutes ago. The car is heading back towards his house. I'll drive by to make sure that's where he goes."

"Thanks Fitz. Stay safe."

"Sure Frankie. Turn your phone off and get some sleep, okay?"

Frankie couldn't help but laugh, "Yep. Night."

Once she got a text confirming Sawyer was home, she went back to bed, falling asleep with Derek's arm flung across her body. She was awakened by the smell of bacon frying and coffee brewing. Frankie laid there listening to the sounds of clanking coming from the kitchen. She knew Derek was trying to make her forget about their conversation. He wanted things to go back the way they were. She slipped out of bed to join him in the kitchen.

The morning went by quickly. Frankie was gathering her things to leave when Derek put his hand on her shoulder and said, "I meant what I said last night. I'll tell her it's over. I don't want to lose what we have."

She wondered to herself if he was serious and if their relationship might be moving in a more permanent direction.

Frankie put her hand on his and said, "That's a start, I guess."

FRANKIE STOOD in the empty squad room and stared out the window. The cold and cloudy scene matched her mood. The morning with Derek had been pleasant but she was still unsettled about the way things were left. The day shift said the phones had been quiet and she hoped the trend would continue. Mia texted and said she was going to take the night off, so Frankie had the office to herself. She loved Mia but was not ready to talk about Derek. She needed time to process everything.

With a sigh, Frankie returned to her desk and pulled out the files on the cases the Perpetrator Information Center had sent to her. One by one she reviewed the reports looking for links to Sawyer or his other victims. She watched videos and listened to audio statements. With a notepad in hand, she made notes on things to follow-up on and interviews to attempt. Although the victims spanned age and race, the pattern was consistent. The victims were all women. All of them were engaged in activities that created some level of vulnerability. An unknown man approached them in a nice car and offered them a ride. If they declined his offer, he would force them inside the car. Most of the crimes occurred at night and all of them occurred within a core area.

Frankie was thinking about grabbing a sandwich when the phone rang, breaking the silence, and causing her to jump in her seat.

"Sex Crimes, Detective Thomas."

She listened as the patrol officer provided an overview of the scene he was dispatched to. Before Frankie could ask any questions, he said, "I've never seen anything quite like this. Not on a rape call."

"Where's she at?"

"They just loaded her into an ambulance. Want me to call Crime Scene?"

"No. I'll call them. Did you get a consent to search signed by the victim?"

"I did not. I'll grab it before they leave then hold the scene for you."

"Great. Thanks. I'll run by the hospital then have Crime Scene meet us there."

"Copy."

Frankie grabbed her coat, bag, and a protein bar and headed out into the cold evening. Frankie pulled into the parking garage of the hospital just as Maggie was being unloaded from the ambulance. She followed the paramedics as they pushed the gurney into the examination room.

"Thirty-four-year old woman with complaints of head, neck, back, and abdominal pain. Probable sexual assault. Pain is at a 6. Pain meds administered en route. No known allergies," the paramedic rattled off information the nurses and doctors would need.

The nurse looked at the broken and battered woman and said, "Maggie?"

A barely perceptible nod was followed by a cough.

The nurse touched her hand and said, "We'll take good care of you sweetie." Turning towards Frankie she said, "She's one of our nurses."

Frankie made note of her name and stood by while the nurse got a medical history. When the nurse assured her Maggie was stable Frankie walked closer to the gurney and said, "Ma'am, I'm Detective Frankie Thomas. The officers out at your house called me. Can you please tell me your full name?"

"Maggie…Lachey."

"Can you tell me what happened?"

Maggie laid there quietly for a few moments without responding. Softly she said, "I'm not really sure."

Frankie sat down on the stool next to Maggie's head. "Tell me anything you can remember."

An involuntary grunt escaped her lips as she adjusted her body. Her voice was hoarse and low, "I took the bus home from work last night. Sometimes I catch a ride from a friend but last night I stayed late and didn't want to make my friend wait. A young boy had been brought in after a car accident. He was scared and his parents were coming from far away so I stayed with him until they got here."

"That was very thoughtful of you."

"He was just a kid…" Maggie's voice trailed off.

"You said you took the bus home?"

Maggie nodded. "I ride the bus all the time. I was about a block from the house when this guy pulled up in his car and tried to proposition me. He thought I was a prostitute, but I told him to buzz off. I ain't no whore."

Frankie nodded.

"I got to my house and that's when things get fuzzy. I felt someone behind me after I got the front door open. It was dark in the house, and he threw me onto the sofa and started hitting me. Every time he hit me, he cursed and called me a name. I don't know how many times he hit me before I finally passed out."

Maggie began to sniffle.

"Were you able to see the man's face?"

"No. It was so dark, and he took me by surprise. He just kept hitting me."

"It's okay. Did you notice anything about his body? Any tattoos, scars, or odors?"

Maggie closed her swollen eyes and lay quietly, tears sliding down her ashen cheeks. Several minutes passed before she said, "He smelled like cologne. It smelled familiar, like I've smelled it before. I'd probably recognize it if I smelled it again. And I think he had a scar or something on his arm."

Frankie had a sinking feeling she knew who Maggie's assailant was.

"What else do you remember?"

"When I regained consciousness, he was gone. My clothes were off, and I felt…he did…something…to me. I had gone to the bank before work so my rent money was in my purse. I thought he might have robbed me but then I saw my purse lying on the floor. I grabbed it to check."

"Was it all still there?"

Maggie nodded and said, "I don't think he even touched it."

"What did you do next?"

"Nothing. I lay on the floor by my purse and cried. I think I passed out again because next thing I knew it was daylight and my neighbor was knocking on the door. I grabbed my scrubs and put them on and answered the door." Maggie took a deep breath and exhaled. "Max lost it when he saw me. He started asking me what happened, but I couldn't really say anything. He sat with me for a while to let me calm down before he called the police. I wasn't sure I was going to call y'all at first, but Max told me it was the right thing to do. I was hurting bad and needed to go to the hospital. He waited with me 'til the ambulance got there."

"What can you tell me about the man or the car that approached you."

"Not much, really. It was a nice car. Not real big. Like a Volvo or a Honda. He was clean cut. Black guy. Pretty big. His head almost hit the ceiling of the car."

"Would you recognize him if you saw him again?"

"Maybe. It was dark inside the car."

"Okay. Is there anything else you can remember about the attack?"

Maggie considered the question thoughtfully before saying, "No. Wait, I don't think he had gloves on."

"Great. I'm going to go back out to the house. I'll stop by when we are done so I can bring you your keys, okay?"

Maggie nodded. "Thank you."

CHAPTER
NINETY-FIVE

FRANKIE CALLED Sergeant Baker on her way to Maggie's house.

"I know it's him Sarge. I don't know how he did it, but I know it's him."

"Did she identify him?"

"I haven't shown her a line-up yet. I suspect she will identify him as the guy that propositioned her, but I'm not sure she can identify him as the guy that raped her. She said she didn't get a good look at his face in the house. Somehow, he figured out the GPS is on his car and disabled it. That stupid……"

Calmly Baker said, "Or it malfunctioned. All we know for certain is that he disappeared for a while. Unfortunately, we don't know where he went during that time. Finish the scene, show her a line-up, then write up a search warrant to get his cell tower information. Maybe we can put him there that way."

Frankie sighed. She knew Baker was right, but also felt like Sawyer was the man who attacked Maggie. Maybe she'd get lucky, and someone would remember seeing him or his car on the block.

The block was dark when she pulled up and parked behind the first responder's car. The house was an old craftsman cottage painted gray with black trim. A deep front porch led to the door. There was plenty of room for someone to hide unseen. The yard was small and there was no garage or cars parked in the drive. Frankie made notes on her notepad as she waited for Crime Scene to get there.

Frankie grabbed a pair of latex gloves and headed towards the house. She stopped on the porch when she saw the Crime Scene van pulling down the block.

"Hey Frankie!"

Frankie turned to see two technicians walking towards her, notepads in hand. Following Rhino was a young man Frankie had never seen before.

"Blake – Frankie. Frankie – Blake." Turning to Blake, Rhino said, "Get used to her face. If shit's going down, she's probably somewhere in the vicinity."

Frankie laughed, looked at Blake, and said, "He's not wrong." She quickly brought the pair up to speed on the current case.

"You think it's related to that other guy."

"I'd bet money on it, but I don't know that I have enough to make an arrest today. This guy is really pissing me off."

"Let's see what we've got," Rhino said. "Maybe he slipped up and left something behind."

Frankie led the way through the front door. She expected the living room to be in disarray but the only thing out of place were the cushions from the couch. "It doesn't look like he tossed the house. She was unconscious when he left. She said her purse with her rent money was still here. I think it's safe to say robbery wasn't the motive."

Rhino instructed Blake on notetaking and photography while Frankie made notes of her own. She didn't touch or move anything until they had documented and collected trace evidence. As they were moving the couch cushions Rhino asked, "You think these are the panties she was wearing?"

Frankie looked where he was pointing and said, "Yea, I'd say so. She doesn't seem the type to leave dirty undergarments lying around."

Frankie was about to put the cushions back on the sofa when a flash caught her eye. She took a second look and noticed a thick gold chain lying on the floor. "Blake, can you snap a picture of this?"

"What do you have Frankie?" Rhino asked.

Frankie had her cellphone out taking a photo, "A gold chain. It doesn't look like a woman's, but I suppose it could be. It could also belong to the suspect."

Once they collected the chain, they did a walkthrough of the rest of the house. There was nothing out of place in the bedrooms or the bathroom. There were two glasses that appeared to have been used in the kitchen. One sat upside down in the sink and the other sat on the counter with water still inside.

"Can we…"

Frankie didn't even get to finish the question before she noticed Rhino taking photographs of the glasses. She watched as he collected swabs from the rims of the glasses and dusted the exteriors for fingerprints.

FRANKIE PUT TOGETHER a photographic lineup of Sawyer and printed off a photograph of the necklace. When the nurse called to say they were finishing up with the exam Frankie asked her to have Maggie wait.

As Frankie walked to the car her cell phone alerted her to an incoming text message.

"Have time for dinner?"

"Working a case. Maybe later this week."

"That's odd," Frankie thought aloud. "Derek never wants to have dinner when I'm working." She didn't have much time to think about it before her phone started to ring.

"Sex Crimes. Thomas."

"Got any sex?"

"Hey Killer. No, we don't have anything to report tonight." Frankie wished she could tell the local news reporter, Gary Kinder, to warn the community about Sawyer but knew she couldn't.

"Okay. Let me know if anything turns up."

"Will do."

Frankie put the car in park and walked inside the Emergency Department, file folder in hand. Maggie was sitting on the examination table, dressed in the clothes the advocate gave her, when Frankie entered the room.

"Thank you for waiting. I just need to show you a few photos. Do you have a ride home?"

Maggie shook her head.

"I can take you wherever you need to go after we finish."

Softly, Maggie said, "Thank you."

Frankie pulled out the photograph of the necklace first, "Do you recognize this?"

Maggie looked at the photograph carefully before saying, "I can't be sure, but I think it might belong to a guy I went out with a couple times."

Frankie masked her disappointment when she asked, "What's his name?"

"Jackson Miller. We only went out a few times before I broke it off."

"When was the last time you saw him?"

Maggie sat thoughtfully.

"A couple of days ago, maybe? He came by my house and tried to talk me into giving him another chance. I was trying to let him down easy, but that night it got a little heated. He didn't like me telling him there was no chance of us going on another date."

"Describe heated."

"He was yelling and cursing at me. I mean we had only gone out a few times and he was acting like we had been together for years. We hadn't even had sex. He finally left when I threatened to call the cops."

"Can you think of any reason why his necklace would be on the floor near your sofa?"

Maggie laughed, "No ma'am. I went on a cleaning frenzy after he left. I was so mad that I had to threaten him. I clean when I get mad and moved the furniture away from the walls and everything. There wasn't a thing out of place when I left for work yesterday."

Frankie nodded and pulled out the photographic line-up. "Do you recognize any of the men in these photos?"

One by one she looked at the photographs. After looking at each one she said, "The guy in number four. I think he was the one that thought I was a whore."

"Had you ever seen him before that incident?"

Maggie shook her head.

"Did you see him after he drove off?"

"No."

"Okay. You've done great. Do you feel safe going back to your house or is there somewhere else you'd like to go?"

"I'll be okay. My cousin said he'd stay with me tonight."

Frankie nodded. Almost as an afterthought she asked, "Did you leave any dirty dishes in the kitchen?"

Maggie furrowed her brows, "I think I might have left a glass in the sink. Why?"

"So, you didn't leave one on the counter?"

"Uh…no I don't think so."

"Would your neighbor have used a glass while he was waiting on the police to arrive?"

"I don't think so. Why are you asking?"

"A glass was left sitting on the counter and it seemed out of place."

Maggie nodded in understanding.

After she dropped Maggie at her house Frankie drove back to her office. She was debating on having officers conduct a residence for Sawyer, but something told her to wait. She had a positive ID on Sawyer approaching her, but Maggie couldn't identify him as the man that raped her. And the type of attack Maggie experienced didn't match Sawyer's pattern of behavior. Frankie wanted it to be him, but her gut told her to hold off on the arrest. She still had some work to do.

CHAPTER
NINETY-SEVEN

FRANKIE DECIDED to do a little research on the guy who owned the necklace they found at the scene. She started by running Jackson Miller in the local and federal law enforcement databases.

"Well, what do you know," she said to an empty squad room. Miller had a long history of assault charges and had spent time in the Illinois State prison system for domestic battery. Miller had gotten out of prison almost a year before and was still on parole. Frankie jotted down the parole officer's name and number. It was a local number so he must have gotten his parole transferred to Jackson County. She made a note to call the officer on Monday.

Next, she looked Miller up in their local dispatch system. She found three calls involving him, but only one where a report had been taken. Frankie pulled up the report and started reading. The initial report said they had been dispatched on a burglary in progress. When they arrived, they found Miller inside the house of a former girlfriend, Dejauna Larabie. Larabie told officers Miller had broken in and hit her repeatedly in the face. Miller was arrested and issued a general ordinance summons to appear in municipal court. The woman got an order of protection issued against Miller, but no violations had been reported.

Frankie looked at her watch. 8:00 PM. She grabbed the report and her keys and headed to Dejauna Larabie's house. Fifteen minutes later she was knocking on the door. She was met by a statuesque woman with the darkest eyes Frankie had ever seen.

"Can I help you?" was the brusque greeting.

Frankie identified herself and explained she was investigating a crime that was possibly related to her assault.

"You think Jackson has hurt someone else?" Dejauna asked.

"It's possible. Can you tell me what happened the day you called police?"

Dejauna's account matched what Frankie had read in the initial officer's report. When she was finished Dejauna rubbed the side of her jaw, remembering.

"Do you know what precipitated the attack?"

"Sure, I do. I told him I didn't want to see him anymore. Actually, I told him that a couple of days before he attacked me. He got really upset, like abnormally so. We had only gone out a few times. Hell, we hadn't even had sex yet."

Frankie nodded, recognizing the similarity between Maggie and Dejauna's cases. "Was there anything you didn't tell the officer that came to the house?"

Dejauna twisted her hands in her lap. After a few moments she said, "I didn't lie to the officer. Jackson did break in. And he did hit me a bunch of times."

"What didn't you tell them?"

She took a deep breath and said, "He was trying to pull my pants off when the officers got to the house. If they wouldn't have got there when they did, he probably would have…"

Dejauna did not finish the sentence, but Frankie knew what she was afraid would have happened.

"What prevented you from saying anything to the officers?"

Looking up from her lap Dejauna said, "I was ashamed. And he didn't really do anything. He just started to pull my pants down and was grabbing my boobs. I didn't think the officers would care about that."

"Thank you for telling me. Other than court, have you seen or heard from Jackson since that night?"

Dejauna shook her head.

"Have you ever known him to wear a gold chain?"

"Yeah. I never saw him without it. He told me his momma gave it to him."

Frankie let out a sigh when she got back to her car. She was glad she had not sent anyone out to pick up Sawyer. It was obvious, to her at least, that Miller was responsible for Maggie's attack. She had been so focused on proving it was Sawyer she almost missed the truth.

CHAPTER
NINETY-EIGHT

DRIVING BACK to her office Frankie called Maggie. On the second ring she heard a husky, "Hello."

"Maggie I'm sorry to disturb you. This is Detective Thomas. Would you mind if I swing by your house for a few minutes?"

"Um," Maggie began to cough. "I'm sorry. I guess so. Is everything okay?"

"Yes, I just wanted to talk to you about a possible development in your case."

"Okay."

Frankie pinched her lips together as she disconnected the phone. She was going out on a limb with what she was about to do, but her gut told her it was the right thing to do. If it worked out the way she expected she would be able to make an arrest in this case tonight. If it didn't, she could be ruining any shot of being able to make an arrest at all.

Frankie glanced down at her watch. 10 PM. Not too late to make the call. If he didn't answer, she'd ask Maggie to try again. She knocked lightly on Maggie's door. Frankie was met by a weary-eyed, battered woman. Maggie had changed out of the sweatpants she wore home from the hospital into pajamas and a soft chenille robe.

"Thank you for allowing me to come over this late."

Maggie nodded. "You think you have a break in the case?"

"Maybe. I know it might be difficult, but can you think about the voice of the man that attacked you. Had you ever heard the voice before that moment?"

Maggie adjusted herself on the sofa. "I'm not sure. Maybe. But I don't want to accuse someone without being 100% sure."

"I understand that. Did the voice remind you of anyone?"

"Yes. I didn't want to believe it though."

Frankie sat quietly, not wanting to push her and possibly damage fragile memories.

"I can't be sure, but I think he sounded like…"

Frankie waited.

Softly Maggie said, "Jackson."

Frankie drew a deep breath through her nose then gently asked, "What about the voice reminded you of him?"

"The guy that attacked me kept calling me names and he had a…a way he said things. It sounded like the way Jackson talked. Especially the night he got so mad at me."

"Good. How well do you know Jackson?"

"Casually. Like I said, we'd only gone out a few times and I realized he just wasn't the right guy for me. I had him over for dinner a few nights ago and decided to tell him it wasn't going to work. He lost his mind and started yelling and screaming. I threatened to call the cops, so he left. I haven't seen or heard from him since."

"Did you know he had a history of assault and is on parole for a crime he committed in Illinois?"

"What? I had no idea. He seemed like a nice guy. Just not *my* guy. Know what I mean?"

"I do. Did he ever threaten to physically harm you?"

"Not really." Maggie paused, then covered her face with her hands. When she looked up, she said, "The night he was yelling at me he told me I needed to be taught a lesson. He called me uppity and said I acted like I was too good for him. I tried explaining that wasn't it, but he wasn't hearing it."

"Is it possible Jackson was the man that attacked you when you got home from work?"

Maggie nodded.

"I have an idea of a way to get him to admit it, but I need your help. Do you think you could make a phone call to him?"

Maggie's eyes got very wide.

"What? Why?"

"I'd be right here the entire time. I have a digital recorder and an earpiece. I'd have you call from your phone and record the conversation. You can tell him you found his necklace and ask him why he came back to your house. You can ask him why he beat you and why he had sex with you while you were knocked out."

"You really think he'd admit to any of that?"

"Yeah. Especially since he thinks he got away with it."

Maggie rubbed her hands together, ringing them in her lap. Frankie waited patiently, giving Maggie time to process what she was being asked to do.

"Okay. When do you want to do it?"

"How about now?"

CHAPTER
NINETY-NINE

FRANKIE SET up the recorder and earpiece then said, "If at any point you decide you need to stop, I want you to tell him your neighbor is at the door. That will be the signal to me that you are going to disconnect the call. Okay?"

"Okay. What do I say when he answers?"

"Say hello, then see where the conversation goes from there."

Maggie cleared her throat, put the earpiece in her ear, and dialed the number. She was about to hang up when she heard a throaty, "Hello."

Frankie saw the fear in Maggie's eyes. She motioned for her to say something.

"Hi. Jackson?"

"Ye…" Jackson coughed and cleared his throat. "…Ah. I didn't think I'd hear from you again."

"Why is that?"

"You were pretty angry the other day. Saying you were going to call the cops and all."

"Oh, that. Yeah, well you kind of freaked me out."

"I'm sorry, I didn't mean to do that. I just wanted you to give me a chance."

"I know. Hey, I found your necklace here when I was cleaning up today."

"Um, uh, well…"

"I think it fell off when you were here last night," Maggie said.

"I, uh, I…" fumbled Jackson.

"I know you were upset with me. I would have talked to you if you wouldn't have jumped out of the dark like that."

Jackson was silent. Frankie was afraid he had hung up the phone. Just as she was about to direct Maggie to hang up and retry the number they heard, "I thought you'd make me leave."

"I wouldn't have." Maggie rolled her eyes at Frankie. "I don't understand why you had to hit me so many times. I mean I know you were upset but why did you hit me so many times?"

Jackson's tone changed. "You needed to be taught…a lesson. You were so uppity to me. I wanted you to know you were no better than me."

"I don't think I'm better. I understand you punishing me but…" Maggie started to choke up. She swallowed and cleared her throat. "But why did you have sex with me when I was passed out?"

Jackson didn't immediately answer. After a few moments of silence, he said, "Because it was mine to take."

Maggie gasped. His response was so cold. Frankie wrote a note and slid it over to her. "Did you at least wear a condom? I mean, what if I'm pregnant? I'm not on any birth control."

Jackson's tone was icy, "Bitch you might want to get something then. I don't wear condoms."

"Oh my gosh, so I could be pregnant?" Maggie's voice lifted on the last word.

"Maybe, but that shit ain't my problem. You said you didn't want to be with me. So, if you are, don't come asking me for anything."

"Jackson my neighbor is at the door. I've got to go." Maggie disconnected the call, put her face in her hands, and began to sob.

Frankie put her hand on Maggie's shoulder and softly said, "You did good Maggie. Real good."

When she calmed down Maggie looked up and said, "He was so cold. So…"

"He admitted to hitting you and to rape. He also admitted he didn't wear a condom so his DNA will show up in your forensic kit. Between the physical evidence and the phone call I'd say he's going to prison for a very long time."

Looking up, Maggie asked, "What happens now?"

"I'm going to send a car to arrest his sorry ass. Hopefully we will get him held on a hefty bond."

"Will you let me know what happens?"

"I will call you when we get him into custody. Okay?" Frankie gathered her things to go to the door. As she was stepping outside, she heard Maggie behind her.

"Thank you, Detective." Frankie heard the deadbolt engaging behind her as the door closed.

ONE HUNDRED

FRANKIE CALLED dispatch and asked for a two-person car meet her in the church parking lot at Gregory and Agnes. She got to the parking lot before the officers and listened to the chatter on the radio while she waited. Frankie couldn't help but smile when she saw the officers that pulled up next to her.

"Hey there! How'd I get so lucky to get you two?" Frankie asked, smiling warmly at Mac and his partner, Maria Payne.

"We may have snatched the call from a dogwatch car. We figured you would appreciate having the A-team on this," Mac said.

Frankie laughed as Payne rolled her eyes at her partner.

"Actually, I *am* glad to have you guys here. We are heading out to 7113 Walrond to do a residence check for Jackson Miller. He beat a woman unconscious to 'teach her a lesson' then raped her while she was knocked out because it was 'his to take.' He is on parole out of Illinois, but I haven't been able to reach his parole officer yet. I didn't find any record of him using guns, but he has a long history of physical assault."

Frankie handed the pair a photograph and said, "This is him."

Mac and Payne took a good look then returned the photo to Frankie.

"Let's get him," Mac said.

The drive to the house was short. A block away they turned out their headlights and parked their cars. They approached the house slowly, careful to stay out of sight of any of the windows. As they entered the yard, Frankie thought she saw a soft blue light flickering behind the blinds. She stood to the side of the door and rapped firmly.

"Who is it?"

"Kansas City Missouri Police Department," Mac's deep voice boomed in the quiet night. "We had a 9-1-1 call from this house."

The door opened to a man of average height and build. "I didn't call 9-1-1. The only call I had tonight was with my girl."

"What's your name," Frankie asked, already knowing the answer.

"Jackson."

Mac asked, "Would you step out here for a moment?"

As soon as Miller stepped onto the porch Mac grabbed him by the arm and put it behind his back. Frankie grabbed hold of his other arm, twisting it behind to meet Mac's hand. Mac put the handcuffs on and said, "You're coming with us." Payne keyed up her radio and said, "242, *start a wagon to 7113 Walrond.*"

Jackson became angry and shouted, "What do you mean I'm coming with you. I ain't done nothing. I've been home all night."

Frankie answered, "Sir, you are under arrest for assault. You and I will talk more when we get downtown."

Jackson suddenly stopped talking. As he was being escorted to the patrol wagon, she thought she heard him mumble, "That bitch."

ONE HUNDRED ONE

MAC AND PAYNE booked Jackson into detention while Frankie worked on the paperwork they needed to hold him. She printed off the photographs she had taken of Maggie and asked Crime Scene to send her photographs of the house. Once she had everything in order, she told the overnight floor detective she was going to be doing an interrogation, started the recording, and went to escort Jackson from the jail.

Frankie attempted small talk with Jackson during the elevator ride from the jail to the interrogation room. Once inside the room she asked him basic, biographical questions, and continued to make small talk – trying to put him at ease.

Finishing up her paperwork, Frankie opened the case file and pulled out a photograph of Maggie's bruised and bloody face. "Do you recognize the woman in this photograph?"

Jackson pushed the photo back towards Frankie and said, "I don't want to look at that."

"Do you recognize her?"

Jackson looked down without answering. Frankie gently pushed the photograph back towards him, letting it rest under his downward gaze. He pushed the photo away, looked up, and said, "Yeah. That's Maggie. I went out with her a few times."

Frankie noted he did not ask how she got the black eyes and swollen jaw. "When was the last time you saw her?"

"A few days ago."

"What happened when you saw her?"

"Nothing really. We had dinner then she told me she didn't want to see me anymore."

"How'd you feel about that?"

"How the fuck do you think I felt? I was pissed. How dare she think she's too good for me."

"Is that what she said? That she was too good for you?"

"Not exactly. But that's what she meant."

"Have you talked to her since that night?"

Jackson looked down and began to clasp and unclasp his hands.

"No," was his quiet response.

"Where were you at around 2AM."

Refusing to make eye contact Jackson said, "In bed asleep."

"Can anyone confirm that?"

"I live alone."

Frankie pulled out a photograph of the house and asked, "Have you ever seen this house?"

Jackson picked up the photograph and said, "That's Maggie's house." Laying the picture back on the table he asked, "What's this about detective?"

"Maggie was attacked when she got home from work last night. Someone beat and raped her. She had to go to the hospital."

Frankie watched Jackson's face as she told him the information. The news had no effect on him.

Brushing his hands along his pants he said, "Like I said, I was home in bed."

"Is there any reason your DNA would be in her forensic kit?"

Jackson twisted his lips and considered his response carefully before saying, "Depends on how long it stays there. I gave her a farewell fuck the other day, so it might be there. I mean I don't know what her hygiene is like."

Frankie wasn't surprised at his response. "When was that?"

"Like four or five days ago."

"Hmm. She told me you all never had sex."

"She lied. She probably didn't want you to know what a whore she is," Jackson smirked.

"When did you say you talked to her last?"

"The other night when she kicked me out of her house."

"Why would she kick you out of the house after you had sex?"

"Like I said, she told me she didn't want to see me anymore."

"So, you haven't talked to her since then?"

"Detective, I told you I haven't talked to her since that night."

Frankie pulled out the recording of his phone call with Maggie. She pressed play and the sound of Maggie's voice filled the room. Jackson sat quietly but his face twisted in rage. After the recording ended Frankie asked, "Do you recognize the man on this recording?"

"Yeah," Jackson said. Without missing a beat, he said, "I want a lawyer."

Frankie nodded, put the photographs back inside the case file, and escorted him back to the jail.

CHAPTER
ONE HUNDRED TWO

DEREK LAID in bed stroking Bear's fur, listening to the news on the television while staring at the ceiling fan. The sound of the phone ringing jolted him from his thoughts. "Hello?"

"Did I wake you?"

"No, I was just watching the news. What's up Jessica?" Derek tried to hide his irritation with the late-night phone call.

"I wondered if you, maybe, uh, wanted some company tonight."

Derek rolled his eyes and sighed.

"I'll take that as a no."

"What, uh, I'm sorry. I'm just tired, that's all. It's been a long day." To himself, Derek thought, *"Tell her you idiot."*

"I bet I can help you forget all about what's bothering you."

"Look, Jessica. I'm sorry if I gave you the wrong idea. I don't want anything serious with you. I thought I was pretty…"

With a huff, Jessica said, "I was just trying to have some fun."

"I'm sorry. It's just, I've been seeing someone off and on…"

"She must not be too important – you didn't seem to mind screwing me…"

"I wasn't trying to hurt you, Jessica. I just…I made a promise this weekend that I'd stop seeing you."

"I thought you said you two were just having fun."

"We were," said Derek. "Or at least that's what I told myself."

"Are you telling me it's suddenly serious? What? Is she pregnant?"

"No, she's not pregnant. I can't explain it. I just know I can't lose her. I made a promise, and I can't break it. I need some time to figure things out."

"Humph. Well, when you get tired of playing with that detective, you know where to find me."

Jessica disconnected the call before Derek could say anything. He lay on his bed wondering if he did the right thing. He wasn't sure he could give Frankie everything she wanted. He didn't want to be a dad. Didn't want to be a husband. Why couldn't she just let things stay the way they were? He was happy with the time they had together. Alone.

Derek lay back against his pillow and continued to stare at the ceiling fan. After a few moments he grabbed his cellphone and sent a text before turning the lights off.

"Sweet dreams baby. XO"

As he dozed off his phone dinged with an incoming text.

"Still working. Wish I was there with you."

CHAPTER
ONE HUNDRED THREE

FRANKIE WOKE up to her cell phone ringing.

"Thomas."

"Frankie, sorry to wake you." Frankie recognized the irritated voice of Sergeant Jeff Kramer, the supervisor of her sister squad.

"It's okay Sarge. What's up?"

"We just tried to get the search warrant signed for Miller's house. The prosecutor refused saying there isn't enough probable cause. She also said she isn't going to charge him. I put a call in to Miller's parole officer to see if he'll violate him but haven't heard back. I'm not letting him go yet– something doesn't feel right about this."

Frankie was suddenly wide awake, sat up, and said, "Let me guess, the prosecutor is Jessica Moon."

"Yeah. I know she's new, but this case is open and shut."

"Hold him. I need to make a phone call. I'll call you back in a few."

Frankie dialed Derek's office number. He answered on the second ring. "Derek Kensington."

"Did you end things with her?" Frankie didn't try to conceal the rage boiling inside of her.

"Frankie? Hold on a second." He got up and closed his office door. "What's going on?"

"Did. You. End. Things. With. Her?"

"Yes. She called me last night and I told her it was over. What's wrong?"

"She's refusing to charge the in-custody from last night. In fact, there are several she is refusing to charge. Sawyer and Stockton to name but two. I didn't say anything at first because I thought she had a little ground to stand on with Sawyer and was even willing to give her a little latitude with Stockton. But not this one. This one is different. We have evidence at the scene, and he fucking admitted everything in a pre-text phone call. Your *friend* refused to sign the fucking search warrant for his house where there could be additional physical evidence. Then she told Kramer she was going to let this batterer go. She made this fucking decision based on you and me and I'm not going to stand for it. I'm going to call her fucking boss and get this handled. The Missouri Bar Association will be my next..."

"Hey, hey, calm down..."

"Don't you dare tell me to calm down. You know as well as I do that this is fucking personal."

"I'm sorry. Let me go look at the case file and call you back. If there's any merit to this, I'll handle it. Okay?"

Frankie was only slightly pacified. "Fine. But if you don't handle that bitch, I'm going to."

Derek hung up the phone, ran his hand through his hair, and called Jessica. "Can you come here for a minute. Bring the file for the sex crimes in-custody."

Less than five minutes later Derek's door opened, and he was met with another angry woman.

"Who do you think you are calling me into your office? You aren't my supervisor and have no right to ask to see anything I'm working on."

Calmly Derek said, "Close the door." He didn't say anything more until his door was closed. "You are right. I'm not your boss and I have no right to tell you what to do on your cases. However, I have been doing this a very long time and I have a very good relationship with the police department. The case detective on the in-custody you are holding has already called me..."

"Oh, for Heaven's sake! She called her *boyfriend* on me?" Venom dripped from the word boyfriend.

"Detective Thomas has never called me on a case before now which tells me there might be some merit to her frustration. You can let me look at it and give a more senior legal opinion or you can let her call Becca." Derek intentionally left out that Frankie was also threatening to call the Bar Association. "But I'll warn you, if she calls Becca, she's going to tell her about all the cases you've declined to charge in-custody and all your cases will be reviewed. If that happens, and she determines you've been letting criminals go because of a personal vendetta, Becca will send you to handle traffic cases. Or worse, fire you. For your own good, let me look at this one, and any others Detective Thomas has worked. I'll give you my unbiased, legal opinion."

"Unbiased my ass."

"It's me or Becca." Derek softened his voice, "It's not too late to fix this Jess."

Jessica's face was flush with anger and embarrassment. She stared at Derek, trying to decide if she should call his bluff. Without a word she stood up, slammed the case file on his desk, turned, and left.

Derek exhaled and called to tell Frankie he was reviewing the in-custody and would be looking at the other cases Jessica had been charged with reviewing. He was going to make this right.

ONE HUNDRED FOUR

FRANKIE WAS TOO angry to go back to bed and she had several hours before she had to be at work. Derek was not going to rush his analysis, so Frankie changed into her workout gear and decided to go for a run.

The air was crisp when she stepped out of her car in the parking lot by the river path. Frankie was glad she had worn gloves and brought a hat and heavy jacket. One earphone in her ear, she blasted Daughtry, and started with a slow jog. As the tempo of the music increased so did her speed. Her anger at Jessica, and at Derek, fueled her run.

To herself she thought, *"If he would have just kept it in his pants."*

Forty-five minutes later Frankie was stretching by her car, thankful she had a bottle of water, when a familiar voice said, "Fancy meeting you here."

Looking up Frankie laughed and said, "Hey Jim. What are you doing?"

"Same thing you are. Did you excise all your demons today?"

Frankie nodded as she took a long drink of water. "Something like that."

"You look like you need to talk. Want to grab some pancakes before you head home?"

"I don't want to keep you from your run," Frankie answered.

"Aw, it's okay. I can run later. Let's grab breakfast."

Frankie nodded and followed him to the City Diner.

Once they had placed their orders Jim said, "Okay, spill it."

Frankie fiddled with the straw in her Diet Coke without saying a word.

"Frankie…"

Frankie looked up into Jim's dark eyes. She hesitated, then told him everything. She told him about giving Derek an ultimatum, about the cases she thought Moon declined because of her, and the case she had worked all night on.

"I've had it. I know she is making decisions because of who I am, not based on the merits of the cases."

"What's he going to do?"

"He said he's going to review all the cases with my name attached and give her an unbiased, senior legal analysis. He wants me to trust him to handle it."

"Do you?"

"What? Trust him? I think so. He's a good prosecutor and believes in doing the right thing where cases are concerned. I think he'll give them a fair assessment."

"Do you think he'll stop sleeping around and give you what you want?" Jim asked. More quietly he added, "What you deserve?"

Frankie looked away from Jim and stared out the window of the diner. She blinked away the tears forming in her eyes before turning back to face him. "Honestly? I don't know. He is a good person, but I think we just want very different things. It was what I wanted and needed for a while but now…"

Frankie's phone began to ring. The caller-id on her phone was for Sergeant Kramer.

"Thomas."

"I don't know what you did, but we were told to bring the search warrant back for signature. Moon also said she is going to issue a warrant for Miller. She's asking for a $100,000 bond."

Frankie sighed, "Thanks Sarge. Did she say anything else?"

Kramer laughed, "Yeah, she said to tell you she'd be in contact with you about a couple other cases you're working. She said you'd understand. Oh, and Miller's parole officer called back. He wants you to call him when you get in."

"Thanks. See you at 3." Frankie looked up at Jim and said, "She's charging the guy from last night and reviewing the other cases."

"Good."

Before Frankie could say anything else her phone buzzed with another incoming call. Looking at the caller-ID she said,

"Hey Derek."

"You were right about the in-custody. There was no reason not to charge him. I did a rough analysis on the Sawyer and Stockton cases. I'm not making any promises, but I think there's a good chance you'll get warrants on both."

"Thank you."

"Her supervisor will take a look at any other cases you might have been involved in and make sure the decisions she made were based on a legal analysis and not a personal grievance."

Frankie and Derek said their good-byes just as the waitress was bringing the check. After they paid for their meals, Jim walked Frankie back to her Jeep.

"What now?"

Frankie looked up at Jim, holding her hand up to shield her eyes from the sun, "I'll finish up the last of the stuff on my cases…"

"No, I mean you and Derek?"

Frankie looked out over the river. After a few moments she faced Jim and said, "Honestly? I don't know."

ONE HUNDRED FIVE

FRANKIE HAD a list of messages waiting for her when she got into the office, but her first call was to Jackson Miller's parole officer.

"Probation and Parole. Harold Cross."

"Mr. Cross, this is Detective Frankie Thomas. I'm investigating one of your parolee's, Jackson Miller."

"How can I help you detective?"

"I was wondering if you could tell me anything about Miller and the case he is serving parole for."

Frankie heard the clicking of a keyboard through the phone. Cross cleared his throat and said, "Here he is. Jackson Miller. Convicted of aggravated assault against a woman he was dating. The notes say he was originally charged with aggravated rape and aggravated assault. It looks like he may have entered a plea deal. His conviction on record is just for the assault."

Frankie feverishly documented what Cross was saying. She wasn't surprised about the plea. It was common for offenders to agree to plead guilty to lesser charges to avoid having to register as a sex offender.

"Looks like there are a few more notes in his file. This guy has some serious rejection issues. The victim in this case was a woman he went out with a few times. She decided to end the relationship and he got angry. She said he broke into her house, beat, and raped her. He was evaluated in prison and is noted as having anger issues, specifically towards women. What's he being investigated for in Kansas City?"

"He is in our custody for assault and rape. I'm waiting on a warrant now. The stories are very similar to what he did time for."

"Stories? As in plural?"

"Yes. We have at least two victims in our city."

"Damn. Okay, I'll start working on a parole revocation."

"Thanks Harold. I'll send you the reports if that will help."

"It will. Thanks."

Frankie looked at the remaining messages. Two were from the lab, confirming the analysis requests she had submitted on the Sawyer cases. The last was from Jerome Connor, Cheyenne's father. Frankie's hands trembled as she dialed his number.

Her call was answered on the second ring, "Hello."

"Mr. Connor, this is Detective Thomas returning your call."

"Oh, hello Detective! Thank you for calling me back. I was sitting here with Cheyenne, and she asked me to call and see if there is anything new with her case."

Frankie felt a huge wave of relief sweep over her body. "How's she doing?"

"She's much better. They said she may even get to go home in a few days. She'll have some rehab, but the doctors said she'll be as good as new before we know it."

"That's great. If you can put her on the phone, I'll give her an update really quick."

Frankie could hear rustling as Jerome handed his daughter the cellphone.

"Hello?"

"Hi Cheyenne. I'm glad to hear you're doing better."

"Thank you."

"Tre was released from the hospital, but he is in jail. I don't think he's going to be getting out anytime soon. They charged him with kidnapping and a bunch of felony traffic violations. His bond was set at $100,000. The prosecutor is looking at the rape case too. When they charge that case, he will get another bond in addition to the one he has now."

"Can his momma bail him out?"

"I suppose she could if she had the money, but I don't think she will."

"Do you think they will charge him with the rape?"

"I sure hope so."

Frankie barely heard Cheyenne say, "Me too." Before handing the phone back to her father, Cheyenne stated, "Detective Thomas?

"Yes."

"Will you please tell that girl I'm sorry I didn't help her?"

Frankie's voice broke as she said "Of course."

Jerome said, "Thank you again for calling Detective, but Cheyenne needs her rest."

"Yes sir. I'll stop by this week and see you all if that's okay."

"That would be nice."

As Frankie hung up the phone, she heard Mia say, "She just hung up. Hold on."

Putting the call on hold Mia said, "It's Jessica Moon."

Frankie felt her blood pressure rise at the sound of her name. Gritting her teeth, she said, "Send her over."

CHAPTER
ONE HUNDRED SIX

"THOMAS."

"Hello detective. I am reviewing the cases you submitted recently and had some questions. Do you have a few minutes?"

Frankie steadied her voice, forcing herself to sound professional. "Sure. Which one are you looking at?"

"Let's start with Treyvon Stockton. I noticed you spoke to several family members and processed a couple cars. Did the victim ever identify the house he took her to?"

Frankie pulled the receiver away from her ear and looked at it. Was she serious? A report had been written clearly stating Sarah identified Georgia's house. Instead of confronting Moon she found the report in her copy of the case file and said, "Yes. If you look at supplemental report 12 you will see she identified Georgia Williams' house as the house Tre took her to. It's also where he switched cars."

"Did you follow up on his alibis? Did you talk to his girlfriend or uncle?"

With a tempered voice Frankie said, "We went to the house where he said the girlfriend lived and talked to his uncle. It's all documented in supplemental report 8. Supplemental report 9 indicates the woman he listed as his girlfriend is deceased. She died in a suspicious fire. I believe the Bomb and Arson Unit are looking at him as a possible suspect in that fire and her murder."

"What about the gas station where Sarah said she was taken."

Frankie didn't even try to hide her frustration. "With all due respect, Jessica did you even look at the case file? Stockton is in custody for kidnapping Cheyenne Connor, the clerk for the gas station where he took the victim, Sarah Smedley. Not only did Sarah identify the store, but we talked to Cheyenne and got surveillance of Tre and Sarah inside the store. Cheyenne reported to us Treyvon came back and threatened her for talking to the police, then later kidnapped her. If you would look at the case file, you would see the reports are all there."

Frankie could hear Moon tapping at the keyboard on her computer. A few moments passed before she said, "Detective I'm preparing a warrant for his arrest. Is there any reason to believe he will bond out today?"

"I don't know. He has a bond set at $100,000. I don't think his mother could bail him out, but it's possible."

"Okay. I'll get this together and walk it through today. Now, about Sawyer."

Frankie took a deep breath. She could tell this one was going to be a battle.

"I have positive identifications by three women and a possible ID by a fourth. You submitted additional cases for review. Have those victims identified Sawyer?"

"No."

"You have a tracker on his car, is that correct?"

"Yes, but..."

"You have a tracker. Go see if the women in the other cases can identify him. Draft a search warrant for the tower information on his cell phone. Once you've done that, give me a call. Depending on what you find, I may be ready to charge him."

Coleman dropped the signed search warrant for Miller's house on Frankie's desk as she hung up the phone. She leaned back in her seat and let out a groan.

"What was that all about?" Mia asked.

"She hadn't even looked at the Stockton case. Even after Derek read her..."

"What?!"

Frankie explained to Mia what happened before their shift.

"Oh my gosh! I thought she was being difficult, but damn!"

"Yeah. She's going to make me jump through hoops on the Sawyer cases. She won't issue a warrant until we have more victims identify him and get his cell tower information. Her rationale is we have a tracker on the car so there's no hurry."

"Great. How many more will there be?"

Frankie sighed. "I need to go search Jackson Miller's house. Want to go?"

ONE HUNDRED SEVEN

"WHAT'S THAT SMELL?" Yang asked as he followed Frankie through the front door of Miller's house.

"Smells like he forgot to take the trash out," Ashley said.

Frankie scrunched up her nose in disgust and said, "Let's get this done so we can get out of here."

The house was small and sparsely furnished. Unlike Maggie's clean house, Miller's had trash, dirty dishes, and unwashed laundry scattered everywhere.

"What are we looking for?" Mia asked.

"The clothes he was wearing the other night and anything that might prove he planned the attack."

"Looking for his clothes is going to be like finding a needle in a haystack."

"Yeah, I'm afraid you might be right. She said it was dark clothing, a hooded jacket and maybe a dark mask." Frankie sifted through the clothes on the sofa, but nothing resembled what Maggie remembered.

"Frankie, you might want to come and look at this," Ashley called from the bedroom.

Frankie dropped the pants she was looking at onto the sofa and walked down the hall. "What the hell? Mia come here."

The room contained an unmade bed and a desk with an open laptop computer. Above the desk were photographs of four different women engaged in various activities. None of the photographs appeared to have been taken with the women's knowledge. There was a red X across the faces of Dejauna and Maggie.

"Was he keeping score, or what?" Mia asked.

"It sure seems that way. I wonder who the other women are?" Frankie looked down at the open computer to see what website he had open. "He has his profile open to a dating website. It shouldn't be too hard to identify these women. I'll get a warrant and see if there's something in his computer that will help get us their names."

"Given his history with rejection, do you think we should wait?"

Frankie stared at the computer screen. If she searched his computer without a warrant anything they found would be inadmissible in court. If she didn't there could be at least two other victims out there.

"I think this would be considered exigent circumstances."

Frankie clicked on the message section of the dating website. There were four message streams. Maggie and Dejauna were two. The women in the photographs over the desk were the other two.

"Cynthia Freeman and Gillian Barnett. Looks like he spoke with both of them within the last seventy-two hours. What do you say we go pay them a visit?"

Mia looked at Frankie and said, "What are we waiting for?"

Frankie got addresses for both women from their in-car computer. Cynthia lived two blocks from Miller and Gillian lived six. "Looks like both are close by. Hopefully neither has rejected them yet."

Within minutes they were knocking on Cynthia's door. Without opening the door, she said, "Who is it?"

"Kansas City Missouri Police Department," the detectives said in unison as they held up their badge so she could see them through the peephole.

"Hold on."

They could hear the deadbolt being thrown and chain being dropped.

"Can I help you?"

Frankie couldn't help but stare at the laceration on Cynthia's high cheekbone. "May we step inside?"

Cynthia stepped aside and let the women walk through the door.

"May I ask what happened to you?" Frankie asked.

She touched her cheek and looked from Mia to Frankie. She sat on the edge of the chair and said, "This? It's nothing. Just a parting gift from a guy I was seeing."

"Was it Jackson Miller by any chance?"

"How'd you know?"

"We arrested him yesterday for assaulting another woman.

Can you tell us what happened to you?

Cynthia's experience matched that of Dejauna and Maggie. The only difference was she did not threaten to call police.

"I told him if he didn't leave, I was going to kill him. After he hit me in the face I ran into my bedroom and grabbed my gun. I told him if he came near me or my house again, I would blow his brains out. He must have believed me because he left."

Frankie smiled and asked, "Did you hear from him again?"

"No. I think he knew I meant what I said."

Frankie got all of Cynthia's contact information then stood to go.

"Is he going to be getting out of jail anytime soon?"

"Not if we have anything to say about it."

ONE HUNDRED EIGHT

GILLIAN'S HOUSE WAS DARK, so Frankie left her business card and headed back towards police headquarters. They hadn't gotten far when her phone began to ring.

"Thomas."

"Frankie, it's Fitz. Sawyer is on the move again. He's on Paseo heading north. Looks like he's almost to the Avenue."

"Okay, we'll head that way."

"Sawyer?" Mia asked.

"Yeah. Let's see if we can catch him in the act." Frankie's phone rang again. "Hey Fitz, do you have?"

"His car isn't moving. It's at Independence and Paseo. Does he ever take girls to motels?"

"We don't have any cases like that, but he may be switching things up. We're about ten minutes out."

"Okay, I'm still a good fifteen minutes away. Let me know if you find him."

Mia drove through the parking lots of the seedy motels located near Independence Avenue and Paseo Boulevard. All three of them were two levels with doors that opened to the parking lot. They each boasted affordable weekly rates and two even offered rooms by the hour, making them frequent hosts to sex workers. Driving through the third parking lot Mia said, "Hey isn't that his car?"

Frankie grabbed the microphone for their police radio. *"1061 on Center Zone."*

"Go ahead 1061," said the dispatcher.

Frankie smiled at the sound of Laura's voice. She and Mac had been her mentors in the Explorer's program.

"Can you have a two-person crew meet me and 1064 at The Admiral Inn at Admiral and Paseo for a residence check?"

"116."

"Independence and Prospect."

"116, meet 1061 and 1064 at The Admiral for a residence check. 2008."

While they waited for the radio car to arrive Frankie and Mia stepped into the office to speak to the night clerk. The small eastern Asian man appeared to be in his fifties. With a barely perceptible accent he identified himself as the business owner.

"You see that car?" Frankie asked, pointing to Sawyer's car. "Can you tell me what room he checked into?"

"Mr. Jones is in room 107," the clerk said.

"Jones, huh? Did he have anyone with him?"

"I do not think so. He usually comes in alone, but I think he has a lady friend who visits him."

"He stays here regularly?"

"I would not say regularly, but often enough that I know him when he comes in."

"Has a lady friend come to visit today?"

The radio car arrived before the clerk could answer.

"Where are we going?"

Frankie turned to look at the officer and his partner who were flanking the entrance to the motel office.

"Room 107 but wait just a minute."

Turning back to the clerk she asked a second time, "Has a lady friend come to visit today?"

"He took a lady out of his car and walked her inside."

"Took a lady out of his car? What do you mean?"

"He had her by the arm. He was pulling her. She walked but was looking around the parking lot."

"Do you have any surveillance cameras?"

"Yes, but they do not record."

"Alright. Thank you. I'd appreciate it if you didn't warn him we were coming." Frankie turned towards the officers, "Let's go knock on this guy's door."

Frankie posted to one side of the door and Mia to the other. The officers stood just behind them. Frankie leaned her ear against the door and listened. Through the door she thought she could hear muffled cries. She used the side of her fist to pound the door. "Police Department, open up."

The muffled sounds became louder screams of, "Help! Help me!"

Frankie stepped aside so one of the patrol officers could kick the door. The first kick was met with resistance. The sound of fists meeting flesh could be heard between screams. The officer lined up and kicked the door again, causing the handle to disengage from the door frame. The sound of a gunshot came as he raised his leg to kick a third time. Frankie looked at Mia and the other officers to make sure they were all okay. Before they could force it, the chain fell and the door opened.

Standing in the doorway was a young woman, hands trembling, holding a gun.

Guns drawn, the officers took a step back and ordered her to drop the gun. Frankie took a step closer and said, "Lorelei, let me have the gun."

Terror filled her eyes as they darted between Frankie and the other officers.

"You know her?"

"Yeah. Lorelei, give me the gun," Frankie said with a bit more firmness.

Slowly Lorelei extended her hand to Frankie. Releasing the weapon into Frankie's hand, Lorelei dropped to her knees and started to cry.

CHAPTER
ONE HUNDRED NINE

"116 START *me an ambulance to Room 107. We have a party down.*"

"*Copy, 116. Ambulance en route. 2018 hours.*"

Frankie and Mia entered the motel room to find Sawyer lying on the floor, bent over holding his knee.

"That bitch shot me!"

"With *your* gun?" Frankie asked.

"It's your fucking fault. You scared her when you started pounding on the door!"

"Mr. Sawyer, I believe it was you that scared her." Frankie looked to the officers and said, "Can you keep an eye on him while I go talk to Miss Rain?"

Outside the room she looked to Mia and asked, "Did you smell that?"

"Yeah, smells like death in there."

Frankie found Lorelei sitting in the front seat of the patrol officer's car. She got into the driver's seat, while Mia called the Crime Scene Unit.

"Can you tell me what happened tonight?"

"You that detective that came and talked to me the last time?"

"Yes."

"You found my book."

"Yes ma'am." Frankie smiled at the memory. Lorelei had a copy of *To Kill a Mockingbird* from the library in a backpack the night Frankie met her. The bag had gone missing, but Frankie was able to find it and return it to Lorelei.

Hanging her head Lorelei said, "He's the same guy. From that night."

"Can you tell me what happened in there?"

Lorelei looked over at Frankie and asked, "I can tell you the truth?"

Frankie nodded.

"I was working when this guy pulled up. I didn't recognize the car at first, but when he put the window down, I saw who it was and started to walk away. He didn't care. He followed me in his car and then showed me his gun. He said if I didn't get in the car, he'd shoot me. Dude's crazy so I got in the car." Lorelei began to cough. When she caught her breath, she continued. "He drove the car here and told me to wait while he got a room. I was going to get out and try to run, but he reminded me he had a gun and would hunt me down if I ran off. So, I waited in the car until he got a room key."

"When he got me into the room, he told me to get in the shower and clean myself up. He stood in the door of the bathroom and watched while I showered and even threw a razor at me and told me to shave. Everywhere. When he thought I was clean enough he told me to get out of the shower and made me get on my knees in front of him. He pulled his thing out and made me suck his dick. He told me if I bit him, it'd be the last thing I ever did. When he had enough of that he threw my clothes at me and told me to put my shirt on, so he didn't have to look at my disgusting body. He shoved me onto the bed and started sticking me. I was crying and tried to tell him to stop but that just pissed him off. He held me by the throat and kept yelling at me."

"What happened next?"

Lorelei began to tap the car door. She looked out the window then back to Frankie. "He had put the gun on the stand next to the bed. When you started pounding on the door, he started punching me and telling me to shut up. He shoved me against the wall and said he was going to kill me. Then he tried to grab the gun. I thought he was going to shoot me, so I grabbed it first. I'd never shot a gun before, but I wasn't afraid to try. We started wrestling for it and it went off. Next thing I know he's lying on the floor. I didn't know what to do so I unhooked the chain and let you in."

"Is there anything else you want to add?"

Lorelei shook her head.

"Would you be willing to go to the hospital for a forensic examination? It's free."

"Will that help get him locked up?"

"It can help."

"Okay, then I'll go."

After directing the patrol officer to take Lorelei to the hospital Frankie stepped over to talk to the paramedics tending to Sawyer. "Is he going to be okay?"

"Looks like a flesh wound but you'd think he was dying," answered the paramedic. "We're going to take him to County, but I expect he'll be released by morning."

"Great." Frankie climbed into the rig and clamped her hand on Sawyer's injured leg. He let out a howl as she said, "Guess we will chat tomorrow."

"Go to hell," was Sawyer's only response.

Frankie stepped out of the rig, turned back and said, "Don't worry, we'll make sure your car is taken care of."

With that she closed the back of the ambulance and slapped the door, indicating they could drive away.

CHAPTER
ONE HUNDRED TEN

MIA WAS STANDING outside the room waiting for Frankie and the Crime Scene Unit when the ambulance pulled away. Before Frankie could say anything, Mia said, "Sawyer rented the room for two hours – two hours ago. The motel owner has signed consent for us to process the room. I tried standing inside to take my notes, but man that smell is just too strong."

"What do you think it is?" asked Frankie.

"Honestly, if I didn't know any better, I'd say it was a dead body, but that room is so small…"

Frankie started to say something but hesitated.

"What? You don't think?"

Frankie raised her eyebrow in response.

The clerk stepped outside the office and asked, "How long will you be?"

"I don't know Mr. Sayed. We are waiting on the Crime Scene Unit to come," answered Mia. "Have you had any complaints about the odor in this room?"

"Detective, my customers are not here long enough to notice an odor." Mr. Sayed turned to walk back to his office. Before going inside, he said, "There was a truck driver who would not stay in that room about a week ago. Made me move him. Said the smell was too strong." With that, Mr. Sayed closed the door.

Yang and Blake pulled in minutes later. After retrieving the information they needed for their reports they began to take photographs of the scene. Mia looked at Frankie then opened the door and said, "Hey Blake, why don't you go in first?"

Blake walked through the door and began to gag. "What the hell?"

Behind him Yang said, "What?" Getting a whiff, he started to dry heave. "Damn, warn a guy, will you?"

"Sorry," Mia giggled. "We honestly don't know what the smell is, but we have a hunch."

"It smells like…"

"Yeah, that's what we thought too," interrupted Frankie.

"Where is it?" Yang asked.

"Not sure, but I have an idea. Once you have collected everything, we can flip the mattress. I think we will find a hollow box frame underneath it."

"You don't think…" Blake asked.

"Maybe," replied Mia.

The color drained from Blake's face.

Frankie touched Blake on the shoulder then grabbed her notepad and started taking notes. Other than the rotten stench, the room wasn't that bad. The bathroom looked like it had been cleaned and the carpets, although stained, appeared to have been vacuumed. She watched as Blake and Yang recovered the bedspread, sheets, and towels from the room. They found a razor on the tub and a spent condom on the floor. Blake recovered both.

After everything had been bagged, tagged, and taken to the van, Frankie looked at Mia and said, "Well?"

"Let's get this over with."

The pair each grabbed a side of the mattress and flipped it off the hollow wooden stand.

"Oh my gawd!" the pair screamed in unison.

ONE HUNDRED ELEVEN

YANG AND BLAKE heard Frankie and Mia scream and ran back into the room. They found the detectives staring into the wooden bedframe that once held the mattress.

"What the…?" Yang asked.

Blake looked inside the box, covered his mouth, and stepped out.

"It's his first body," Yang said by way of explanation.

"Damn, what a way to break in," said Mia. "I'll go check on him."

Frankie grabbed her notepad while Yang grabbed his camera. Inside the wooden box frame lay two women in advanced stages of decomposition. Both women wore a black miniskirt and red tank top, but neither were wearing shoes. There were no obvious signs of trauma, which left Frankie to wonder how they died.

"What's that say on their tops?" Frankie asked.

Yang snapped a photograph from different angles, stood back, and said, "I think it says, 'Shady Lady.'"

Frankie squatted down next to the box and looked closer at the women. Both were young.

Yang asked, "How old do you think these girls are?"

Frankie looked at the two young girls and said, "They don't even look like they're 18." She was about to stand up when something caught her eye. She carefully reached in and looked at the inside of the right wrist on each woman. "Hmm."

"Does that mean something to you?" Yang asked.

"I don't know. Maybe. I need to make a couple phone calls. Have you called the coroner yet?"

"No, I'll do it now."

"Thanks." Frankie stepped outside the hotel room and breathed in the semi-fresh air. Mia walked up just as she was about to call Jim. "How's Blake?"

"He'll be okay. What are you thinking?"

"That this might be related to Katarina Schlovik. Both women are wearing tank tops with 'Shady Lady' on them. And they both have a rose tattoo on their right wrist."

"Didn't Tessa have a rose tattoo on her right wrist?"

"Yep. So did Katarina. I'm going to call Fitz and Jim. They need to see this."

Within half an hour both men were at the scene waiting for the coroner to remove the bodies. Fitz had called the Homicide Unit and told him the Intelligence Unit was going to work the case.

"I'd bet a paycheck they are related. I'm curious what the cause of death was," Fitz said.

"Me too," Frankie said. "Will you go to the autopsy?"

"Yeah. I'll let you know what they say."

Jim stood quietly, evaluating the scene. They were just starting to move the first body when he suddenly said, "Wait." Jim squatted by the box and stared.

"What is it Jim," Frankie asked.

With gloved hands he extricated a charm bracelet from one of the women's skirt pockets. The delicate silver chain held four charms.

"Looks like the clasp is broken so she put it in her pocket to keep from losing it." Jim held the bracelet in his hand and looked at the charms. "A camera, dog, ballerina, and a pony. She can't be more than eighteen."

The coroners lifted each body onto a gurney with care.

Jim didn't move until both bodies were gone. Frankie waited until the coroner was finished before she asked, "Do you guys mind if Mia and I take off? I need to finish up my reports and am kind of hoping they release Sawyer from the hospital tonight."

Jim looked up from the box and asked, "Do you think he'll talk to you?"

"No, but it's worth a shot."

"Want some help?"

Frankie looked from Mia to Jim and said, "Why not? Maybe the photographs of these women will loosen his tongue. I'll call you when he gets brought in."

"You don't really think he had anything to do with it, do you?" Jim asked.

"No, but I don't mind letting *him* think we do."

Fitz laughed and said, "You are ruthless. No wonder I like you!"

Frankie and Mia laughed all the way to the car.

ONE HUNDRED TWELVE

"SEX CRIMES, THOMAS."

"Detective Thomas, this is Jessica Moon from the prosecutor's office. You paged me?"

Frankie rolled her eyes. Of course, *she* would be the one on call. "We have an in-custody. Actually, it's Sawyer."

"What? Never mind, tell me what you have."

Frankie gave Moon the details, including the bodies, and waited.

"Do you think he has anything to do with the dead women?"

Frankie thought about lying just to make Moon question herself but instead said, "No. We actually think it's related to another set of unsolved homicides. The Intelligence Unit is working that angle. All we have on Sawyer is kidnapping, aggravated assault, and rape."

"Write it up and get it to me in the morning. Are you going to need any search warrants signed tonight?"

"I don't think so. If he doesn't give us consent to process him tonight, we can get a search warrant in the morning."

"Okay. If things change, let me know."

Frankie looked at Mia and said, "Suddenly she wants to do something."

"I guess we should be thankful. The hospital just called. Sawyer is being released and transported to the jail. Do you want them to bring him here?"

"No. Let's let them book him. I want to go find Allie and see if she can identify him."

Thirty minutes later Frankie and Mia were on the way to the last known address for Allie Wheaton. While Frankie drove, Mia looked up the reports on Allie's bus accident.

"Looks like Tucker recovered a surveillance video." Minutes later Mia had him on the phone.

After listening to the one-sided conversation, Frankie said, "Well…"

"Tucker said Allie was definitely pushed. The bus stop is in view of the Family Dollar Store camera. He said you can clearly see a black man get out of a gold Honda, walk over, and push Allie into the path of the bus."

"Damn. Can he send you a still shot so we can see if it's Sawyer?"

"I'll send him a text and see. He said he's had a hard time getting her to respond to his calls. I'm sure he'd appreciate the help."

Frankie parked the car across the street from Allie's last known address and waited until Mia received the text from Tucker.

"You think she'll be able to identify him?"

Mia's phone dinged with an incoming text, "Take a look."

"Looks like Sawyer to me."

"Me too. Hopefully she'll be able to pick him out of a line-up. Let's go."

It only took a moment for Frankie's knock to be answered. The door was answered by a hulk of a man filling the doorway. A voice so deep and gravely it was almost a growl asked, "What you want?"

"We need to speak with Allie."

"What you want with her?"

"We think we have the man that attacked her in police custody and want to show her a photographic line-up."

"All – ee," boomed the man.

Frankie smiled at the woman who was dwarfed by the man standing next to her.

"Hi detectives. Like, what do you all need?"

"We have some photographs we need you to look at," answered Mia.

"Okay."

Frankie and Mia sat with Allie at the kitchen table. They laid the file folder containing photographs on the table.

"I want you to look at each photograph carefully. If you recognize any of the men, I want you to tell us where you recognize him from."

Allie opened the folder and carefully looked at each photograph. She waited until she had looked at each one before pulling out Sawyer's and saying, "That's him."

Mia handed her a pen and asked her to sign the photograph.

"Like, what happens now?"

"He's in police custody for another case. We will present your case to the prosecutor in the morning and hopefully she will set his bond high enough that he won't be able to get out."

"Will I, like, have to go to court and like, testify?"

Mia looked to Frankie and then said, "Maybe."

Allie sat quietly for a moment before saying, "Okay."

Mia touched Allie's hand and said, "You did good."

ONE HUNDRED THIRTEEN

AS SOON AS they got back to the office Frankie texted Jim.

"Getting ready to pull Sawyer out. You in?"

"Be there in ten."

True to his word, ten minutes later Jim was walking into the squad room.

"Are you guys ready to get a confession?"

Frankie smiled and said, "I'd be happy for a few admissions. Mia, I think you and Jim should take this. Sawyer thinks of me as his enemy. It might help bringing in some fresh faces."

"Are you sure Frankie?"

"Yep. He can't say much about Lorelei other than maybe it was consensual. Get him locked into a story then pull the pictures of the dead women."

Mia laughed, "The look on his face is going to be priceless."

Mia and Jim went to the Detention Unit to retrieve Sawyer. As they were getting onto the elevator Sawyer asked, "Where's the other chick? The one with the boy's name?"

Mia stifled a smile. "She's dealing with something else right now."

"Harumph."

Mia asked Sawyer a bunch of questions she already knew the answers to while Jim sat back and listened. When Mia pulled out the

Miranda Waiver for Sawyer to sign Jim grabbed the paper and said, "Allow me."

Jim made a production of reading the document, first to himself, and then aloud to Sawyer. Playing up his southern drawl he said, "Now, you don't have to sign this, but if you don't that means we can't tell the prosecutor the truth."

Sawyer sat up a little straighter and looked over the form Jim had laid in front of him.

"You see I know how these bitches are. I mean, have you even had a chance to talk to a man about all this or have you only talked to these here little ladies?"

"As a matter of fact, they haven't let me talk to a man. I mean these girls; they've got it all wrong. That whore's just trying to put a case on me but that's not how it is."

"I'd really be interested in hearing what you have to say, but unfortunately I can't talk to you unless you sign this," Jim tapped the waiver.

Sawyer looked at the form then back up at Jim. He picked the pen up and signed his name.

"I don't know why you all arrested me anyway. I'm the victim here. That bitch shot me."

Jim handed Mia the form and said, "Why don't you tell me how it *really* is."

Sawyer leaned back in his chair and rubbed the stubble on his face. He pursed his lips and said, "That bitch and I had a deal. I rented the room, and she was supposed to give me head and pussy. And everything was going fine. She was giving it up when that other chick started pounding on the door. That whore got freaked out and started screaming. Next thing I know she pulled out a gun and shot me."

"Whose gun was it?" Jim asked.

"She must have brought it with her. You know how them whores are. Bitch was probably going to rob me."

Jim nodded. He motioned for Mia to hand him the photos of the women under the bed. He left them face down on the table.

"Do you always use that same room when you pick up whores?"

"What are you talking about?"

"The owner said you go there regularly with a lady friend. I assume it's where you take your whores. Do you use that same room every time?"

"It's not against the law to rent a room."

"Nope." Jim noticed Sawyer was avoiding his question. "How often do you get a room there?"

"Every now and then."

"Did you notice any kind of smell or anything in the room?"

Sawyer didn't immediately answer, but instead nodded at the papers lying on the table and asked, "What are those?"

Jim and Mia kept their eyes trained on Sawyer as they flipped the photographs over one at a time.

"What the hell is that?" Sawyer shouted. He stood up, shoved his chair back from the table, and pushed the photographs at Jim, "Seriously, what the hell?"

"Do you know either one of these women?"

"Fuck no! Where did you take those pictures?" demanded Sawyer.

"In your motel room. Your regular room."

It suddenly dawned on Sawyer that he was a suspect in a double homicide. He bellowed , "You think I fucking did this! I ain't never killed anyone. I might beat up whores once in a while but I ain't no fucking killer."

ONE HUNDRED FOURTEEN

FRANKIE AWOKE to the sound of in incoming text message from Derek.

"$250,000 bond on Sawyer. $100,000 bond on Stockton. You did it babe."

"Woo hoo! We did it!" exclaimed Frankie.

She grabbed her phone and called Mia to tell her the news. After lots of "good jobs" and "we did its" they hung up. Frankie flopped back onto her bed and stared at her ceiling fan. She couldn't wait to find the women Sawyer and Stockton assaulted to tell them both were in jail and weren't going to get out.

Frankie picked up the phone and stared at the screen. She punched in the numbers and waited.

"If it isn't Francesca Thomas!"

Frankie laughed. "We did it. Sawyer is being held on a $250,000 bond!"

"Fantastic! It's about time, huh?"

"Seriously! I'm sure there will be some follow-up, but it feels good knowing he's off the streets."

"I guess Derek got through to Moon."

Frankie thought she heard something catch in Jim's voice when he said Derek's name. "Yeah, but your work in that interrogation didn't hurt."

Jim chuckled, "Thanks. Hey, Fitz just got here. We have a meeting with the prosecutor about the Schlovik case. Want to go for a run tomorrow?"

"Sounds good." Frankie smiled as she dropped her phone onto the bed thinking to herself that for once the good guys won.

ONE HUNDRED FIFTEEN

"JIM CRAVEN. DEREK KENSINGTON."

Derek extended his hand first to Fitzmeyer then to Jim. If Derek recognized Jim, he didn't let on. Gesturing to the table in his office he said, "Please have a seat."

Jim sat down and, while waiting for Derek to get to the table, sent Frankie a text message.

"Did you know Derek was the pros Fitz was working with?"

"No. He didn't mention it."

"Call you when I leave."

"K."

Derek laid his legal pad onto the table and asked, "Did you find out whose DNA was in Katarina Schlovik's rape kit?"

Fitz looked at his notepad and said, "Two male profiles were identified. One belonged to Jeremy DiCapoli. He was one of the guys found in the trunk with her and is believed to be one of Finnegan's soldiers. The second guy in the trunk hasn't been identified but his DNA has been excluded from the kit. The second sample belonged to an unknown male."

"Did you say DiCapoli? What's the last known address on him?" Derek asked.

"Yeah, why?" Jim asked.

"I went to school with Johnny DiCapoli. He had a little brother, but I can't remember his name. He was a couple years younger than me. There were rumors the DiCapolis were tight with the Finnegan's but…" Derek's voice trailed off.

Fitzmeyer scanned his notepad but didn't see any mention of a Johnny DiCapoli. "There have been new developments since I brought you the case file."

Derek looked up from the notes he had been taking.

"Two more bodies were found last night."

Fitzmeyer pulled out the photographs of the women from the motel.

Sucking in his breath Derek said, "Damn. How the hell did they get in there?"

"We don't know. Sex Crimes was busting a serial they had been working and lifted the mattress because of the smell."

"You think the guy they busted had anything to do with it?"

Jim quickly answered, "No. He's a prick but I don't think he's a killer. It doesn't match anything else he's done."

Derek glared at Jim and said, "You seem pretty familiar with the case."

"Yeah, the detectives working it are friends of mine."

Fitzmeyer looked from Derek to Jim then said, "There's something else."

Derek broke the stare and asked, "What?"

"We noticed…"

"Actually, Frankie noticed," Jim corrected.

"Detective Thomas noticed both women have a rose tattoo on the inside of their wrist. Same as Katarina Schlovik. We worked another case with Thomas recently and one of those girls had the same tattoo. That makes four women with the same tattoo on the same wrist. Coincidence?"

"I don't believe in coincidences." Derek stood up and walked to his desk.

"Me either," Fitzmeyer said.

Derek picked up the phone and dialed. He said, "Can you come here a minute?"

Hanging up the phone, Derek returned to the table. Before he could explain, Jessica Moon walked into the room. Jim and Fitzmeyer stood when she walked into the room, both appraising what they saw.

"You needed me?" Jessica looked at both men appreciatively, smiling as she spoke.

"The other night you said you had a case with a woman who had a rose tattoo on her wrist."

Jim didn't miss the fact Derek referred to the other *night*.

"Yeah. I think we're waiting on DNA to come back."

"Can you grab that case file and come back in here?"

"What's going on?"

Jim flipped over the photographs of the unidentified women from the motel.

Jessica gasped, covering her mouth with her hand. She reached down and picked the photograph up from the table. With her hand still over her mouth she said, "Oh my gosh." Tears filled her eyes.

Derek looked at her with concern, "What's wrong?" Jessica dropped the photograph and left the room.

Derek got up to follow Jessica and said, "I'll be right back."

ONE HUNDRED SIXTEEN

"JESSICA, WAIT. WHAT'S WRONG?"

Jessica was rummaging through the files in her desk drawer. "Where the hell is it? Dammit!"

"Jess, talk to me."

Throwing the folder onto the desk she looked up and said, "I fucked up, okay? Is that what you want me to say? It's my fault that girl is dead."

"What are you talking about?"

Jessica plopped into her office chair and let out a deep sigh. She opened the file folder and pulled out a photograph of a young girl with long curly hair.

Derek stared at the girl in the photograph.

"Her name is Andrea. I caught the case last summer. The fact pattern was full of challenges. She was a dancer high on meth. She identified the suspect in a line-up, but I didn't feel comfortable charging anyone until we got DNA back. Maybe if I had she wouldn't be dead."

Derek reached his hand across the desk, covered hers and softly said "Or maybe she still would be."

Jessica looked up and said, "You think?"

"We don't know who murdered her. It may not be related to her rape." Derek stood up and said, "Come on. Let's go see what else they have to say."

Jessica looked into Derek's dark eyes and said, "Thank you, Derek."

Derek nodded and walked out of the office.

Jessica smoothed her skirt, wiped her face, and followed. Before Derek could say anything, she looked at Jim and Fitzmeyer and said, "I'm so sorry. I needed to find this file. One of the women in your photograph is Andrea Tucker." Jessica opened the file, pulled out a photograph, and said, "As you can see, she had a tattoo of a rose on her wrist when this report was made last summer. The suspect in the case was identified as Richard Hinckley. We were waiting on DNA to come back to charge him."

Fitzmeyer was taking notes while Jessica spoke. Jim looked from Derek to Jessica.

Derek asked, "Is there any reason to suspect Hinckley is connected to the Finnegan or Marzullo families?"

Jim and Fitzmeyer shook their heads in unison.

"What are you guys thinking?"

Jim stood up, looked at Fitzmeyer, and said, "We need to go catch a killer."

Fitzmeyer followed Jim's lead and said, "Thank you for meeting with us today."

Derek extended his hand to both men and said, "Anytime." Grabbing two business cards and handing one to each man he added, "Let me know when you are ready to get warrants. My cell is on the card."

"Thanks Derek. We'll be in touch," Fitzmeyer said.

Once Jim and Fitzmeyer were in the elevator Derek looked at Jessica and asked, "Are you okay?"

"Honestly? No. I could really use a drink right now."

Derek closed his office door, opened the bottom drawer of his desk and pulled out two glasses and a bottle of Johnny Walker Black. He poured a finger in each glass then handed one to Jessica.

She looked from the bottle to Derek before taking a deep swallow of the amber liquid. When they had both drained their glasses, he poured another finger into each glass. The pair sat in silence and watched the sky darken and the street lights illuminate outside the window.

CHAPTER
ONE HUNDRED SEVENTEEN

"FRANK-EE!" Jim's voice boomed in the quiet office. Frankie and Mia erupted in laughter.

"What are you guys doing here?" Mia asked.

"We just left Kensington's office and wanted to see if you guys would help us out. Again," Fitzmeyer answered.

Mia raised her eyebrow as she looked at Frankie.

Jim and Fitzmeyer detailed the meeting they had, leaving out the part about Jessica's emotional response. When they were finished Jim said, "So we were hoping you would give us a copy of the file on Andrea Tucker. And maybe tell us who's working the case."

Within seconds Mia said, "Coleman's working the case. I'm printing a copy now. Do you think the murder is related to the rape?"

Jim sat thoughtfully for a moment before saying, "As much as I'd like to say yes, I don't think so. I think it's just a fluke."

Frankie asked, "Did you ever get an ID on the other girl?"

"Not yet," Fitzmeyer answered. "They are doing the autopsy tomorrow. We'll get a copy of her fingerprints and run them then. Or there is another option that might be a little faster. Or at least a little more fun."

Frankie's forehead wrinkled with question.

"We could go talk to Tessa Kemp. All the women had a rose tattoo on their wrist just like Tessa. It's too much of a coincidence not to be related."

The corners of Frankie's mouth began to rise, "I'll make a few phone calls." Looking at Jim she winked and said, "Maybe you should go see her. You do seem to have a way with the ladies."

Laughing, Jim said, "I think she's immune to my charms."

"She never bailed out," Mia said. "Maybe we can get into County and talk to her tonight."

Fitzmeyer looked from Frankie to Mia to Jim and asked, "You all want to help us find a killer?"

Frankie's eyes brightened as she said, "Hell yeah."

ONE HUNDRED EIGHTEEN

FRANKIE AND MIA sat across from Tessa in a small interview room at county lock-up. After making it very clear they were there to speak to her about something unrelated to her charges, Frankie pulled out the file folder containing photographs of the three dead women. She pulled out the photograph of Katarina first and asked, "Did you know this woman?"

Tessa touched the photograph and said, "Yes. That's Kat."

Frankie noticed Tessa did not ask what happened to Katarina. She displayed the second photograph. "What about these women?"

Tears filled Tessa's eyes. Pointing to one of the women she said, "That's Andi. Andrea. Andrea Tucker." Pointing to the other woman she said, "And that's Nicki. Nicole Andrews."

"I couldn't help but notice you have the same tattoo as these three women, so I have to ask - how do you know them?"

Tessa looked up and closed her eyes. With moist eyes she looked back towards the photographs. After a few minutes she said, "We all used to dance together. There was a group of us that worked the club but also did private parties. We kind of lost touch when I went to work for Stevenson."

Frankie nodded as Mia asked, "What's with the tattoo?"

Tessa looked from Mia to Frankie before standing up and saying,

"I'm done talking here." She walked to the door and slapped it with her hand, "Guard."

Frankie gave Mia a questioning glance. She shrugged her shoulder in response.

Ten minutes later they were driving quietly past the courthouse on the way back to police headquarters. Mia suddenly asked, "Hey isn't that Derek's car?"

Frankie looked in the direction Mia pointed just in time to see the car pull out of the parking lot with a woman in the passenger's seat.

THE SOUND of the tires rolling across the pavement echoed in Heather's ears. She twisted her body but couldn't loosen the duct tape binding her hands and feet. She took slow, deep breaths, trying not to panic as the trunk walls close in around her.

Heather felt the car begin to slow down and eventually stop. She could feel her heart pounding in her chest. She listened to the muffled voices but couldn't quite make out what they were saying. The doors of the car creaked open, then slammed shut. She waited.

After what seemed like forever, Heather heard the doors of the car open again. The car shuddered as the engine turned over and roared to a start. Laughter echoed from the backseat as tears rolled down Heather's cheeks.

Heather felt the seat back move against her head, then the center console lower. A rush of cool air forced its way into the hot, cramped trunk. Heather gulped the fresh air and fought the urge to scream.

"Drink this."

Heather saw a straw sticking out of a white Styrofoam cup. She hesitated, afraid of what might be inside. Tentatively she sipped the amber liquid, sighing with relief at the familiar taste of cola. The cup was moved abruptly from her mouth causing the liquid to dribble down her chin.

Heather pleaded when the console started to close, "Please! Leave it open. It's so hot back here."

She heard the men chuckling in the backseat, but the console was left down.

"Where are you taking me?"

Heather lay there listening to the sounds of the radio, waiting for an answer to her question. She twisted her hands to loosen the tape, but her efforts were futile. If anything, the binds felt tighter.

"Let me out of here. Why are you doing this? Where are we going? Just let me go." Heather continued to ask questions, barely stopping long enough to take a breath.

Once again Heather felt the car slow. When it came to a stop, the radio went silent. The chatter within the car came to a lull and the car door creaked open. Heather heard steps thump on the pavement then come to a stop at the back of the car. The latch holding the trunk closed was released and the lid popped open. Heather wriggled her body and tried to sit up.

"Please let me out of here. I won't tell anyone if you just let me go."

Corey looked at her and laughed a deep, sinister laugh. "You aren't going anywhere." He grabbed a pillowcase from the trunk. He pulled Heather into a sitting position and started to put it over her head.

"Please don't! I promise, I'll be quiet! Please don't cover my head. I won't be able to breathe!"

Corey put the pillowcase over Heather's head and grabbed the duct tape. She continued to plead until he removed the fabric but took a strip of tape and covered her mouth. He hesitated before shoving her back into the trunk, dropping the roll of duct tape next to her body.

Heather twisted her body and moved her head from side to side, trying to get the tape off her mouth. But the more she twisted the more the tape pulled against her hair. She finally stopped moving and lay quietly wondering why someone she thought was her friend would do something like this to her.

ACKNOWLEDGMENTS

To my children. Thank you for the years of support and sacrifice – both when I was on the job and now. I hope seeing me go for my dreams will be the inspiration for you to pursue your own.

To all of my family and friends who continue to believe in, support, and encourage me on this writing journey, thank you. You keep me moving forward.

To Rachel, my sister from another mister. Together and separately we fought for those who could not stand up for themselves. The good times were better, and the rough times more bearable, because of you.

To Joanne Archambault and Dr. Kimberly Lonsway. I will always be grateful for your advice and mentorship throughout my professional career and for your continued friendship.

Thank you to Christine and Sarah for holding me accountable to my writing goals. I appreciate your dedication to our little writing group! Your encouragement is appreciated more than words can say.

To my editors Kimberly Hanson and Dave Cohen. Thank you for the time, effort, skill and patience you had with me and my manuscript. I value your time, insight, guidance, and contribution. This novel is the polished piece it is, in part, because of you.

To my cover artist, Jaycee, at Sweet N' Spicy Designs. Thank you for listening to my vision and using your talent to create a cover that sent chills down my spine and exceeded my expectations.

For more information on how to respond to victims of sexual assault please visit www.startbybelieving.org.

ABOUT THE AUTHOR

CJ Johnson was born and raised in the mid-west and spent over ten years working for a major metropolitan police department with the last six spent as a detective in the Sex Crimes Section of the Special Victims Unit. Passionate about her work, she fought hard for justice for every victim – especially those others often overlooked.

In 2012, she left the high-stress, fast paced career of law enforcement investigations to spend more time with her family. As a nationally recognized subject matter expert on sexual assault investigations, she focused on developing and executing training curriculum focusing on sex crime investigations to law enforcement agencies and their officers for the state of North Carolina.

She continues to play an active role in her mission to end interpersonal violence through training, volunteerism, and leading a team of investigators for an organization with an aligned mission while working on the *City of Fountains* series.

BOOKS BY C.J. JOHNSON

FEATURING FRANKIE THOMAS

Thorns of Deceit

No Stone Unturned

Across State Lines

Moonglow Road

Visit:

https://www.cjjohnsonbooks.com